Stoke the Flames

An Orphans of St John's Novel
Book Two

By Monica Misho-Grems

First paperback edition February 2021

Book cover design by A. R. Williams and Monica Misho-Grems

http://authoratheart.com

Table of Contents

To my husband. You're my Angel.

Mom & Dad, please skip Chapter 17, except the last paragraph. For all of us. Thanks.

Prologue

March 21st, 2004

St John's Catholic Church and Orphanage

"Where is Felicity?" a disgruntled nun looked down quizzically at the blonde-haired, blue-eyed nine year old who looked so much like Shirley Temple in her outfit that it was comical.

"She...she-" tears began to well up in her eyes as the nun's gaze bore into her soul, scaring the little girl out of her wits. She'd experienced the nun's wrath and didn't want to set her off, it was an incredibly special day.

"Felicity went to the library, Sister. Sophie tried to stop her, but she said there was a book she was waiting to come in that she just had to read. I'm sorry, Sister." The nun looked down at the little boy who spoke to her. She'd never met a child so well-mannered and kind-hearted while working at the orphanage. It bothered her.

"I was not asking you, boy! I asked this one, here!" she turned her glare back to Sophie as she pointed a finger in the small girl's direction. "If you ever plan on being adopted, you'd better start speaking up instead of crying. Or you'll always just be a victim, waiting for some 'man-'" she cut a glance at the bronze-skinned eight year old, "to rescue you. You'll always be at the mercy of a man if you-"

"Sister Meredith? Could you please come look over the chair arrangement one more time? I believe one of the children may have moved some chairs while sweeping."

The nun quickly turned from the two children and looked past the nun speaking to her. She rushed off in a huff, muttering something that was likely to be rather ungodly of her. In her absence, the other nun filled the room with her radiant energy, relieving the two children before she could even say a word.

"Oh children, I am so sorry about Sister Meredith. You know how she gets on adoption day. It's a stressful time for all of us here at St. John's. We all just want the best for each of you." She looked over to Sophie and kneeled down, "And don't you worry about what she said. You are a strong, beautiful young girl who will be such a special young lady when you grow up. Any family would be lucky to have you." She winked at the small child as she pinched her rosy cheek, which made Sophie giggle. "That's more like it. Now-" she stood up, "let's get ready to go meet your future families! Oh, I'm so excited!"

"Thank you, Sister Gloria!" the kids shouted as a sprightful Sister Gloria bounced out of the room. Sophie looked at the boy who had come to her rescue. He always seemed to be there when she'd needed back up, and somehow she never minded. She was a very capable young girl, but there were times when even she felt that she needed help. And when her "big sister" Felicity wasn't around, he'd always pop up.

"Thank y-" Sophie was cut short of her thanks as she felt a sudden burst of air underneath her dress against her nylon-clad legs. She quickly turned and saw exactly who she'd hoped not to. Zachariah was a lean, shorter-than-average fourteen year old, who loved to prey on the younger girls. He didn't like to mess with Felicity, there was something unnerving about her to him. But Sophie, she was one of his favorite targets. He loved to wait in the shadows until she was alone and try to lift her dress or pull her shirt up. Whenever the girls would tell the nuns, they would just say it's boyish pranks, and that the girls shouldn't even think of such things, as that's not lady-like, that they would go to hell if they even thought of entertaining his desires. He'd been caught several times pinning girls down and touching them, but somehow he never got into trouble. He was Sister

Meredith's favorite, since she'd been the one to find him on the church steps and was the one who named him. Any time a girl would tell her, she would blame them for tempting him.

"Oh Sophie, your panties match your eyes," Zachariah remarked snidely, a perverted grin on his face.

"Stop, you bully!" The little boy jumped between Sophie and Zachariah. Zachariah quickly pushed the boy to the ground.

"Ugh, you stupid - what did Sister Meredith call you...oh yea - you stupid beaner! Go mind your own business, or I'll-" before he could finish his statement, Sophie gave him a swift, yet powerful, kick to the groin. She grabbed the little boy's hand to pull him up and the pair ran off, Zachariah screaming after them in the distance.

"You know you don't always have to stick up for me. I can do it on my own. You're going to get yourself hurt one of these days!" Sophie pleaded with the boy.

"I know, but if that's what I gotta do to keep you safe, then that's what I'm going to do!" The boy stared into Sophie's eyes. She stared back, surprisingly enjoying the staring contest. Then they both looked away, eyes burning, blinking rapidly, laughing in unison.

Their laughter was cut short when they looked over and saw a boy, about thirteen, sitting quietly in the corner. He was looking at them... but more so looking through them. "Oh, sorry River. We didn't realize you were in here. We can g-"

"No, it's ok Sophie. You two can be in here. I think I'll go get ready," River said, without batting an eyelid.

"Get ready?" Sophie asked.

"The nuns believe it's time for me to participate in Adoption Day again."

"But River..."

"It's ok, guys. Really." He gave them both a weak smile. He slowly stood up and slinked towards where he and the older boys shared a room.

After about half an hour, the nuns were bustling about the orphanage, wrangling up the children to come to the main hall. Sophie and her protector emerged into the grand hall and saw hundreds of unfamiliar faces, with a few familiar ones mixed in. As she walked to her spot where she had to stand on display like a life-sized Cabbage Patch Kid, she overheard a couple of the familiar faces speaking.

"No Charlotte, I promise, this will be the last time. If we can't find a child that we feel a special connection to, we will stop coming."

"Oh Rick, are you sure? We've been coming here for more than two years, and still haven't found our special one. Maybe we just aren't meant to be parents."

"Charlotte, honey, I promise you. This time will be different. I feel it!"

Sophie arrived at her spot and looked around. There were so many adults in one room! Some families looked really smart, some looked fun, some looked rich, some looked happy, and some...looked at her! She couldn't believe it. As she looked around, there were two families looking back towards her! One couple wore shiny, bright smiles; nice, neat clothing; and an expression that could only be described as "loving." The other couple on the other hand...were the opposite. The man had on a greasy white tank top that was visible through his open mechanics' shirt. His beard was a disheveled red mess with patches of gray in it. He had a greasy face and a scowl that didn't seem to go away. His wife - Sophie presumed - was definitely half his age. She was tall and slender, with a nice updo, and fake diamonds. She had a smile on her face, but something about her eyes worried Sophie. She looked as if she were screaming for help.

Sophie saw the happy couple coming towards her and began to get very excited. Just as they were within earshot, Sister Meredith swooped in and told them that she had the perfect child for them. She took the couple over to Zachariah who threw on the same charm he used on her. They seemed to buy the act. Within minutes, they were leaving together, along with Sophie's last hope of a happy family.

With sadness in her heart, Sophie looked around some more. She saw a beautiful couple heading towards her protector. She became happy for him, although a bit confused. Sister Meredith had always said that "white families only want white children, black families only want black children, and brown people only want little brown bastards." Sophie was very confused why this happy black couple would want her protector. He was a very nice, sweet, brave boy...but he was brown. Sister Meredith said no one would want him. She could see the look of shock and disgust as the couple walked with him - hand in hand - towards Sister Meredith. Sister Meredith quickly left the room before they could reach her. Just in time, Sister Gloria came to them and ushered them away to sign the paperwork. A few minutes later, they all walked out, happy as could be, leaving Sophie without her protector. But she was happy for him.

After nearly an hour of standing there, Sophie began to think she was never getting adopted. She often heard people pass her by saying things like "She's too pretty." "She looks a bit spoiled." "Oh, I bet she's such a flirt with the older boys. No, thank you, that could be a lot of trouble." With only a few kids and families left, her hope was almost nonexistent. Suddenly she looked up and saw a really handsome man with a serious look on his face. He had a tattoo on his neck, but he was dressed in such nice, slick clothing - that's what Sister Gloria called really nice suits. Sophie figured he had to have a lot of money to afford a suit like that. There were rings on his fingers, and he even had a cellphone on his hip, as well as a two-way pager. She thought this man could be her new father. She stood there with the biggest smile plastered on her face, hoping he would notice.

The man looked around a little longer, and with a defeated look on his face, he turned around and walked out of the orphanage. Sophie could hear the roar of his car's engine from inside of the orphanage and wondered what kind of car he drove.

Sophie snapped out of her thought bubble and noticed the nice-looking but sad couple, Charlotte and Rick, were still there. She didn't think they'd choose her, since they'd been there so many times and never noticed her. Sophie's thoughts changed rapidly when they looked towards her, looked at each other, and smiled the biggest smile. This was it! Sophie found her family! Sister Meredith approached the couple and asked if they had found someone. They nodded yes and pointed towards Sophie. Sister Meredith loudly exclaimed, "That one? Really? Are you sure?"

Charlotte replied, "Yes, we're very sure. He is the one. He's the child we've been praying for!"

Sophie's heart dropped! *He? He!? I'm very clearly a girl... They're not talking about me. Wait, if they're not talking about me, then they must be...* Sophie whipped around to see River, all alone, in a chair, a melancholy expression on his face. The couple, escorted by Sister Meredith, approached him, and Sophie caught a glimpse of a smile on his face for the first time in over two years.

Well, I guess today just isn't my day. But at least River finally got a family. I'm so happy for him. Besides, I won't be alone. There are these other kids. And Felicity! I still have Felicity!

Just as Sophie began to feel ok not being adopted, a stench of cheap gas station cologne entered her nostrils, and a firm hand painfully landed on her shoulder. She was forcefully spun around and saw the greasy man from earlier. He had his hand wrapped around his wife's hip and said to Sophie "Would you look at that? We get the prettiest one after all. Isn't she beautiful, sweetheart?"

"Yes, Papa. The perfect little sister." The man kissed the teenage girl on the lips and went to find a nun, leaving the two girls alone. "Hi, I'm Laurie. I'm going to be your big sister. Papa takes good care of us. We've got two more sisters at home with our big brother Danny. They're eleven and thirteen. Danny's twenty, but we're all awfully close. I'm only fifteen, but Papa says I'm the woman of the house."

The girl said all of this with a smile, so Sophie couldn't sense the pain within every word spoken. *Sure, this isn't the cleanest family, but maybe they're really nice,* Sophie thought. The man came back with Sister Gloria, who looked slightly concerned.

"So, how much do I get from the gov'ment for taking this one?"

"Well," Sister Gloria reluctantly spoke, "I don't really keep track of that, since my main focus is finding a loving home for all of our children. You can always contact the Department of Human Services with more questions. Now that you've signed the paperwork, it should be in the copies that I've given to you."

"Well," the man thought, "Good enough. Come on Laurie, get your new sister and let's go home!"

Home! Sophie thought to herself. The thought of having a home made tears come to her eyes. She looked at Sister Gloria one last time as she walked out. To her surprise, she didn't see the happy face she was expecting. *Hmmm, that's odd. Maybe she's just going to miss me.*

As Sophie got in the car, she could see a tall, slender girl with dark hair and glasses walking down the sidewalk, headed towards the orphanage. She watched as her best friend went back to the place she hoped never to set foot in again, with a bitter-sweet taste to go with her bitter-sweet feeling.

Felicity walked quickly down the sidewalk towards St. John's absent-mindedly. *I can't believe I did this again! I got so wrapped up in reading, I missed Adoption Day. Sister Meredith is going to be so upset with me! Oh well, Sophie and I will just sit there and laugh about it later. I hope she's got good stories about how many families passed up Zachariah. That always cheers me up. Hey, wait a minute...*

Felicity looked up and noticed a blonde-haired girl with a periwinkle dress getting into the back of a random car. That's Sophie's favorite dress! She only wears it on Adoption Day and Christmas. Felicity looked on with tears forming in her eyes as her best friend left the home they shared together. Though she was happy her friend finally had a family, she now had no reason to want to come back to the orphanage - for Sophie was her family. Now, her only friends were located at The Arlington. Maybe she would see Sophie again...

1

June 2021

Sophie sat at her half of the large central desk she shared with her friend and boss, Felicity Johnson, at the John Arlington Library. Her chair was whirled around by the back, unexpectedly, her limbs flailing as she tried to grasp something - anything - to hold herself steady. "Whoa! Felicity, what are you doing?"

"You're still coming tonight, right? I need you there. I've never had a dinner party and it's mostly Cage's employees, so I need you." Felicity's face was pink and slightly sweaty, and her eyes were wide like a deer caught in headlights, her anxiety was on full display. How long had she been stressing out without Sophie noticing? Had Sophie really zoned out that much?

"Yeah, I'll be there." Sophie kept her words calm and cool and collected, even though she felt the opposite on the inside. She hadn't ever met these people. She'd never been to a dinner party. That was for rich people. She'd been too busy scrounging for meals and making sure she had a roof over her head to ever even think of attending a dinner party.

Since she reunited with Felicity, she had been well taken care of. Felicity was a nurturer. She was a giver - a caretaker. Felicity gave her all to everyone she cared about, which included Sophie. Sophie couldn't have been more thankful for everything Felicity had done for her in the last two months. She had given her a job with a very fair wage, helped her find an apartment, helped her find a good quality, used, bicycle - not that Sophie ever used it since Chicago wasn't necessarily friendly to bicyclists. She spent hours talking to her about nothing. Felicity became her best friend faster than she'd ever thought possible.

"Do you want me to come early to help set everything up? We both know I'm no good in the kitchen." Sophie's tone was jovial and jokingly self-deprecating, but all she felt deep down was dread. The one thing Sophie wasn't excited for, the damn dinner party at Felicity and Cage's house. The invite list was small, but still too big for Sophie's taste. Felicity, Cage, Sophie, and three of Cage's closest friends, who also happened to work for him at his security company. She was already anxious.

Sophie was always wary of new people. Her adopted family made sure of that. She shuddered at the thought of them. *Forget about them, Sophie. You're safe now.* Sophie shook the thought from her head, tossing her platinum blonde curls about before starting her weekly task of contacting the patrons with outstanding fees.

Sophie stood in Felicity's dining room looking over the table. She counted the place settings, six in total. Each one was perfectly aligned, all the silverware set neatly over a white linen napkin. Each setting had a glass for water and wine. "Hey, Felicity, can you come check this out? I feel like it's missing something." Sophie rubbed her chin, a pensive gaze on her faerie-like face. *There is something missing.*

A whoosh of air next to Sophie alerted her of Felicity's arrival in the dining room. "Looks great to me, Soph." Felicity rushed out of the dining room and back to the kitchen again.

"Candles!" Sophie said as she finally realized what was missing. "Felicity, where are your candles?!"

"In the closet in the hallway!" She shouted from the kitchen.

"'Kay!" Sophie jogged to the hallway and found the closet she was looking for. Tall, white candlesticks. *Where's the holders?* She shuffled through the items in the closet until she found the neat, clean cut, glass holders. *Perfect*! She brought the candles back to the dining room and set them in the center of the table. *We'll light 'em just before everybody gets here... Now - to check on Felicity.*

A loud crash made Sophie jump out of her skin, but she was calmed by the cursing that followed - at least Felicity hadn't died. She jogged into the kitchen, which she soon realized was a mistake. It was chaos. There were pans, cooking utensils, and food everywhere. Sophie gasped as she covered her mouth. Felicity was somehow wrangling the circus of her cooking and pulled a decorative pan of stuffing out of the oven. "Holy cow, Felicity. There was a tornado in your kitchen! Are you okay?"

"It's fine! I know it's a mess! Good thing no one can see it from the dining room! Can you set out the appetizers? Alex, Theo, and Benjamin should be here any minute!"

"Where are they?" Sophie asked as she tried to peer past the mess of dishes and find the appetizers in question.

"Fridge," Felicity said as she set about checking the temperature on the two chickens still roasting in the oven. Sophie searched for the plate of bruschetta in the over-sized, crowded fridge and took it to the set table.

Sophie had learned over the last few months that Felicity was an amazing cook. She often brought leftovers to the library for Sophie that were to die for, she'd never had such delectable meals. She was often envious that Cage got to eat it all freshly cooked.

The doorbell rang throughout the house, echoing against the hardwood floors. "I got it!" Cage's voice came from the entryway. Sophie heard multiple new voices mingling with Cage's familiar tones. They all sounded excited about something. Sophie tried to figure out what but couldn't pick out any comprehensible words, despite the fact that their voices carried through the halls to the dining room.

Her heart began to race at the idea of being around so many people. What if she said or did something that made her look ridiculous? Her palms began to feel clammy, and she could feel the tingling in her skin that preceded her regular perspiration at the idea of being around people she didn't know, especially men. New people - new men - were unpredictable. She didn't know how to handle the suspense of not knowing how it would go. Could she leave now and risk disappointing Felicity? Would Felicity understand? Sophie heard multiple sets of heavy footsteps in the living room coming toward the hallway, which would eventually lead to the dining room she stood frozen in.

The room started to feel too small for six people to fit in. She scrambled down the hallway to the bathroom, fortunately able to avoid the group of men coming toward the room she felt trapped in. Why was she running like a scared, timid, little kitten? She rested her hands on the edge of the white marble vanity and glared at herself in the mirror.

She hated the way her nose was so tiny, like a button, her lips were too full for the size of her head. Her eyes were the worst shade of blue, not like Felicity's perfectly bright green, emerald-like eyes. Hers were an ugly grayish shade of blue that made it hard to tell if they were blue, gray, or green. Her naturally platinum blonde hair was too light for her light skin tone. She hated everything about how she looked, from her hair all the way down to the way her pinky toe was crooked. What was it her therapist had said when her thoughts were taking over?

Fight back. Aggressively praise yourself against the bad thoughts. Sophie squeezed her eyes shut and tried to think of something she liked about herself.

Felicity's face flashed in her mind. Her friendly smile lit up the darkness that clouded Sophie's thoughts. "I'm a good friend for being here even though I hate it," she whispered to herself. "It doesn't matter what Cage's friends think of me because I'm a good person for being here for my friend." She took a deep breath, forcing her lungs and heart to slow back to a normal cadence. "I'm a good friend to Felicity, who in turn is a good friend to me." She looked her reflection in the eye and felt her confidence return just enough to be able to walk out of the bathroom and meet Cage's friends.

She put her hand on the doorknob and turned it, only to come face to face with a tall, handsome man with smooth skin - the color of aged cinnamon bark - and kind, deep brown eyes.

"Oh, I'm sorry. I didn't know anyone was in here. I can wait," he said quickly as he turned to walk away.

"No, it's okay. I'm done. It's all yours." She left the room and pressed herself against the wall of the hallway to let him pass. He dwarfed her tiny frame as he walked by.

He smelled like expensive cologne, a scent that permeated her brain and caught her off-guard. It was familiar. It smelled like the man she saw at the orphanage as a kid. The one with the tattoo on his neck in the slick suit. She was perplexed by the memory. That was the worst day of her life.

The man closed the door after him with one last glance and smiled at the woman who now stood in the hall outside the bathroom.

Sophie slowly walked back up the hallway toward the dining room she'd spent so long readying for this exact reason. She peeked around the corner of the wall, surveying the room before entering. She spotted Cage and Felicity talking to two other good-looking, muscular men. She recognized Benjamin; the brunette cutie Felicity was giving a hug to. Felicity had told her about him when he visited the library a few months before. He was Cage's cousin, as well as his employee. He had the same blue eyes as Cage, tropical ocean blue with a dark ring around the iris. The same smile too. They could almost be brothers. *Murphy genes must be strong.* Sophie wondered briefly what a baby from Cage and Felicity would look like.

Sophie didn't know if the one with perfectly messy brown hair and green eyes was Alex or Theo. She hesitated for a few more seconds, hoping to glean a hint at what his name could be, but was startled by a hand on her shoulder. She gasped when she found the man who'd accidentally scared her witless at the bathroom door.

"I'm so sorry, I promise I'm not trying to scare you. I'm Theo by the way," he said sincerely as he smiled, showing off his brilliant, perfectly straight teeth. His attempt to put her at ease had failed. She felt uncomfortable at his touch, something she hadn't felt in a long time. It wasn't a bad uncomfortable. It was like she enjoyed it more than she thought she should have. He was gorgeous and seemed sweet. He held out his hand for her to shake, an expensive looking silver watch hung from his wrist.

"It's fine." Her tone was short, but only because of the fact that it was the second time he'd startled her in the last few minutes, and she was sure she looked like a lunatic, being as easily startled as she was. "I'm Sophie," she told him, making sure her tone was more kind than it was at first. She took his hand, making a note in the back of her mind about how wonderfully warm it was against her palm.

"Well, we should get in there." He gave her a sympathetic smile and walked into the dining room.

Yeah, here goes nothing, she thought as she straightened her spine and pushed her shoulders back, trying to appear more confident than she actually was. She brushed out the skirt of her light blue dress, steadied herself and walked into the dining room. She was met by the gazes of each of Cage's guests. Benjamin smiled and waved at the familiar face.

"Hey, Sophie!" he said cheerfully.

"Hi," she said quietly as she waved back.

"Sophie, it's a pleasure to meet you," said the man with perfectly messy brunette hair as he took her hand and kissed the back of it. The unexpected physical affection sent her mind reeling. Sophie couldn't shake the gross feeling it left on her hand, like she needed to go wash it with soap and scalding hot water. *He must be Alex,* she thought. *Definitely gonna have to stay away from him.*

"Alright, calm down, Casanova." Cage's jovial attitude cut through the tension in the room she felt when she walked in, and all eyes landed on her. "Felicity worked hard on this meal, so let's dig in. Anyone want some wine?" he asked. Everyone nodded and he grabbed the bottle from the middle of the table to open and pour.

Here goes nothing, thought Angel as he opened the door of his pickup truck. It was his first day at the firehouse. His first day as a firefighter. He'd graduated his fire safety program and was finally ready to start serving his community.

He thought of how proud his parents were when he walked across the stage to receive his Bachelors degree. His heart swelled in his chest at the thought. They were the loudest in the crowd. He fought back tears as he received his degree from the Dean of the University of Chicago. He'd come so far, but it was all because of them.

Camille and Lester Harris adopted Angel when he was eight and loved him despite the fact that he was actually Latino, and they were - as his cousin Lonnie would say - "South Side Black." It had been drilled into him by a horrible nun that he would only ever be adopted by parents the same color as him, which he now knew was ridiculous and horribly racist.

His parents loved and cared for him every day since they adopted him, and he couldn't be anymore grateful for the life they gave him. They raised him to be hard-working, caring, and strong. They also showed him how to be empathetic, sympathetic, and above all else they taught him to question everything. "Always ask questions, because it's the only way you'll ever learn the answer," his father told him, usually multiple times a day.

Angel pulled the door open and stopped at the office just inside the entrance, then knocked on the door. The fire chief, Anderson Stevens, opened the door and Angel watched as his small, polite smile stretched into a grin that spread from ear to ear.

"Angel! Glad you're here. Now, let's go introduce you to your team." The tall, broad shouldered man with silver hair clapped him on the shoulder then led him down the hallway, talking all the way. "These are the men and women you'll work with every day. Get to know them, because you'll be spending the majority of your time with them while you're on. It's important you understand that we're like a big family. We always watch each other's backs." He stopped just before what Angel assumed was the kitchen and turned to face him. "You'll be like family soon enough, kid."

Kid. Angel had to fight back a frown when he heard the word.

Before he could protest and inform the Chief he was far from a child, the Chief pushed open the door and ushered Angel in. "Come meet your new family..."

Two men sat in recliners facing the television, lounging. A woman was sitting at a long metal dining table, typing away on a laptop with papers spread all around her. One more man was in the kitchen cooking, and another sat at a breakfast bar chatting with him. Every one of them turned toward the door Angel and the Chief had just entered.

Angel smiled his friendliest smile and waved to everyone. "Hi," he said in the most inviting tone he could. A chorus of hellos greeted him back before everyone turned back to what they had been doing, seemingly uninterested by the new face they'd be seeing around the fire house. The Chief steered him toward the two men in recliners in front of the old flat screen television.

"Angel, this is your Captain, Jamieson Jacobs. Been the Captain for me ever since I took up the position as Chief, which was, oh let's see here, about 14 years ago?" he said as he tapped his chin with his finger. The balding man in the recliner stood up to greet his new underling. He was about six inches shorter than Angel, but his personality was a whole lot bigger than that.

"Long as you fall in line like the rest, we won't have any problems." The balding man's voice was gruff, and his eyebrows were knitted together so tightly that they almost made a unibrow. When he took Angel's hand it was immediately obvious to Angel that he felt intimidated by the younger, taller, new recruit. He squeezed hard, hard enough to make Angel's knuckles grind together for a moment before he could squeeze back.

He'd experienced men doing this sort of thing most of his life. He always saw it as a kind of pissing contest that smaller men would impose on larger men, a way to prove their strength and therefore their worth and their place among the pack, as it were. It didn't bother Angel. He knew he was the rookie now. The lowest on the totem pole. He'd prove his worth with kindness and perseverance, rather than follow suit with his so-called leader.

Angel just smiled as he shook the man's hand. "A pleasure to meet you, sir. I look forward to learning everything I can from your extensive experience." A perfectly kind compliment to pay a perfectly annoying Captain who would read into it and likely take it as an insult on his age.

"There's a lot to learn, but that takes time, boy." Jamieson's voice was gravelly. Angel could tell he was lowering it on purpose, adding an air of authority that wasn't needed.

Boy. More egotistical crap.

"I'm a quick study," Angel assured the man before they each let go of their grip with a final shake and squeeze. Angel was far from a boy, he knew this, as did his Captain. But the word still rang out in his mind as the Chief led him to the next set of introductions, ignoring the second man who'd stayed in his recliner.

Angel later learned that this man's name was Tony. A strong, gentle, giant who loved fishing and playing pool.

Jonas stood at the stove, a warm and friendly man with curly, blond hair and an inviting smile.

The man at the breakfast bar was Todd, the newest recruit before Angel. He was just around the same age but had bright red hair and looked a lot like a certain pop singer to Angel, with his round-shaped head and blue eyes.

Both were friendly in their greetings, neither made his hand hurt when they shook it, which Angel was glad for but would never admit out loud.

The woman sitting at the dining table was Michelle, or Elle as she stated she preferred to be called. She was the crew's jack of all trades. She managed their union contracts, was the public liaison, the liaison for the mayor, and was the general head of human resources for the firehouse. She did it all and did it with a smile.

She was older, around 50, but she was obsessive about her fitness and diet. She told Angel later that day that her body is her temple and so she must treat it as such, because you only get one body for this lifetime. She also turned out to be the crew's physical trainer, keeping them in shape for their rigorous duties as firefighters. She could've easily outworked everyone in the firehouse at any time. The sparkle in her brown eyes made Angel want to test it out, see if he could best her. He knew it would take a lot of work to be able to do it, but one day he'd try.

Angel spent the rest of his time getting oriented with the layout of the fire house and setting up his sleeping area that came equipped with a bed, a desk, and a chair for the desk. He set up two picture frames, one of his parents, the other of the three of them at his college graduation.

He put some extra clothing away in the dark green trunk he'd been assigned. He sat in the chair once he was done and smiled. He'd done it. He'd made his dream of being a firefighter come true and he couldn't have been any prouder of himself in that moment.

2

"I'm so excited you agreed to come out with us tonight, Sophie. You're gonna love this place. It's small and not too crowded. Maybe you and Theo will really hit it off! He's a good guy. You deserve a good man in your life, especially after the losers you've told me about!" Felicity was babbling again.

Her mission in life it seemed - now that she was engaged - was to find Sophie a perfect mate as well. And Theo was the target.

Except, Sophie knew all too well that perfect men didn't exist. Cage seemed pretty close to perfect, but he was Felicity's and Sophie wasn't interested. Sophie was extremely happy for Felicity, but she had no hope for herself.

She was too broken for any man to handle, something Felicity had been unaware of and would never find out if Sophie had anything to say about it. Sophie really didn't mind being alone, either. She was content in taking care of herself. She didn't need anyone else to take care of, that would just be more stress for her. The same reason she'd decided to never have kids. She didn't need the added responsibility of another life on her conscience when she could barely take care of her own.

Sophie spent the rest of the day reminding herself why she didn't need a man in her life and when the time came to head home and get ready to go out with Felicity on their double date, Sophie was headstrong in her resolve to die a crazy, old, cat lady. Who was she kidding? Sophie hated cats. *Maybe I will be a crazy, old, dog lady*, she mused.

Sophie enjoyed the sun on her face as she started her short walk to the bus stop a block down the street from The Arlington. She had taken the same bus, down the same route every day since she'd moved into her apartment. It made things easy. She knew exactly how long it would take to get home each day and she could depend on the fact that her bus driver, Carla, was never late.

Carla was a stout, middle-aged woman with ebony skin, bright and sparkling amber eyes, and the most beautiful halo of kinky, curly hair Sophie had ever seen. Carla always offered the same friendly smile every time Sophie climbed up the steps and swiped her bus pass, and a "How ya doin', darlin'?".

To which Sophie would always reply with, "It's been a good day, how about you Carla?" That day was no different. Sophie sat in the closest open seat, careful to make sure no one else needed it first, then plugged in her headphones and played her favorite Pandora playlist, a collection of funky pop songs that was always sure to hype her up.

After three songs, Sophie saw her building come into view. She packed away her headphones and prepared to leave the bus. Her apartment sat in a tall, old, brick building that was about a ten minute bus ride away from the library. It was within walking distance on nice days, if Sophie was in the mood to do so, but it wasn't one of those days for Sophie. She was dreading the night to come, and her mind was too busy thinking about that to walk all the way home.

While Felicity paid her a good and fair wage for being an assistant librarian, it wasn't enough for anything lavish in the city of Chicago. Sophie enjoyed her studio apartment, though. She could lay in bed and watch TV, but could also sit in her plush recliner - which she often fell asleep in. Sophie smiled at her little apartment, it made her heart feel so full of pride that she had a place of her own, paid for by her own money.

Sophie walked into her bathroom, half of which served as a closet, the other half housed the actual bathroom. She sifted through her mountains of blouses, skirts, pants, and dresses before settling on a silky white dress with spaghetti straps that fell over her body and made her feel like Aphrodite, the Greek Goddess of Love.

It was one of her favorite dresses. It gave her the confidence she needed to go out and about and made her feel like a Hollywood actress would when she stepped on the red carpet. It also complimented her platinum blonde hair and blue-gray eyes.

She let her hair out of its bun so it could fall around her shoulders in the perfect, messy waves her bun had created. She ran her fingers through the silken strands to neaten them up a bit and checked her appearance in the mirror over her sink.

Perfect, she thought. Just enough to make Felicity think she was actually looking for a boyfriend, but also to feel confident enough to go out into the world of the night.

Her cell phone buzzed just as she was applying her lipstick. Felicity's name flashed across the screen. *Time to do this thing,* Sophie thought. She picked it up and answered. "Hey, I'll be down in just a minute." She swiped the stick over her plump bottom lip, applying just enough of the natural pinkish red to color her lips and added a light layer of gloss to make them pop.

"Perfect, see you soon!" They both hung up and Sophie went to pull on her silver heels, admiring her look in her full length mirror once she was done.

Sophie snapped a cute selfie with her bent over and blowing a kiss to the mirror to post on Instagram later and walked out of her front door, making sure to pull it fully closed and locked it before taking off down the hallway towards the old elevator that made noises that creeped her out.

Every time she rode it, it felt to her as if the steel box would fall by the time the doors closed in front of her. She'd learned to ignore the sounds the elevator made as it creaked and groaned on its way down to the first floor.

She'd been adamant when she moved in that it needed to be checked by a technician, that the sounds the moaning metal made could not be normal for a fully functional elevator. Building management assured her that they had it checked once a year and it always had a clean bill of health, so to speak. She was skeptical but didn't push the matter further. It would be their money on the line when it did actually fall and caused a huge lawsuit.

When she entered the lobby from the creepy, old elevator, she spotted Cage's car parked on the street just in front of her building with the back passenger door open and waiting for her to climb in. When she pushed open the lobby door she heard Felicity.

"Sophie, you look amazing! You're gonna knock Theo off his feet!" Felicity complimented as Sophie slid into the back seat.

Sophie heard Cage chuckle from his spot in the driver's seat, a sound that said she probably wouldn't need to try awfully hard to seduce the man in question.

Sophie jokingly rolled her eyes at Felicity's comment and Cage's chuckle. She pulled out her phone to take a picture of the three in the car and posted it to Instagram, along with her mirror selfie, after tagging her companions in the post.

They arrived at the small lounge and were seated at once. Cage clued the women into why they had received such swift entry into the popular bar, he told them about how he'd helped design the security system in the building so the owner put him on the eternal VIP list.

The lighting was dim and soft pop music played from hidden speakers. It was a nice spot. The dance floor was an expansive stained wood structure that was elevated above the rest of the floor by about a foot with a half-height glass wall surrounding it to make sure overly inebriated visitors wouldn't fall.

The open areas surrounding the dancefloor were lined with booths and tables for patrons to relax. The bar was huge, spanning one entire wall, long enough for six bartenders to be behind it comfortably and still be out of reach of one another with their arms outstretched.

The waiters and waitresses were busily shuffling back and forth between the bar, the kitchen, and the tables in their white button ups, black slacks, and black ties. After finding an open booth, the trio ordered drinks to get started as they waited for the fourth member of their party.

Theo arrived soon after their first round of drinks were gone. He looked great in his pristine cobalt collared shirt with ivory buttons holding the silk fabric closed, hiding what Sophie could only imagine was perfectly toned muscle, and surprisingly tame beige slacks. His broad shoulders were accentuated by the clean cut lines of his shirt, which Sophie figured he'd had tailored.

He spared no expense to look good, which she didn't mind. She did briefly wonder how much Cage paid him, though. Then she wondered how much Cage paid himself.

Theo slid into the booth next to Sophie and greeted her with a dazzling smile. "Good to see you again, Sophie. You look beautiful." He took Sophie's hand in his and pressed a warm kiss to the back of it, sending little butterflies soaring around in her chest. After greeting Sophie, he bumped fists with Cage and said hello to Felicity.

Sophie was flattered that he'd taken a moment to really acknowledge her, give her his full attention and compliment her. She felt a blush rise in her cheeks as she smiled at the handsome man who's smile, and eyes sparkled in the dim lights of the lounge. She let the smile on her face grow into a grin. *Such a charming gentleman. Maybe Felicity is right...* Sophie thought. *Maybe he deserves a chance...*

"Your drinks are on me tonight, sweetheart," Theo told Sophie as he rested his arm on the booth behind her. "What would you like?"

Sophie didn't drink much, not that she didn't enjoy tasty mixed drinks and beer, she'd just had too many encounters with annoying drunken men who had a hard time taking "No" for an answer. Sophie got the feeling that Theo wasn't like that. He was sweet, a gentleman.

"Oh! Mr. Big Shot, huh?" Cage teased Theo as he laughed. "You buying my drinks too, tonight?"

"Just trying to be polite. You should take notes," Theo replied jokingly as he shot a playful wink to Sophie, who blushed in response.

Felicity laughed as Sophie thought over her options while tapping her chin pensively. "I think I'll have another Fuzzy Navel," Sophie told Theo.

He took the rest of the group's orders and left them momentarily to give them to the bartender, before walking back to the table. Sophie took the time he was gone to see how he interacted with others. He kindly excused himself when he bumped into other patrons, was polite to the servers and let them pass in front of him and was also kind to the bartender taking the order. She even spotted him leaving a hefty tip on the bar for the man.

Sophie took the chance to really look at him. His cinnamon-colored skin was smooth and blemish free. He was tall, but not too tall. His smile was just as dazzling as it had been when he first walked in. His lips were luscious. He was muscular, but lean, not stocky. He was absolutely gorgeous, the kind of handsome that could've just walked off the cover of a magazine. As cliché as it sounded, it was true.

The couples shared a few more rounds of drinks before deciding to dance on the crowded floor. Theo took Sophie's hand and led her up the stairs and into the middle of the crowd. He spun her around before pulling her close to him, her chest pressing against his abdomen, feeling the taut muscle beneath his shirt. She could feel her body heat up with the closeness his dancing commanded.

She felt her cheeks tinge pink as their bodies moved together to the beat of the song - one Sophie didn't recognize, but Theo seemed to. So, she followed his lead. She let him move her as the music moved him, their bodies touching the entire time.

If sex could be performed clothed and standing upright in the middle of a dancefloor, that's what they were doing. Sophie didn't care, though. The alcohol had kicked in and her inhibitions were out the window. She was ready to forget her past and have a little fun for the night. She never let her guard down enough to do that anymore.

When they'd finished their dancing, they took their seats at the booth again, parched, and ready for some more drinks. "Where'd you learn to dance like that?" Sophie asked, the smile plastered on her face gave away how much fun she was having with the man she was starting to get to know a little better. Maybe she'd even begun developing a little crush.

"You'll never believe me!" He told her. His smile mesmerized her, almost making her forget her question.

"Now you really have to tell me!" Sophie playfully demanded as she smacked her hand on the table, excitedly waiting for an answer.

"My favorite movie as a kid was Dirty Dancing. I'd dance around the house like Patrick Swayze. Told my mom I wanted to be a dancer when I grew up. Don't laugh! I'm serious," Theo told her as he laughed along with her. "I took lessons until I was in middle school, and it wasn't cool anymore," he revealed.

He's so cute! Sophie thought as they shared another smile.

Out of the corner of her eye, she caught a glance of a man in a dark jacket. It was the bomber type of jacket that pilots wore in the early 1900s. His was dark blue, though, and not made of leather. But it had zippers on both sets of pockets, the ones on his chest and by his hips. The man also wore a Chicago Cubs baseball cap that was pulled down and covered his eyes.

Sophie had assumed he'd been looking at her, but when she didn't catch his eyes she figured he wasn't actually watching her. *Just some guy waiting for his drink.* She brushed it off and turned her attention back to Theo, who hadn't noticed she'd even looked away.

Angel had been in the firehouse a whole 12 hours and had already been bombarded with more than a prank an hour. He sat in the chair at his small desk with his head in his hands. It was more annoying than anything. He knew he had to endure it, or he'd never live it down.

Don't let them see you sweat, he told himself each time.

He hadn't even been in the firehouse for an hour before the first one hit him. The Chief had just finished showing him around and he'd finished setting his things up and one of his new crew mates, Jonas, asked him if he'd wanted some coffee.

Angel, being just out of college and highly addicted to caffeine, said, "Of course!" He followed Jonas down to the kitchen and was handed a huge mug of freshly brewed hot, magic bean water. He brought the mug to his nose and inhaled the aroma of roasted coffee beans and took his first sip.

Angel's eyes went wide before he spit the entire drink out all over the counter. He choked on the half swallowed, half spit out, entirely disgusting coffee as the rest of the crew laughed hysterically. Jonas had replaced the sugar with salt.

Then, hour two rolled around. Angel was trying to finish his new employee paperwork when he heard a scream echo down the hall. He ran towards the gym and found Elle lying on the ground, trapped under a barbell with way too much weight on it for her to have been lifting. He struggled to move the weight but had shifted it just enough to get her free. Only to find out - after Angel insisted she needed to be checked for broken bones - once she started laughing, that Tony had helped her with the set up.

"I'm sorry, kid! I couldn't resist!" She cackled as she held her sides from laughing so hard.

He almost wished he could laugh with her. He did manage to force a chuckle as he left the gym.

Once he got back to the sleeping quarters he decided he'd try to stay away from everyone for a while, maybe take a nap to pass some time and hope they decided not to mess with him anymore.

He'd had hope until the second he sat on his bed and immediately sank to the floor. Someone had pulled all the slats off of his bed frame and he was now tangled up in a mess of sheets, blankets, and cold metal. Angel had to admit, that one was surprisingly sneaky and a great idea. He wondered for a moment just how they'd gotten his mattress to stay up without the slats underneath it but decided not to ask.

This went on *all day long.*

Twelve *hours.*

More than a dozen stupid high school level pranks.

It was *his* turn.

How would he get everyone back? Angel thought long and hard about how he could possibly get every single one of them back at once.

Thirty minutes later, he had a plan. Maybe it wouldn't be today, or tomorrow. *No.* He had to let some time pass. Let them think he'd forgotten *everything.* All the stupid initiation pranks. *No.* He'd let them get *really* comfortable. They wouldn't even know what hit them!

With a plan in place, Angel went about his day. He worked out with Elle, just to get a feel for how she ran things. He was not surprised to see that she had out-worked him easily. He took a shower after that, then set about making some dinner for himself. Nothing fancy, just a burrito bowl recipe his mom had shown him.

Once it was time to sleep, Angel laid in his bed slowly and carefully. He had to make sure they hadn't taken out the slats again.

He smiled once the light was out. His crew had no idea who they'd messed with. Angel was known for his pranks in college. His fraternity had some of the best times pranking each other. They had a YouTube channel of all the pranks they'd pull.

Angel was well-versed in the art of a good prank. They'd messed with the *wrong man.* And they would pay for it. They wanted pranks. They would get them.

Angel had a knack for picking out people's weaknesses. He'd watch his new crew. Learn what made each of them tick. Things they liked, things they hated.

He'd noticed that most of them had steered clear of any spicy food, so far. He'd keep an eye on that. Was there some background info there? Did they just not like spicy food? Was there a reason for the lack of hot sauce in the firehouse? Angel would find all these answers and more.

Then, he would get his revenge.

Sooner than they would ever see coming.

Sweet, hot, spicy revenge.

3

Sophie pulled open the glass door to the library as her head throbbed. She'd tried coffee, aspirin, a greasy breakfast burrito, and four glasses of water. Nothing had helped the headache that pounded behind her eyes.

Felicity liked to keep some of the lights off in the morning, so patrons could tell they weren't quite open for business and Sophie had never been more thankful than she was that morning. She plopped into her chair – which was a mistake as it only intensified the throbbing – and clocked in for the day.

"Soph, you look like Hell. You wanna take the day off?" Felicity asked as she took a seat in her chair. The squeak the chair made as Felicity sat down and turned toward her made Sophie cringe.

When Sophie's eyes met Felicity's, she could see the empathy laced through the green irises staring back at her. "How are you not just as bad as me right now?" Sophie asked as she rubbed at her temples, again. She hoped beyond hope the torturous hangover would end before the library opened. *The aspirin or the breakfast or water should kick in soon, right?*

"Cage has a cure. Swears by it. It's the most disgusting thing on the planet. To be honest, I'd take a hangover over that God awful concoction any day, but he makes me drink it. Something with spinach and turmeric and lemons, I don't know. It works though. Want me to see if he'll bring some by before he goes to work?" Felicity offered.

"Sounds gross. No, I'm good. I drank some water and took an aspirin, which should kick in at any time." Sophie sighed as she gently rested her forehead on her crossed forearms. She could have gone home and gone back to sleep if it weren't for the massive book signing they had planned that afternoon. Sophie knew she couldn't leave Felicity alone with a frenzied mob of readers all clamoring in line to meet their favorite author, Scarlett Phoenix. At least she had a few hours before it was time for the chaos.

Sophie picked her head back up a minute later to find Felicity struggling to get the tables set up for the signing. She was trying to lift a particularly heavy one, and was about to drop it, when Sophie sprung up out of her chair and rushed over to help.

"Thanks! Don't know what I would do without you," Felicity said as she stooped with her hands on her knees and struggled to catch her breath. It wasn't often the pair of them had to do things like move heavy furniture such as the tables, but when a popular local author asks to have a book signing at her favorite local library, it's hard to refuse that kind of publicity. Even when heavy tables are involved.

Sophie had read the author's newest books, the ones she was sharing at the signing. It was an adventure-based, smutty, romance series about a couple who faced evil after evil, but always managed to come out the other end more in love than they were before.

Sophie finished the whole series of four books in - an almost record breaking - four days. Really, she'd just been trying to keep up with Felicity who finished all four in two days, which was just a couple of days after the author had requested the signing event be held at the John Arlington Library. The pair figured they should know who they're letting hold events at their library.

The series had pleasantly surprised Sophie. She was kept engaged by the beautiful prose and the fully fleshed out characters that each had their own distinctive arcs throughout the series. She was also a sucker for the main heroine, who was such a badass! She handled business like Sophie always wished she could with a sassy phrase and a swing of her hair. She and Felicity had been spending their idle time at the library comparing notes and discussing the series, both getting excited for the signing more and more as each day passed and the event grew closer.

Sophie unfolded the white table cloth and aired it over the table, making sure each side was evenly covered before starting to set out copies of the book for patrons to buy. The author, a tall, slender woman who Sophie thought resembled an Amazonian warrior queen – with her lean muscles, long black hair, and honey-colored skin - was kind enough to drop off all of the supplies to set up the tables, without actually offering any help with the set up herself.

Sophie had found that to be rude initially, but then scolded herself for the judgmental thought. She didn't know this woman, she didn't know how busy she was, or that she'd done it to be rude at all. Perhaps, she was used to each place setting up their own displays.

Sophie stepped back and took a look at her finished display. It was almost perfect but lacking something. A vital element she'd left out but couldn't put her finger on exactly what it needed.

Sophie vaguely felt like this feeling was a recurring theme in her life. Almost perfect but not quite. Her life ever since she left that terrible place she'd been adopted into was just that, almost perfect but not quite. Perhaps she was doomed to live that sort of mediocre existence, the same one she'd been born into, adopted into, and now thrust into after fleeing the house she'd been adopted into. Sophie stared at the table as she thought of all the ways her life had never been quite as spectacular as she'd hoped.

For years, she dreamed that the little boy from the orphanage would come and rescue her. They'd ride off into the sunset together. The musings of a silly little girl. The one who would always need a man to save her, according to Sister Meredith.

Ironically enough, men hadn't done anything but throw her life so completely off track she'd had to pick up and start over, multiple times, from square one.

Flowers! That's what the table needs. The covers of the books had been adorned with beautiful watercolor flowers. It only made sense to include them on the table. Sophie pulled her light jacket on and told Felicity she'd be right back, that she had to run to the florist down the street.

"Okay! Be safe!" Felicity shouted from the store room where the rest of the display books were being held.

"Be back soon, mom!" she said as she opened the glass door and started heading down the street.

Moving the tables had distracted her long enough for her headache to resolve by whichever one of her many treatments had worked. She stood in the bright, morning sunlight for a moment, taking in the vitamin D the sun gave her, before heading left towards the flower shop.

It was a cute little mom n' pop shop that had been around for ages. Carson's Carnations was the perfect place to get the flowers she needed. As she approached the building, the sign reminded her it'd been around for exactly 79 years.

The paint had long since peeled away, revealing the graying wooden sign underneath. Founded in 1942 by Kitty and Reginald Carson, now run and operated by their daughter, Lori. Every so often, Sophie would see Kitty and Reginald stop by when she came to get her weekly bouquet for the library. Something about a fresh vase of flowers made the aging library feel a little homier to Sophie. Felicity didn't mind either, and Sophie had even gotten compliments on the flowers she picked out.

"Good morning, Lori! How are you doing today?" Sophie asked as she perused the rows of bouquets on the display floor.

"I'm doing well. How about yourself, Sophie?" the portly woman behind the counter asked as she smiled at the cute blonde, her face almost split in half from the wide grin she gave so freely to all of her customers. Lori was such a sweetheart.

"Same. We're having a book signing for Scarlett Phoenix today, so I figured some flowers would look nice on the display table; something small that won't take too much attention away from the books."

"How about this one?" Lori held up a small bouquet of forget me nots twisted with chamomile and other bright green foliage to fill in the empty spaces.

"Her books have more red in the covers. Got anything red or pink?"

Lori held up a finger and waddled into the back room where she assembled all the bouquets and brought out a small, but gorgeous bouquet of red, pink, and white carnations. "This one?" she asked but knew she didn't have to once she saw Sophie's face.

"They're perfect!" the blonde squealed as she held her hands out to take the flowers. Sophie held the flowers up to her nose and inhaled the sweet floral scent. Fresh flowers were her favorite smell. "How much do I owe you?"

"Ten dollars even, my dear."

Sophie handed the bill to the florist and left a tip in her tip jar. "Thanks, Lori! Come by the library if you wanna meet Scarlett and pick up a book or two, yeah?" Sophie waved at the woman behind the counter when she got to the door, then left the small shop. She took a right and headed back toward the library.

The early morning rush of traffic was just starting. Cars were zooming past her as she walked down the sidewalk. She passed a bus stop, one she often used if she needed to head downtown, then by a large telephone pole with layers and layers of flyers stapled to it. All the layers were so thick, it made it to where she couldn't see the original wood of the pole where it was within reach of having a flyer pinned to it. Sophie always saw things like that as artwork. All the colors blended together in different shapes; it was like the stuff they put in museums and called it all abstract.

She was drawn for a moment by a flyer about a missing puppy. She studied it, trying to commit it to memory just in case she saw the little dog anywhere. She pulled out her phone and snapped a picture of it. *Just in case*, she thought as she slipped her phone into her back pocket.

Sophie looked up just as she was about to start walking towards the library again, but a dark figure with a familiar silhouette on the other side of the street caught her attention out of the corner of her eye. She whipped her head to the left to find the shadowy figure, but a car passed and when she was able to see the sidewalk again there was no one there.

She knitted her brows together in confusion. She was sure there was someone there just a second ago. She watched the sidewalk for a moment and looked down either side - finding nothing out of place - before resuming her walk.

She walked faster than she had before. She wasn't exactly sure what she'd seen, so why had it frightened her so much? Why was it driving her adrenaline levels through the roof? Why was her heart about to pound out of her rib cage? Sophie felt as though the figure was breathing down her neck. Her strides became longer, and she was surprised to find herself almost running back to the library.

When she made it back she was out of breath from the exertion of her almost running for as long as she had. Sophie was not what one would consider athletic. She was only thin because her metabolism had decided to make her that way. She assumed it would slow as she got older, and she'd fill out a bit more in time.

She was just about to set the flowers down on the central desk when her phone rang and buzzed in her pocket, making her jump. She held a hand over her heart for a moment before she pulled the phone from her pocket. "Theo" blinked on her screen as the phone buzzed again. She pressed the answer button and held it to her ear.

"Hello, this is Sophie." *Ugh, too formal. You know it's him! What's wrong with you?!*

"Hey, it's Theo!"

"Oh, hey. Sorry, didn't check caller ID before I answered. How are you?" Sophie internally rolled her eyes at herself. *Idiot.*

"I'm feeling alright after all those drinks, which is outstanding. How are you feeling, though? I think you had the most of anyone." Theo chuckled into her ear, sending goosebumps erupting down her arms. Flashes of them dancing, laughing, and drinking played across her memory.

"Better after some aspirin," Sophie replied as she giggled. Felicity caught her eye and mouthed a question, which Sophie couldn't understand. Sophie waved her hand at the green-eyed woman as if to shush her and shoo her away so she could focus on her phone call.

"Good, good. Well, beautiful, I was wondering if you'd like to come to lunch with me this afternoon. I'm off at one o'clock and I was hoping you'd join me for a bite, to make up for your hangover. What do you say?"

Sophie was thrilled he was asking but nervous to be alone with the man. In the time she'd spent with him up to that point, there had been buffers. Buffers named Cage and Felicity, to be specific. Could she handle being alone with him? Would she clam up? Like she was now? *Shit! Answer him!* "Yeah, sure. That sounds great. You wanna pick me up at the library?" Sophie asked in her best flirty voice.

Felicity beamed at her, understanding finally who had called and what they wanted. She pumped her fists triumphantly in the air as she watched Sophie struggle not to laugh out loud.

"Sounds good. See you soon, gorgeous."

Sophie blushed as she squeaked out a goodbye before hanging up.

"Was that Theo?!" Felicity asked a little too loudly. She got an angry glare from one of the patrons who was quietly reading one of the books set up on display. "Sorry!" Felicity whisper-yelled to the patron as she gave an apologetic wave.

"Yeah, he's gonna pick me up at one for lunch. That okay? I won't be long. Maybe half an hour?" Sophie asked cautiously. The event was supposed to start at two o'clock. She had to make sure she was back by then to help Felicity control the crowd.

"Of course! Ugh, you guys are so cute! Obviously, you'll have to let me know how it goes."

"I promise, I will."

The two librarians giggled quietly with each other until it was time for Theo to pick Sophie up at one. Ever the gentleman, he opened every door for her as he led her out of the library to his car. Some fancy new sportscar she couldn't remember the name of. He'd mentioned it last night, but she couldn't pick out the exact name from the fuzzy memory. Too much alcohol.

Besides, cars had never really fascinated her the way old literature had. She was a full-on nerd for the Bronte sisters and Dickens. One of her most prized possessions was an early copy of Mary Shelley's *Frankenstein* from 1892. She could picture the book that sat on its own special stand on her shelf. The corners were worn and bent. Some of the pages had holes in the edges. Sophie loved and cherished it all the same. There was a sort of camaraderie between her and the worn book. She felt like if she were a book she would look the same way, old and beat up from her rough history.

The pair engaged in meaningless small talk on the way to the restaurant that when they pulled up had made Sophie feel like she wasn't quite dressed up enough for. She pushed the thought out of her mind and followed Theo inside. They were quickly seated by a woman in a white blouse who had short black hair and piercing brown eyes that she'd tried to soften with her smile.

"What can I get you two to drink?" she asked kindly, using her best customer service voice.

Theo looked at Sophie and waited for her to order first. Sophie looked back at the woman and asked for water.

Theo, on the other hand, requested a mimosa. When Sophie gave him a funny look, he simply replied with, "Hair of the dog," and smiled brightly at the blonde sitting across from him. When the waitress left to go get their drink, Theo tossed another smile Sophie's way and began to speak. "I'm really glad you came out last night, Felicity had said it'd be a long shot. That you don't go out much. Can I ask why?"

"Would you be offended if I said men?" Sophie asked as she peered into his brown gaze, looking for any hint of aggression or anger there.

"No, honestly that would not surprise me at all. A beautiful woman like you is bound to get a lot of unwanted attention, unfortunately."

"So, you get it," Sophie chuckled as she looked down at her intertwined fingers.

"It's sad. Men nowadays can't ever seem to understand the word no. I'm sorry you've had to deal with that." The sincerity that filled his voice made Sophie wish it made a difference.

Sophie simply nodded in agreement, hoping he'd change the subject. She didn't have to hope for long before he seemed to read her mind. "So, tell me more about you. We didn't get to talk much last night with Felicity and Cage there."

"What do you want to know? I'm an open book," she said as she sent a tight smile his way. That was a lie. She was far from it, and she knew he could sense it.

"How did you get into literature?" Straight for her passion.

Sophie was shocked by the question. That meant he had paid attention to the things she'd mentioned at the dinner party. He must have if he'd really just asked about her love of literature. "Well, Felicity actually got me into it as a kid."

"Oh, I didn't know you knew each other before you started working at the library."

"We were at St. John's together for a number of years. Orphans usually tend to stick together in those kinds of places. She really took me under her wing. Taught me how to read and really kick-started my love for books and literature. One day, she brought home a book called *Frankenstein*. She'd refused for a few days to read it to me because she thought it would scare me."

"The classic *Frankenstein*? By Mary Shelley?" Theo questioned as he leaned in closer, clearly engrossed in the conversation.

Sophie nodded. Just then the waitress dropped off their drinks and took their orders. Sophie got the house salad, while Theo got a gourmet burger.

Once the woman walked away, Theo's attention was right back on Sophie, awaiting an answer to his earlier question. "Yeah, the classic. Eventually she read my annoying, younger self the book and I was in love. Couldn't get enough. Once I really learned to read by myself, I started reading them all. *The Great Gatsby*, *Great Expectations*, *To Kill a Mockingbird*. All of them. Books were a way of escaping reality for me, especially after I got adopted when I was nine."

Sophie could tell Theo wanted to pry, but he'd been intercepted by the waitress bringing out their food. Most of the rest of the lunch was silent. They knew they had to hurry and eat because Sophie was due to be back at the library soon.

Once finished, Theo set a few bills on the table and let the waitress know she could keep the change for a tip. Surely their meal could not have cost $80. *That's what he set on the table. Was he flaunting his money on purpose?* Trying to appeal to a possible gold-digging side of Sophie that really honestly didn't exist. Money had never been important to her. You made it and you spent it. Everyone did. Some just had more to spend was all.

Sophie was unimpressed but was polite as he smiled at her, and she smiled back. She let him lead her with his hand just above the small of her back, warming her skin through her shirt. He, again, opened each door for her from the restaurant all the way back to the library.

"Thank you for coming to lunch with me. I hope we can do this again, soon." His voice was smooth and confident. Sophie could tell he was sure he'd wooed her by the smile that covered his face when he thought she wasn't looking. She stood on her tippy toes and pressed a chaste kiss to his cheek and muttered a quick "thank you" before going back inside the library. She waved at him from her spot at her desk and he waved back, a silly smile plastered across his face. *He is a pretty sweet guy*, Sophie decided, even if he did think she was materialistic.

4

Todd stood at the stove, preparing breakfast for himself, when Angel walked into the firehouse kitchen. "Smells good," he said as he dramatically sniffed the air and sat at the breakfast bar.

"Prosciutto, mushroom, and gruyere omelet. Want one?" Todd glanced behind him at Angel to await his answer.

"Please!" Angel almost begged. The smell was heavenly, he could only imagine what it tasted like. "Anyone made coffee yet?"

"Yeah, fresh just a couple minutes ago. I'm usually the only one up this early, not many other guys like getting up at five in the morning."

"There's nothing wrong with it, right? I've had enough salty coffee to last a lifetime." Angel narrowed his eyes in suspicion. Jonas had been the one who contaminated his coffee the first time, but that didn't necessarily mean Todd was off the hook.

"No, I didn't mess with it. Promise." Todd's eyes shifted to the floor before they turned back to the omelet he was cooking.

A pang of guilt settled in Angel's chest. He hadn't meant to make Todd feel bad. "I'm sorry, man. Everyone has been messing with me. I know it's supposed to all be a joke, but you can only handle so much, you know?"

"The only reason I'm not still going through it is because you came on. Fresh meat," Todd flipped the omelet as he gave a resentful chuckle, as if those were the exact words his crewmates had used to describe him.

"I'm sorry, I didn't know." The guilt grew and began to take over Angel's whole body. He shouldn't have said anything about the damn pranks.

"If it helps, I know how much it sucks. So, I haven't pulled any." Todd slipped the omelet out of the pan and onto a plate, which he handed to Angel.

"Thanks, I appreciate it."

"The food or the pranks?"

"Both."

"Well, you're welcome."

When Todd sat down at the bar with his own omelet, the pair fell into easy conversation. Angel was so relieved to not have to worry about every single member of their crew pulling tricks at all hours of the day. Even though Todd was just one person, Angel was happy to feel safe around him.

Angel found that in the weeks following his conversation with Todd, the pranking lessened more and more each day. Angel had tried his best to not let each trick they pulled do much more than surprise him for a few seconds. Perhaps his crewmates had gotten bored with the less severe reactions and therefore were starting to leave him alone. He sincerely hoped so.

Angel sat with his parents at the dining room table as they ate the surprisingly common grandiose dinner his mom had cooked for them. He liked the food that they cooked at the station, but nothing compared to his mother's cooking: Slow-cooked pot roast with just enough fat on it that the flavor was intensified, garlic mashed potatoes with a gravy made from the roast, roasted Brussel's sprouts, a carrot-broccoli-cauliflower sauté that only Camille Harris could make, homemade buttermilk biscuits, with blackberry jam that Angel helped can years ago, and some fresh iced tea.

Angel wondered how his mother was able to make such amazing dishes daily, even though she'd picked up a part-time job a few years ago to help Angel not have to go into student loan debt. He truly owed them the world.

He looked around at the dining room and couldn't help but smile. He'd eaten dinner in that room almost every day for nearly twenty years, and he thought of each day as a blessing. Lester caught him looking around and chuckled to himself.

"So, Angel, how's the apartment hunt going?" his father asked.

Angel, slightly embarrassed, snapped out of his reverie. "Well, one of the crew needs a place, too. His name's Todd. He and his girlfriend want to move in together, but she's in school to be a nurse and he can't afford to support them both in their own apartment. So, we decided to pool our resources and rent a little house on the outskirts of the city near the fire station."

Camille shot Lester a smirk while Angel spread jam onto his biscuit. "Oh, honey! That sounds amazing. Have you already put in the application?" his mom asked. He could tell by her tone that they must have both been excited for him to finally move out.

He'd lived there since he was adopted and all the way through college. He couldn't blame them. Every parent he'd ever known was ready for their kids to move out the second they went to college; his were kind enough not to express it out loud. But he was determined to move out so that his mom could stop working and start doing what she loved to do before...even if he never quite knew what it was to begin with.

"Yeah, we put in for it yesterday. They said we were the first ones, so hopefully we will get it."

"How could they not? Two firefighters and a nurse!"

"Studying to be a nurse."

"Yeah, yeah. Will you let me help decorate?" Camille asked with a raised eyebrow and slight grin.

"Of course, mama." With his parents satisfied that he'd be moving out soon, they fell silent as they ate.

It only took a week to get approved and be handed the keys to move in. Camille was ecstatic. Angel and Todd were excited, but nothing could compare to Angel's mother's enthusiasm for making sure her son's first place was absolutely perfect for him. She'd gone so far as to convince the landlord to let her paint the shutters and front door a "better color than the baby shit green" they were when Angel and Todd had signed the lease.

To Angel's surprise, she hadn't gone nuts with the inside of the house. She kept everything neutral and homey, a lot like a model home he'd seen on TV. The kitchen, living room, and dining room were all open to each other, which Angel knew his mom loved. There was nothing better than an open floor plan to Camille Harris.

Angel watched as she walked around, looking at the area from different angles and tapping her chin and taking notes in a small notepad.

"Alright, boys. You'll need a couch, a love seat, an accent chair, both a coffee and dining room table, a couple end tables, at least two rugs, and some little decorative accents that I can pick out. Let's go shopping!"

Angel and Todd kindly opted out but offered up Todd's girlfriend, Melody, as a volunteer. Luckily enough for them, she was happy to go. As the two women left, Todd and Angel got to work unloading their personal items from the moving truck they'd packed all their belongings into.

Angel set up his bed, dresser, and desk in his bedroom. It was the smaller of the two bedrooms in the house, but Angel didn't mind giving the couple more space. He didn't need much anyways.

He unpacked his clothes into his dresser and his toiletries into the bathroom. He was just about to start on setting up his computer when he heard his mom and Melody return from their shopping adventure. He rushed out to the living room to see them carrying in dining room chairs.

"Don't be shy, go help Todd with the couch." Camille Harris was a force to be reckoned with. Angel was glad she was on his team in life. Without missing a beat, Angel and Todd unloaded the rest of the furniture and décor Camille and Melody had purchased.

They unpacked for the rest of the evening and ordered pizza once they were done. Angel sat at the table as he sipped his beer and munched on his pepperoni pizza. Todd and Melody had excused themselves a few minutes earlier, leaving Angel alone in the dining room area.

He looked around, taking in the sights of his new home. It would definitely take some getting used to, not being in the comfort of the bedroom that had been his ever since he was adopted. His parents were at least nice enough to let him take the furniture with him, but he had a feeling that was because his mom had wanted to redecorate the newly empty space once he left.

He'd done it. He'd moved out. He was renting his own place with his own roommate. Angel felt the pride swell in his chest. He'd graduated, gotten his dream career started, got his own place. He was making it. He chuckled as he realized he could finally think of himself as a *real adult*. The kind of adult that worked and lived independently. He couldn't help the grin that broke out on his face.

Angel looked around the room again. There was only one thing missing. His own girlfriend. The thought wiped his smile away. He was happy for Todd and Melody, who'd been together for a while before moving in together. He felt that little green monster sneak into his mind every now and again. He wanted someone to love and to love him back.

One step at a time, man, he reminded himself. *It'll come eventually.* Angel finished his beer and tossed his empty plate in the sink. He walked to his bedroom and flopped back onto his bed, which he sank into. His last thought before falling asleep was, *you made it!*

"Sooophieee!" Felicity sang out into the library from the office where she was supposed to be working on the accounting for the library. Sophie smiled and rose from her chair. Just as she stepped out from behind the central desk, Felicity called out to her again.

"Coming!" Sophie shouted back and quickly jogged to the office. "What's up?" she asked as she popped her head in and spied Felicity sitting at the desk, her head bent over a small stack of papers.

"Come in, sit," she said as she gestured towards the chair across the desk from her. Sophie did as she was told but couldn't help the anxiety that started pumping through her body. Had she made a mistake? Was she in trouble? She couldn't pinpoint any mistakes she'd made recently, which made her heart pump even harder.

"Did I do something wrong?" Sophie asked, her voice wavering slightly. She'd never been one to deal well with conflict. She supposed it was likely because of her childhood. Any time anyone did anything wrong, they all got in trouble, especially if she and her other adopted siblings fought with each other. Sophie learned quickly to avoid any types of conflict by becoming invisible and working hard to make sure everything was taken care of without having to be asked.

"What? No. I wanted to ask you something," Felicity said as she smiled excitedly. Sophie's tensed shoulders relaxed as she waited for Felicity's question. "I just wanted to know what you're doing in exactly seventy-five days?"

"I have no idea, why?"

"Because... I was wondering... if you'd..." Felicity started, her voice anxious, like she was searching for the right words to say. "Liketobemymaidofhonor?" She finished in a rush to get the words out in whatever way they might come. It was almost like she could feel Sophie's own reservations about having to stand in front of a crowd and make a toast and be in a crowd that big in general. Sophie wrestled with the decision in her head silently for a moment while Felicity waited impatiently twiddling her fingers. "Theo is gonna be the Best Man, if that helps at all?" she offered, knowing why Sophie was hesitating on giving an answer.

Sophie chuckled; she knew there was no way she could say no. She'd do it for the amazing, strong, generous woman in front of her, pleading silently for her to say yes. Sophie nodded as she replied, "Yes, of course I will. I'd do anything for you, Felicity."

What was expected of her? Did she have to give a speech? Did she need to plan anything? What was she going to do if she had to give a speech? She didn't know anything about Cage's family, what if she had to talk to them? What had she just agreed to?

Felicity wrapped her arms tightly around Sophie's shoulders and squeezed. "Thank you so much, Soph. I don't know if I could be in front of all those people without you next to me," Felicity said quietly into Sophie's ear.

Tears filled Sophie's eyes. She couldn't not be there for her best friend. The only person who'd truly cared about her, ever. The person who still cared every day. She knew that if she ever got married, Felicity would be her Maid of Honor. There was no one else. No bridesmaids. Just Felicity. Felicity and Sophie against the world. And soon, it'd be Sophie, Felicity, and Cage against the world. She could not have been happier for her friend but fighting off the anxious thoughts of what was to come would be a battle she had to win, for Felicity's sake.

5

Another long day of returning books to shelves and helping the elderly navigate computers had wiped Sophie out. She was completely exhausted. The visitor count in the library had picked up since Scarlett Phoenix's book signing event, something Sophie was glad for but also secretly hated. Big crowds meant fielding more questions, putting away more books, and more angry patrons who couldn't check out that one book they'd been looking forward to reading. If one more person complained about not being able to find a book by the time she had clocked out, she thought she might've exploded.

Sophie sat at the bus stop, waiting. She was looking forward to her bus ride home, where she could plug in her headphones and tune out the world. She just needed a break from all the noise of the city. Just a few more minutes and she'd be officially on her way home. Carla was never late.

She couldn't help but feel the same prickling at the back of her neck as she waited. Sophie studied the street and sidewalk around her. Nothing seemed off. So, why was her body acting like she was about to be devoured by an invisible predator? She glanced behind her towards the library.

A familiar figure in a dark jacket and a baseball hat covering his face stood out at once to her. She whipped her head around, looking away from the darkly clad man. When she looked back, she saw him again. But he didn't look the same. His jaw was more rounded and his hair a lighter shade of brown. It had to be someone else. It was definitely not the same man from the bar, the same man who had followed her from across the street.

Her hammering heart began to slow at the realization that it was a different person. At least, she was fairly sure it was. She was sure enough to stay right where she was and wait for Carla and her big, dark blue bus.

Carla's contagious smile did make her feel better after the exhausting day and terrifying encounter at the bus stop. Sophie couldn't help but shoot her a quick smile back. She sat in her usual spot on the bus and put on her headphones. She scrolled through her music, waiting for Carla to take off. When she didn't Sophie glanced up at the front of the bus to make sure no one was harassing her favorite bus driver.

To Sophie's absolute horror, it was the man who she'd been seeing around town entirely too often for it to not be on purpose. He kept his face hidden from her view with his dark hat. He took a seat at the back of the bus, behind Carla. Sophie watched intently; her music forgotten. He pulled a newspaper out of his dark bomber jacket and brought it up, covering the rest of his face.

The blood pulsed in Sophie's ears, making the headphones uncomfortable. She ripped them out of her ears and shoved them in her bag. She swallowed, hard, trying to get the lump of fear out of her throat. What could possibly be making this man follow her? She was the most uninteresting person in the world. She literally went to work and went home. Occasionally, she would go out with Felicity. That was it! Why would anyone want to follow her? The thoughts raced through her mind as she tried to solve the mystery of the man following her. She ran through every possibility imaginable by the time Carla pulled the bus up to her stop.

She contemplated not getting off and just taking the bus all the way to the garage and asking if Carla could drive her home. She decided that she didn't want to burden the bus driver, though. If he were any sort of danger to Sophie, she couldn't live with herself if something were to happen to Carla. Stalkers could be unpredictable; impossible to know how serious their obsessions were and just how far they would take things. No. Sophie couldn't endanger Carla, too. She just needed to get herself home safely.

She rushed off the bus at the last second hoping he wouldn't have time to follow her, but the man made it through the doors just in time. Sophie did the only thing she could think of to get away from him as quickly as possible.

She sprinted into the street, in the middle of traffic. Drivers laid on their horns, making her eardrums ring. She knew she must have scared the wits out of them, seemingly appearing from nowhere right in front of them. One car's tires squealed as they came to a stop just before hitting her.

Sophie just kept running. She ran until she reached the front door of her apartment building. When she turned to look for the man, she was relieved she didn't see him.

Once inside her apartment, she secured all of the locks on her door and finally let her body relax. She rolled her shoulders to try to release the tension created by the fear of seeing the man who'd been following her.

What was she going to do about this? Was there anything the police would do? Probably not. She'd heard horror stories of women being told that there was nothing the police could do because the stalker hadn't done anything. Yet. Sophie didn't want it to get to the 'yet' part. Cops were off the table.

What about Theo? He was a professional security guard. *An expensive one, considering his car and clothing. Okay, Theo is out too.* Sophie couldn't afford anything like that. Not to mention that she didn't even know if this guy was dangerous. And she barely knew him. She wasn't about to just drop all of her problems on him, that'd scare him away. *He'll end up leaving anyway once he learns everything. Ugh. No. Not the time for that.* Sophie rubbed her temples as she plopped into her recliner. *Not Theo.*

Perhaps Cage would have some advice for her? Like a free consultation? Sophie would have to find a way to make sure Felicity didn't overhear the conversation, though. She'd make Cage put a full security detail on her 24/7 and that was the opposite of what Sophie wanted. She just wanted to keep herself safe. That was it. Was that too much to ask?

She rolled her neck from side to side, releasing more of the tension that had continued to build in her muscles. *Having a safe and normal life shouldn't be this hard.*

She jumped a mile into the air when her phone rang, alerting her that someone had wanted to get ahold of her. *Who would even be calling me right now?* Sophie wondered. She picked up her phone and was surprised to see Theo's name crossing her screen as the phone rang. Sophie didn't have the energy to answer and pretend to be okay. She let it go to voicemail. She tossed her phone onto her bed but winced when it ended up bouncing off and hitting the floor. *Of course.*

Sophie made up her mind. She'd talk to Cage once she could get him alone for a minute. She didn't want Felicity mothering her about anything. Felicity was busy enough as it was, running the library, planning a wedding, and being the most amazing best friend there ever was. Sophie probably would have died if she hadn't met Felicity again. She wouldn't ever be able to repay her.

Sophie didn't have it in her to make an actual meal. She tossed a frozen dinner in the microwave and restlessly waited for it to be ready. She just wanted to go to bed. She was so tired it was making her entire body feel heavy. The adrenaline had cleared her system, leaving her dead tired. She almost fell asleep waiting for her food to get done heating up. Luckily, the high pitched beeping of the microwave woke her up just enough to eat the bland, moderately nourishing food.

With a full belly and an achingly tired body, she got in bed and curled up under the covers. Sleep came swiftly.

The next morning Sophie was awoken by her alarm. She felt as if she hadn't even slept. She usually only felt like that when her sleeping mind was plagued with nightmares of her childhood. She couldn't recall having any dreams at all. She rolled onto her back after turning her alarm off and stared at the plain white ceiling of her studio. The warm, morning sunlight streamed in her window, slowly helping her body adjust to waking. She grabbed the remote from her bedside table and turned on the small television.

She liked watching the news in the morning, mainly to see what the weather would be like. She really liked the chipper anchor, as well. The woman had deep umber skin and a gorgeous head of silky curls. What Sophie would do for curls that had some structure like that. Ever since she first cut her hair short as a kid, her curls had grown back uneven - wavy in some spots and spiraled in others.

Sophie's heart lurched as she remembered the night before. She looked to her front door, checking the locks. All still in place. She took a deep breath, trying to calm her nerves. It didn't work very well. She checked the time on her phone before dropping it on the table next to her bed. A quick shower was just what she needed to get her mind off of everything for a little bit.

She wrapped her hair up in a towel and put on a little makeup.

Theo had called her last night. She was sure he'd be dropping by the library since she didn't answer. He seemed like the type to check in on someone who doesn't answer. Caring. Felicity always told her she needed someone who cared about her. Sophie would usually reply with a quip about her and Felicity getting married instead of Felicity and Cage, because Felicity *definitely* cared. They'd end up in a fit of giggles, as always.

Sophie unwrapped her hair and used a large round brush to blow dry it, section by section. She'd watched a lot of YouTube videos about how to do your own blow out, like what they did in salons after haircuts to make your hair look extra perfect. She'd gotten rather good at it over the last few years.

That'll do, pig.

She made sure that she was dressed by the time she had to leave to catch the bus. Unfortunately, Carla wasn't her morning bus driver. It was usually one of two people. Isaiah, a younger man who was rather uninterested in everything. Very monotonous. Sophie didn't mind him. He wasn't creepy. Just completely apathetic. About everything.

Then, there was Lilah. Lilah was a former southern-belle and pageant winner. Sophie never did find out just how she'd found herself in Chicago, though. All she would talk about is all her trophies. That, or she'd be yelling at the kids on their way to school to 'Quit makin' such a ruckus on my bus before I make ya walk right alongside it.' Sophie usually got a kick out of how heavy her accent came out when she got mad at passengers, but she did not like when she yelled at the kids. It triggered the same shame and guilt she'd feel when the nuns at the orphanage would yell at her.

Sophie hoped Isaiah was the driver today. She didn't know if she could handle Lilah that morning. She was still so tired from the day before. Sophie pulled on her sneakers, specially worn just in case she needed to run home from the bus stop again.

She stopped at the entry doors to her apartment building and looked out to the bus stop. It was deserted. Just how she'd hoped it would be. She took her normal route to the stop, her head on a swivel the whole time. No sign of the man she'd been followed by yesterday. She let out a sigh of relief.

She let out another when she saw Isaiah pull up to the bus stop. "Morning," she said quietly to the young man in the driver's seat. His dull, brown eyes blinked once at her before he turned back to face the windshield. Sophie took her seat silently and waited for the bus to take off.

She pulled out her phone and absent-mindedly checked her emails. All junk. Spam. She deleted them all. By the time she'd finished, they were pulling into her stop. She looked out the window before getting off the bus to make sure the coast was clear.

She made it into the front door of the library without incident. She tried her best to look calm and unafraid. Felicity could usually pinpoint exactly how she was feeling just from looking at her. She put a happy face on as she walked up to the central desk to take her seat. "Morning Felicity!" she said cheerfully as she sat in her chair.

Felicity hardly looked up from whatever she was bent over. "Mornin' Soph." Her short reply caught Sophie off guard. Felicity wasn't usually so short with her.

"You okay?" Sophie asked as she clocked in for the day and put her bag away in the locking drawer at the bottom of her desk.

"The rehearsal dinner is this weekend and I feel like it's going to go horribly. I don't have any food picked out yet, and Cage is too busy with work, and I don't even know what to wear!" Felicity unloaded as she turned toward Sophie. She had tears in her panicked eyes and her cheeks had started turning pink.

"It's at that little Italian spot right? Giano's? They have amazing lasagna, with or without meat and the best desserts. Can't beat a good cannoli."

"That's such a great idea Sophie! You're such a lifesaver. I don't know what I'd do without you."

"Who all is coming?"

"Cage and I, obviously. George and Martha, Mrs. Arlington, and Cage's parents. Small. I don't think I could handle anything big right now. I never thought planning a wedding would be so hard and time consuming."

"Isn't Cage helping?" Sophie asked. She'd always thought he'd be incredibly involved in planning their wedding, but she could have been wrong. He just didn't seem like the type to leave everything to Felicity.

"He is, he's just been really busy with his clients the last couple weeks. We're finally going out on a date for the first time since we did that double date at the bar. He's taking me to this new pizza place down the street for lunch. Oh! You can come if you want to?"

"No, no. You enjoy your alone time. I can handle myself for an hour."

"Okay, if you're sure. I'll bring you some. I know you love pizza."

This is why we're best friends, Sophie thought. "Thanks," she said as she turned to her computer and started on the work for the day.

The clock dragged as Sophie waited for Cage to arrive to take Felicity to lunch. She was hoping to catch him for a minute and talk to him about her potential stalker issue. Noon finally rolled around, and a familiar figure walked in the front door of the library. Cage smiled when he saw Felicity and sent a friendly wave to Sophie. "Hello, ladies. Felicity, you ready for lunch?" he asked.

"Almost, just gotta finish unloading that cart really fast, then we can go." Felicity pointed to an almost empty cart on the other side of the desk.

Sophie wanted to stop her and offer to do it so she could leave and go to lunch, but then she wouldn't get the minute alone with Cage. She waited for Felicity to walk away before saying anything. "Hey Cage, can I ask you a question?"

"Of course. What's up? Are you okay?" Concern painted his handsome face, dimming the shining of his blue eyes.

"You can't tell Felicity. We both know how much she'd freak out, but there's this guy. I think he's been following me. I've seen him a couple of times now. I just wanted to know if you had any advice to try to get him to leave me alone?"

"Wow, are you sure he hasn't done anything but follow you?"

"Pretty sure. I've only seen him a few times, I just wanna try to shake him, you know? Make sure he doesn't find out where I live."

"Do you take the same route home every day?" he asked.

"Oh, I probably shouldn't, huh?" Sophie felt a pit in her stomach. That is probably how he knew to get on and off the bus at the same time as her. She took the same bus down the same route and walked the same way every day.

"That's the easiest thing. If you're not comfortable with taking the bus, I could always have one of the guys give you a ride home. I'm sure Theo wouldn't mind."

"No! Don't tell Theo either. I can handle it. I'm probably just being paranoid. I'll just change up my route and I doubt I'll see him again." Sophie tried to brush it off, like it hadn't been scaring the living hell out of her for weeks. If Cage could tell she was that nervous, he'd tell Felicity he was worried, then his whole company would be assigned to Sophie's detail. She wouldn't be able to go anywhere without someone attached to her at all times. Sophie was not about to live that way.

"Okay, if you change your mind the offer stands. Let me know if anything else happens, okay? I'm fairly good at my job, you know," he joked, letting it go.

Sophie smiled at him, trying to reassure him that she would be fine. "Alright Mr. Bodyguard."

Felicity came back just as they ended their conversation. "Ready to go?" she asked as she snaked her arm into Cage's.

"Definitely. I'm starving. I nearly died as you put those books away," he said as they walked out the front door. Sophie watched the door close behind them. She was tempted to go lock it but knew that she'd probably forget, and Felicity would ask questions. She kept her eye on the door as she worked, though, making sure no uninvited guests came in.

Sophie stood in the dressing room, feeling the satin of her Maid of Honor dress softly caress her skin as she twirled the skirt around. The blush colored dress fell to the middle of her calves, a length that was usually unflattering on her shorter than average self but was redeemed by the color and fabric. The pinkish tone brought out the warm undertones in her skin and complemented the flawless, dewy makeup she'd had done at the salon with Felicity earlier that day.

The makeup artist had also styled her hair in starlet waves and pinned one side back, leaving the rest to fall over her opposite shoulder. She studied herself in one of the multiple mirrors that lined the dressing room walls. Felicity had told her she looked like an old-timey Hollywood star. While Sophie, of course, disagreed; she had also been told so by the other salon workers and George. She supposed she fit Felicity's vintage speakeasy themed wedding perfectly.

While Sophie had shocked those around, it was nothing compared to the breath-taking metamorphosis Felicity had undergone. Her shiny, dark hair was pulled back into a low-lying bun that hung loosely just above her shoulders. She'd adorned a crystal encrusted, lace headband and a matching crystal necklace that had a chain that hung down her back, accentuating the backless gown she wore. The silk and lace gown hugged her body in just the right places and hung loosely at her lower back, with a crystal brooch pinning the fabric in place. She looked like a goddess.

Every time someone walked in to wish her luck in her marriage, they were stopped in their tracks and left breathless. Sophie couldn't have hoped for more on Felicity's big day. She had been planning meticulously for months. It would most definitely go off without a hitch.

There was a soft knock on the door. Sophie rushed to it as she'd been placed on guard duty.

Cage had been chomping at the bit to see Felicity and had already tried to sneak in twice, once through the window. He was lucky Felicity was in the bathroom, so no bad luck would befall their marriage because of his impatience. Sophie could understand why he was so anxious. They hadn't gone a night apart until the night before their wedding; which also meant Felicity had slept over at Sophie's.

Because of that, Sophie couldn't sleep. Having someone in her bed had been a difficult experience for her. She couldn't remember the last time she shared a bed with another woman. Probably in that shit-hole she'd been adopted into. Felicity's wedding wasn't the time to think about that place. It was time to have fun. This was a day of celebration! Sophie planned on getting drunk and letting go. *No safer place than with a bunch of elite security guards around, right?*

Upon seeing George's smiling face with Madeleine Arlington, Mr. Arlington's widow, close behind. Sophie ushered them in quickly, checking the hallway to ensure Cage hadn't snuck up behind them. She closed and locked the door once they were safely inside.

"Oh, Felicity. You look absolutely breathtaking, dear!" Mrs. Arlington told her as she gave her a tight hug, careful to avoid her hair and makeup. Once she let go, George gave her a tight squeeze as well.

In a whisper that Sophie was sure she wasn't supposed to overhear, George said something that dampened the mood in the room; "Ya know, John always hoped he'd be the one to walk you down the aisle. Even though I'm the one people are seeing, I know he wouldn't miss this day for nothing."

As he pulled away he let a big grin cover his face. "It's just about time. Are you ready?" George asked as he held her hands in his. Mrs. Arlington wrapped an arm around Felicity's shoulders and pulled her close.

Sophie watched Felicity as she blinked away happy tears and nodded. She'd been especially quiet since they woke up. Sophie could tell she was near tears every time she looked at her. It was a huge day for Felicity, to marry the man she'd fallen so hard for in the months since she'd come home.

In the time leading up to the wedding, Felicity had revealed very little about how she and Cage had met. Since she and Sophie had reconnected, Felicity did let it slip that he'd saved her life many times, in more ways than one, and she his. Sophie had a feeling she meant this literally from the grave tone in her voice each time it had come up.

There was a knock on the door before a cheery, red-headed woman unlocked it and bounced into the room. She had a wide smile stretched across her face. "Sophie, time to get lined up for the procession. Then, Felicity and George. Remember, this is your day, darling. You look gorgeous. He's gonna be knocked right off his feet!"

Sophie heard the quiet notes of a piano floating through the venue. Cage must have been walking up to the altar. Sophie grabbed her bouquet and walked out to her spot. She waited patiently for Theo to arrive, they were set to walk down together, arm in arm.

She peeked around the corner and spied Cage standing at the altar, his face calm but smiling. Sophie wondered how he could be so calm on such a big day, perhaps he had gotten a lot of practice keeping his cool in his profession. Elite security work couldn't be an easy thing, protecting someone's life with your own. Made sense.

Sophie turned as she heard footsteps approaching from behind her. Her gaze was met by Theo's soul-piercing, dark brown eyes. He looked dashing in his freshly pressed tux. He let a smile creep across his face when their eyes met.

"Wow, you look amazing! That color makes you look like a cute, little pixie." Theo pressed a warm kiss to Sophie's cheek. The gesture was not unwelcome but made Sophie's skin prickle. She hardly knew the man, granted they'd been on a few dates but nothing more than that, and he'd just kissed her cheek. They hadn't even kissed for real yet. Maybe he was saving it for later?

"Thanks, I guess. I don't know how most grown women feel about being called pixies, though," Sophie said as she chuckled.

"Well, you're the most beautiful pixie I've ever seen, so hope that makes up for it." Theo offered his elbow to her. "Ready? It's almost our turn."

Sophie smiled before sliding her hand into the crook of his elbow and held up the bouquet in her hand before they set off down the aisle. *Maybe this is a sneak peak of my future? Theo is a good guy*, she thought as they walked toward the altar.

Sophie didn't think she'd cry like she did during Cage and Felicity's vows. It made her heart long for a love like theirs as she listened to them talk about their souls being one. Not just soul mates, but twin flames. One soul split into two at creation, longing for its other half.

She was glad she'd opted for waterproof makeup and a lot of setting spray. She'd never been to a wedding before, so she hadn't thought that she would be so emotional about it. The whole ceremony was beautiful. Not a dry eye in the house as her eyes swept over the small crowd in the church pews.

She hooked her arm in Theo's again to head back up the aisle after Cage and Felicity. The recession was the easy part. She just had to deal with all the people at the reception for the rest of the night. *Easier said than done*, she thought. She felt a warm hand cover hers as Theo stopped just beyond the entrance to the hall where the ceremony had taken place.

"Want a ride to the reception? Felicity mentioned you had taken a cab to get here. It's the least I could do for calling you a pixie earlier." A cheeky grin spread across his face, showing off his pearly-white smile, in contrast with his dark, rich skin. A smile that left Sophie thoroughly dazzled.

She nodded in answer before she could stop herself. Theo was one of the only people she was actually semi-comfortable with, best to just go along with it. "Yeah, let's go. We should leave now to beat the rush there."

"Okay, follow me, mi' lady." Theo laughed as he led Sophie out to the parking lot of the church. He opened the door to his fancy car, of which Sophie still could not remember the name of, and let her sit in the passenger seat and buckle in before closing the door and walking to the driver's side and getting in. "That was such a beautiful ceremony, wasn't it?" Theo asked as he glanced away from the road to Sophie, whose gaze was fixed out the window watching the buildings fly by.

"Mhmm," Sophie agreed. The wedding had stirred up deep and conflicting feelings of happiness and loneliness in her chest. Happiness for her best friend, who'd just married the one for her, but the longing and loneliness burned her heart with its white hot, molten tendrils wrapping around every vessel in her body.

What she wouldn't give to have a love like that; to know someone will always be there for you and never leave or abandon you. Perhaps she could find that in Theo if she'd just open her heart up a little and let him see all the ugliness on the inside, the bruised and broken parts of herself she tried so hard to never share with anyone. She hadn't even shared them with Felicity.

"You okay, Soph?" he asked as he rested his hand over her knee. He could feel her loneliness, the ache in her heart for that kind of connection.

She couldn't remember the last time she'd even considered loving someone. "Yeah, just hope that I get that someday, you know?" The tears welled up in her eyes and she felt her chin tremble. She willed the tears away. Crying would just scare Theo away, leaving her to start all over again from square one. Hell, square zero, square negative five.

"Yeah, me too. They really are a beautiful couple. They fit so well, like pieces of a puzzle. Like they'd always been together. I'm glad he found someone to deal with his grumpy ass." Theo's chuckle rumbled through the car. He loved his friend and was genuinely happy for him, if not a little jealous as well.

He must have the same loneliness, Sophie guessed.

Minutes later, the pair arrived at the reception venue. Only the wedding planner had shown up before them. When she heard Theo's car she rushed outside, which was almost comical. Sophie watched as she took tiny baby steps so fast in her stilettos it made her whole body bounce, her curly red hair was not excluded. It was a wild mess around her face, like she'd been rushing around all day trying to get everything ready, which Sophie had supposed was the case.

"Oh great! You're here early. Come help me set out the last of the chairs!" She demanded. Sophie and Theo followed her into the dining room.

It was all Sophie could do to not gasp audibly when she entered the expansive room. The high vaulted ceilings had three ornate chandeliers hanging in a row, giving the room an ethereal glow, almost like candle light without the flames, casting shadows throughout the room giving it the feel of an old, gothic library.

Sophie walked up to a table and studied the centerpiece. It was a glass stand with a mirrored top that held candles and a small, crystal vase that almost looked like an ornate decanter with a single rose in it. On each table there were similar stands, all were set on top of a stack of aged books. It was breathtaking and perfect. Felicity would love it; Sophie was certain she would.

"Come, come. We don't have long until everyone else arrives. Chairs, please!"

Sophie was ushered towards the small stack of chairs that hadn't been brought out to the tables yet. "Okay, where do they go?" she asked.

"The back corner over there," the wedding planner said as she pointed toward the far corner of the room.

No wonder it wasn't done yet. She'd been trying to do it in those ridiculous heels. Sophie understood why she needed help. Not that Sophie herself would be much more help. She was in the same kind of shoes. Theo however, man-handled four chairs at once, leaving only one for Sophie to carry.

"Show off!" Sophie joked as she followed him to the table in need of seating. Theo lifted the chairs like weights while grunting like they were difficult to curl, making Sophie laugh.

"Gotta show the lady what I'm capable of!"

"Oh, you don't have to show off for me," Sophie scoffed as she set the chair down at the table.

Theo placed the chairs as he replied, "Oh, you thought I was showing off for you? No. No, definitely not. It was for Miss May over there." Theo pointed to the wedding planner mumbling to herself near the cake, placing flowers in just the right places in order to accentuate the artistry that had gone into making it.

The naked cake almost looked like a birch tree with how it was iced. It added a rustic element to the romantic, gothic vibe of the reception hall. Sophie laughed along with him as they watched her fuss with the cake table a little more before the first guests started trickling in.

It wasn't long before the room and tables were full, and Sophie was ushered to sit at the wedding party table with Theo and Cage's parents, George and Martha, and Mrs. Arlington. Music filled the room before the doors opened to reveal the newly wed bride and groom.

Felicity was glowing, like her heart was so full of love it was shining out of her pores. Cage was grinning like an idiot as he led his bride to the table at the front of the room, making sure to go slow so everyone could get a good look at the happy couple. As they passed the wedding party table, Theo reached out his fist and Cage fist bumped it. The perfect bro moment to make everyone laugh.

Dinner was delicious and the cake was even better. Plenty of hilarious, heart-felt toasts later, everyone was drunk and ready to party till all hours of the night and morning. Sophie sat at her seat at the table and watched as Cage and Felicity smiled and danced the night away in the middle of the crowd. She was startled by someone taking the seat next to hers.

"What's a girl like you doing alone?" a woman she didn't recognize asked. She had long, perfectly straight, platinum blonde hair and flawless ivory skin. Sophie wondered why she hadn't noticed her during the ceremony, she was gorgeous and looked like a runway model.

"I could ask you the same..." Sophie raised a curious eyebrow as her voice trailed off into silence, trying to indicate to the woman she should introduce herself.

"Mia, Mia Murphy."

"Murphy as in Cage's family?"

"Yeah, I'm his younger sister. I was late to the ceremony, figured I'd better be on time to the reception. Work stuff, no biggie. He'd understand." The woman flashed a perfectly glittering smile at Sophie. "So, what were you doing over here by yourself again?"

Sophie's cheeks blushed as she thought about what a terrible dancer she was. "Just trying to save myself from some embarrassment is all."

"You think that would matter with Cage out there? I mean, look at him. He's such a dork!" They laughed as they watched him attempt what Sophie thought was dancing. Felicity was cracking up, fully enjoying her new husband's ability to make her laugh.

"Guess you've got a point there. What about you? Why aren't you up there?" Sophie searched the woman's stunning face for an answer.

"Because I'm about as good at dancing as he is, sweetheart. Go enjoy yourself a little. That's what weddings are for." With that Mia left the table after shooting Sophie a flirty wink. Sophie watched her walk back to the bar and start talking to the bartender, a pretty, petite brunette whose cheeks immediately started turning pink as they talked.

Seconds after Mia left, Theo plopped down on the chair she'd left vacant. "What do you say, you up for a dance with me?"

"Surprised you'd still want to dance with me after the club. I'm a terrible dancer."

Theo waved off her self-deprecating remark and grabbed Sophie's hand and pulled her to the dance floor. "You're not a bad dancer. I would know." He pulled her close, their bodies touching as he swayed and rocked her along to the rhythm of the song. "See?" he whispered in her ear. "You're not that bad. Cage stepped on my feet way more than you ever have." He pressed a warm kiss to her neck, just below her ear. The touch made her skin tingle.

Sophie pulled away just enough to look into Theo's eyes. They were glazed over, likely from the freely flowing champagne. *Fuck it,* Sophie thought. *I do need to have a little fun every now and then. Weddings are the perfect time to let go. The perfect time for new romance, maybe.*

Sophie ran her tongue over her bottom lip, keeping her eyes locked on Theo's. But his eyes were certainly not focused on hers. His attention had been drawn lower to Sophie's plump, perfectly glossy and inviting lips. Theo's hand ran up her back and came to rest on her cheek where his thumb brushed her cheekbone. He pulled her lips to his in a gentle kiss. The world melted away and it was just them, lips locked on the dance floor. Even drunk, Theo was an amazing kisser.

They were only brought out of the kiss after getting bumped by a stumbling George. "Oh! So sorry, you two. This champagne is just hitting me hard. Time to see if Martha will drive us home, I think. You two have a good night," he said as he shot them an exaggerated wink.

Sophie's jaw dropped as her cheeks burned in embarrassment. Was it that obvious? "Oh, my God. Did that really just happen?" She asked as she covered her cheeks and buried her face into Theo's muscular chest and tried to disappear from the room. A laugh rumbled in said chest as he wrapped his arms around her, holding her close to him.

"It sure did. At least he's the only one drunk enough to say anything," Theo said quietly into her ear. "I'm definitely not sorry though."

"Me either," Sophie said as she pulled away from the strong arms holding her to the warm, muscular body that was intoxicating her, making her mind go fuzzy and making her want more than she should. Or maybe that was the champagne. Sophie wasn't usually much of a drinker, but it was a night to let go. Perhaps she'd had more than she thought, surely it wasn't Theo making her feel a little dizzy and off-balance. "It's getting late. I should start heading home."

"I wish I were smarter. I would've not had so much to drink so I could drive you home. Felicity is just so good at picking out the most amazing whiskey. At least let me call you an Uber?" Theo asked as he followed her off the dance floor and back to their table.

"Yeah, sure. Thank you." Sophie found Felicity and Cage again after grabbing her small clutch purse. She said a quick good night and thank you. She told Felicity she would see her after the honeymoon. Theo walked her out to the curb where the Uber waited for her.

"I'll see you soon, okay?" he asked as he pressed a kiss to her hand. "Text me when you get home?"

Sophie nodded as she pressed a quick kiss to his cheek. "Thank you. I'll text you when I get home."

"Have a good night, Sophie."

"You too," Sophie said with a wave goodbye as she lowered herself into the car.

7

Trigger Warning: graphic description of rape and child abuse

"Good party?" the Uber driver asked as he glanced in his rearview mirror and caught Sophie's gaze. His light hazel eyes were curious as they searched hers for an answer.

"Yeah, my best friend got married. It was such a beautiful wedding." Her words came out a little more slurred than she'd thought they would. She chuckled at herself and turned to look out the window as they passed building after building. They slowly made their way through the traffic and the city, back to Sophie's apartment building.

"Congrats to your friend. Sounds like it was a good night," he said kindly as he slid his eyes back to the road.

Every once in a while for the remainder of the ride, Sophie felt his eyes on her again and again. She assumed it was because she was still all done up from the wedding. Maybe he thought she was pretty. She thought she looked pretty, nowhere near as gorgeous as Felicity, but she definitely ranked in the pretty category with the hair, makeup, and dress.

Did Theo think so? He did kiss her. *Man, what a kiss it was!* Sophie felt her cheeks heat up more than they already were. He chose not to go home with her, though.

Sophie rolled that thought around in her brain for a bit. Why? They'd been going on dates and getting to know each other for a few months at that point. Why hadn't he even tried? Was he not that interested? Was she not interesting enough? Sophie supposed that was likely the case. She didn't do much besides work and go home.

She could see how Theo wouldn't find her enticing enough to go home with. He was flashy and dazzling on a regular basis. He had an exciting job, where she just worked in a boring library, no action or adventure there. *Unless you count the James Patterson section. Dear Lord, he has so many books.*

Then, there was the fact that Theo drove a gorgeous, fancy, expensive car; Sophie didn't even have a car. She sighed as she rested her forehead on the window, her head felt like it had been weighed down by all the thoughts she couldn't seem to stop.

She yawned and let her eyes slip closed, just for a moment. The feeling of the car rolling down the street had begun to lull her to sleep. She could hear the tires against the pavement below them. She could hear the wind rushing past the car as they crossed an intersection. She felt the bumps in the road jostle her slightly. It was all kind of relaxing. She could fall asleep at any moment if it weren't for the thoughts of Theo racing through her mind. Was she just not good enough? That was usually the case when it came to her relationships.

She felt herself slip into a daydream where everything was perfect. She and Theo were in the kitchen of their gorgeous, sleek, modern house, cooking breakfast in the pristine all white kitchen. He was only in his pajama pants, his glorious, muscular body contoured and highlighted by the morning sunrise streaming in the window. Sophie's arms were wrapped around his waist, her cheek resting against his back as he fried bacon. She could almost smell the bacon mixed with his delicious cologne. She wondered briefly what he wore, his signature scent. He always smelled really good, like expensive man cologne. It probably *was* expensive. Everything about Theo *screamed* expensive.

Sophie was broken out of her daydream by her head bumping on the window when the car jolted over a speed-bump. "Ow," she said quietly as she rubbed her forehead. It could have been worse.

"I'm sorry. I tried to take it gently, but it was a huge pothole," the driver told her as he caught her eyes in the rearview mirror again.

"It's alright, it could be worse. Just bumped my head, is all. Not your fault." Sophie leaned back against the seat. "Are we almost there?" she asked. Sophie was ready to fall into her bed and slip into a deep sleep. She was so tired from the long day mixed with the alcohol and the anxiety caused by wondering what Theo's intentions with their relationship were, if that's what it even was.

"Yeah, GPS says just a couple more minutes."

"Good, it's been a long day..." Sophie yawned again, which only emphasized her point.

The car finally rolled to a stop in front of Sophie's building. She looked up at the brick structure. Her apartment seemed so far away. She sighed as she felt her arms and legs go heavy, like she wore shoes and boxing gloves lined with lead and concrete.

Who knew a wedding would be so exhausting? She should have figured that with all the people and the interacting with them that she had to do, she would be tired. Not to mention the shoes and the waking up early for hair and makeup and all the prep that crazy-haired lady made her help with. It was a day full of everything that made her anxious. People touching her and talking to her and directing her on what to do and where to go and how to do all of it.

"Thanks for the ride," she said quietly as she opened the car door and yawned. Her feet ached as her high heels met the concrete. She reached behind her to grab her small purse off the seat and turned to stand and step up onto the curb, but the toe of her shoe caught the concrete edge and she stumbled forward. She nearly fell to her hands and knees but caught herself just before her face met the sidewalk.

The driver rushed out of the car and to her side. He held her forearm and curled an arm around her waist, holding her steady against him until she was standing upright. "Are you okay?" concern laced his voice. He let go of her arm and waist but kept his hands out, ready to catch her in case she tripped again.

Sophie thought it was sweet of him to care, but that she was an idiot for tripping like that. *Damn heels.* Sophie couldn't wait to get to her apartment and take them off. "Yeah, just these shoes. I don't wear heels too often. I'm like a baby deer," she said as she chuckled and tried to make light of her situation. She could feel her cheeks warm as the man studied her face.

She noticed for the first time that he was wearing a baseball cap. It was darkly colored, and that realization poked at the back of her mind, making her feel a little wary about the man holding her upright.

"I'm okay really. Just the shoes and a little too much champagne," she assured the man with a nonchalant, drunken wave of her hand.

"You're sure you're okay? Do you want me to walk you up to your apartment, so you don't fall?" His brows were knitted together, and Sophie could tell he was truly worried about her well-being. This eased her mind, so she nodded, agreeing to let him help her.

"Everyone needs help every now and again," isn't that what my therapist would say? "It's always okay to accept help when it's offered if you need it."

"Yeah, sure. That would be nice. Thank you." She smiled and the driver slid his arm around her waist while pulling her arm over his shoulder, to keep her steady as he also pulled her close. Sophie glanced at him as he walked her up to the front doors. He wore a dark jacket that reminded her of something important. What was it though? Why did his jacket set off those red flags in her brain? She tried to reach for the root of the idea her mind was trying to give her, but it felt too fuzzy from the champagne to pick the exact reason why she felt that way. *Whatever. I just want to go to bed.*

The walk to the elevator felt like a hike - uphill both ways - as she tried to figure out exactly what it was about the man that was beginning to make her regret her decision to let him walk her up to her apartment. He pressed the up button on the wall outside the elevator and they waited for the creaking, old, death trap to arrive.

"What floor?" he asked. Sophie reached out and pressed the button for him. Too tired to talk. She rested her head on his shoulder and braced herself for the rocky ride to her floor. By the time the doors opened she was beginning to feel nauseous from the elevator's jerky movements. She hated it. She wished she were in the right, sober enough, condition to have taken the stairs up.

"Ugh," she groaned. She willed the contents of her stomach to stay down. *Do not puke in front of this kind man who is helping you get home.* She swallowed hard, forcing the bile back down. *I'm never drinking again.*

"Hey, you okay? We're almost there. Which one?" he asked her as he held her up.

"972," she told him. He was lucky she got that out without vomit following.

He held her up, supporting most of her weight as he practically carried her to her front door. "You have your key?" he asked. Sophie nodded and held up her purse to open it and dig for her key. She was so glad there wasn't much else she could fit in there. It made finding the key easy enough. She pulled it out and brandished it to the driver in victory.

"Found it! Thank you for helping me. I'm sure it's totally not in your contract for Ubering, but I appreciate it." She pulled away from him to open her door, hoping he got the message that she was good from there. He didn't quite seem to get it, he stayed in place. "I'm good now, thank you again."

"Of course," he told her. He turned away and she pushed the key into the lock and opened the door. As the door swung open, Sophie stood trying to maintain her balance just enough to close the door and get to bed. *I should really take this makeup off. Screw it, I'll be fine. I'll just go to bed.* Just as Sophie finally composed herself to take a step, she felt a hand fist into her hair and push her into her apartment. Before she could scream a hand covered her mouth, muffling the noises she managed to make. She stumbled over hers and a second pair of feet as she tried not to focus on the aching in her scalp.

The fear and adrenaline coursing through her veins started to override the fuzziness the champagne created. She knew exactly what was happening. She wasn't about to make it easy on him, though. Sophie grabbed at the hand covering her mouth to pry herself free. He was strong, much stronger than Sophie. She couldn't get out of his grip. She reached behind her head and grabbed onto the hand in her hair. She tried to dig her nails in and pull away, but the man was too strong for her to over power.

No, no, no, this can't be happening. Please, don't let this be real, she begged silently as she was forced deeper into her apartment, struggling to get free all the way. Tears fell from her eyes as she was dropped on the bed face first. She tried to roll over to gain the least bit of leverage to try and fight him off, but he held her down with his body over hers.

"No point in fighting so much," he told her as he pulled up her dress, letting the material bunch up around her waist, exposing her lower body to him. Sophie tried kicking, screaming, and clawing at her attacker. He was just too big, too strong for her to take control of the situation she'd found herself in.

She felt him tear at her panties, taking away the last shred of protection she had against his attack. She cried into his hand as she continued struggling. It was all she could do to keep trying to save herself. She had to save herself. She was the only one who could save herself from this man.

He pulled her up off the bed by her hair. Sophie felt some of her hair rip out of her scalp. She sobbed into his hand still covering her mouth. She tried to grab the hand wrapped in her hair to pull it away.

With an angry grunt, he flipped her onto her back and after she landed on the bed with a small bounce, he threw a stiff punch at her cheek. His fist caught its mark. It wasn't quite enough to knock her out, but it rattled her brain, making her instantly dizzy and tired. Sophie saw stars as she stopped struggling for a moment. The impact of his fist hitting her cheek made her dizzy, but it also felt strangely familiar. It definitely wasn't the first time she'd been hit by a man much larger than she was. As she struggled to keep her eyes straight and maintain consciousness, she saw what she was afraid to see: the dark baseball cap

He pushed the skirt of her dress back up around her hips as she struggled to get her arms to move the way she wanted them to. A familiar searing pain ripped through her body when he pushed in between her legs, tearing her open at her core. Sophie felt a strange sense of calm wash over her body then. Her eyes glazed over, and reality seemed to slip away as she was lost in a memory from a time she'd rather have forgotten.

She was taken back to that stinking shit hole she'd been adopted into. The cushion below her was lumpy and uncomfortable, but Sophie stayed where she was. Daddy had already left for work, so she'd been sat on the couch while her new sister told her about how things worked in the house the morning after she arrived.

"And Daddy needs dinner cooked by 6 o'clock every night. He's tired after work, so it needs to be ready when he gets home. Otherwise, he gets mad."

"What happens if it's not done?" Sophie asked, her voice small and meek. She felt nervous, she didn't want to upset anyone.

"Don't you worry your pretty little head over it. Just make sure you don't make him mad." Her new sister booped her on the nose before she pulled her off the couch and started taking her on a tour of the small house.

Sophie understood she was not to upset her new Daddy for any reason. She did not want to find out what happened when he got angry. She followed her sister around all day, learning about where everything was, what she was expected to do every day, and how to take care not to make Daddy angry. Sophie was the youngest of the bunch but was expected to help with everything just the same.

She was excited when she got to meet her new family. They'd been in bed when she got home the night before. She had an older brother, 20 year old Danny, 13 year old Madeline, and 11 year old Violet, and of course Laurie, who had come with to adopt her the day before.

Danny scared her a little. When Laurie had taken Sophie to his room she realized Danny was different from other boys she had known in the orphanage. He wore a t-shirt and a ratty, holey pair of jeans. His hair was long - down to his chin - covered his eyes, and looked greasy, like he needed a shower.

Sophie peeked around the rest of the messy, cluttered room as Laurie introduced the two new siblings. He was lucky. He got a television in his room! She saw a poster on the wall that was unlike any she'd ever seen before. She had seen the other girls in the orphanage change their clothes, but the poster on Danny's wall was different. The lady was completely naked, and her body was posed in a way that made her look curvy, like a snake. Danny had pushed them out of his room after being introduced, frowning the whole time, and then slammed the door in their faces.

"He just likes his privacy," Laurie chirped before leading Sophie back to the living room. "Danny is Daddy's only biological son. The rest of us were adopted after Danny's mom passed away when he was 12. I was 10 when I was adopted, I think Danny was 15 at that point. But I got the most responsibility, even though I was the youngest. I get to be like the mom of the house. Then, we adopted Violet a couple of years later, then Maddie a year after that. Now, you." Laurie was chattering excitedly about how they would be the best of friends as she taught Sophie that day.

It was nearing 5 o'clock when Laurie brought Sophie to the kitchen to start cooking dinner. She was going to make spaghetti. "Daddy's favorite dish," she told

Sophie as the ground beef sizzled away, browning in the pan before she added canned spaghetti sauce. "Now, it needs to simmer while we cook the noodles."

Sophie watched as Laurie filled a pot with water and set it on the stove to start boiling. "How long do we have to wait for the noodles to turn into spaghetti?" Sophie asked. She glanced at the clock, seeing it was almost 6:00. She began to get nervous the food wouldn't be done in time. Laurie said it had to be done by 6 o'clock, and they had four minutes before then.

"Shit! They won't be done in time. You!" Laurie shouted as she pointed her finger accusingly at Sophie. "This is your fault! Everything took too long to teach you and now he's going to be mad it's not done!"

Tears welled up in Sophie's eyes. She hadn't meant to make dinner late. She was just trying to learn. "I'm sorry! Please don't tell Daddy it was my fault!"

The two stopped as they heard the front door open, and slam closed. The sound made Sophie jump. She didn't want to make him mad. She just wanted to do everything the right way. Heavy footsteps neared the entry to the kitchen, each one making Sophie's heart beat harder in anticipation of what would happen because dinner wasn't done in time.

"Is there a goddamn reason my food isn't on the table waiting for me?" Daddy shouted at the two girls tending the pots on the stove. Sophie whipped around to look at the man the voice came from. He was covered head to toe in grease and dirt. His denim overalls had gone from the clean blue they were that morning when he left, to a dingy blue-brown that smelled like Danny's bedroom and a gas station.

"She asked too many questions and slowed me down! I told her it was all her fault. She should be punished." Laurie's voice was nearly a hiss as she threw Sophie directly under the bus immediately. Sophie's body trembled as she cried.

"I'm s-sorry, Daddy. I was just trying to make sure I learn everything the right way. Please, don't get mad!" Sophie said as she cried. She wrapped her arms around herself, trying to make sure she didn't make him any angrier.

He stomped up to Sophie and grabbed her by the collar of her shirt. "I'm already angry, you little brat! Why would you make my dinner late on purpose?" he yelled, the stink of his breath hit Sophie like a freight train. She flinched away, which only made Daddy's wrath worsen. "Don't you try to get away from me!" he said as he slapped her across the face.

The pain of his hand across her cheek radiated throughout her body. She was in complete shock. No adult had ever hit her like that before. Her cheek felt like it was on fire. Before she could stop it, sobs wracked her body. They were coming so fast she couldn't breathe, and her chest ached. She tried to tell him she was sorry again, but she couldn't speak through the fear.

"Stop your damn sniveling and finish my fucking dinner!" Daddy shouted as he threw Sophie to the floor. Her elbows hit first, causing a shooting pain down both arms to her fingers, then her back hit the floor. Her body ached immediately. She watched silently as Daddy left the kitchen. Tears were still streaming down her face as she turned to look at Laurie who was draining the pasta in the sink.

Laurie turned to Sophie and shrugged her shoulders while saying, "I told you not to make him mad." Sophie's bottom lip trembled as she cried silently, afraid to make a noise, laying there on the kitchen floor. She felt so tiny and scared. Was this what being a family was really like? "Get up, take this plate to him. Stop crying first, or he'll be more upset."

Sophie tried to get her lip to stop trembling as she stood up from the floor. Her back and elbows hurt so much. She tried to ignore the pain. She didn't want to make it worse. She wiped her eyes and took the plate from Laurie. She took a deep breath before leaving the kitchen, careful to not trip on anything and face the wrath of Daddy for accidentally dropping his plate.

As Angel's engine pulled up to the scene, the gray sedan was fully engulfed in flames. He had hoped it'd be a pretty quiet night, as he'd been on twenty-four seven duty for the last week and a half. It wasn't too hard work, but he'd hoped to sleep through just one night. It was no one's fault but his own since he had volunteered to take on the extra shifts. *I can't let them think I'm lazy. I need to show that I'm truly dedicated*, is what he'd originally thought. Now, on the other hand...

"Well, I'm not really a fan of the car either, but I don't think giving it a Viking funeral was the best way to get rid of it," Jonas quipped. He was always good at making sure everyone got a chuckle before diving into the situation.

"Alright team looks like an average vehicle fire. Todd, Angel, go hook up the hose and get this contained. Jonas, search the area for any starters. This is a newer vehicle, with no passengers. Clearly this was no accidental fire. Thankfully, this is small enough to contain being just the four of us. I'm gonna contact McDavenport with CPD and see who called this in."

"Got it, Captain!" The three men got to work.

"How considerate of the arsonist to leave this so close to a hydrant," Todd joked.

"Yeah, that's pretty interesting. I don't think I've heard of a considerate criminal in Chicago before. Must be from out of town." Angel and Todd laughed. He was happy that he and Todd were still pretty great, even after moving in together. It actually made their work chemistry even better. They got the fire put out in less than two minutes because they were so in-sync.

Todd and Angel cleaned up their equipment while Jamieson and Jonas checked out the car for any starters.

"Hey, Angel. What do you say we take a vacation sometime next month? These month-long twenty-four seven shifts take it out of me. I need a little r-and-r, ya know? Plus, between these shifts and Melody's shifts at the hospital between classes, I feel like I haven't seen her in years. I think the three of us should take a trip somewhere. What do you think?" Todd asked as he rewound the firehose.

Angel put the tools back in the lockbox on the truck and latched it. "That honestly sounds great, but after all of this, I just want to see my folks, maybe eat a Camille Harris special meal, and sleep in my own bed. Plus, one of us needs to watch the house. You two should definitely take a trip though. Maybe hit up Niagara Falls. I hear August is when the tourist season starts to wind down."

"Niagara Falls' tourist season is year round, but nice try. You just want that special candy from the gift shop."

"Guilty!"

"Ha, I knew it! But that doesn't sound like a bad trip. Maybe we'll head up to the Falls and then see her uncle and aunt that live in Buffalo. They've been asking for us to come back ever since I made them my famous chili a while ago."

"The secret is the sun-dried tomatoes. Sounds like a good trip. So, it's decided?"

"Yes sir! Now I've got something to look forward to. And don't worry, I'll bring you back some candy."

"Oh, I'm holding you to that!"

"Hey, you two done over there? We've found the starter. As expected, another Molotov. I can't understand who'd waste a perfectly good bottle of Hooch!"

"Captain, you were born after prohibition, right?"

"Alright you youngins, let's head back to the station. I've got CPD heading down here to tow the car. We'll have Tony head over there tomorrow and try to work with them to find our arsonist, though with a Molotov it's unlikely we'll track them down. If we leave now, we might be able to get some shut eye before Elle comes through with the morning workout."

They all groaned.

8

The bright morning sun streaming in through the window woke Sophie early the next morning. Memories of the night before hit Sophie as she tried rolling over to look at her clock. She ached everywhere, especially her face and between her legs. She curled up in a ball on her bed as painful sobs shook her small frame.

She wished it were just a horrible nightmare, but the evidence her body provided told her it wasn't. She cried until she couldn't cry anymore. She'd run dry - physically and emotionally. A person could only cry so much until there was nothing left. She was numb.

She sat up on the edge of the bed, careful not to aggravate her injuries with too much movement. She stood and walked to the bathroom; her gait uneven as she tried to compensate for the pain she felt all over. She left the light off. She couldn't look in the mirror. She couldn't look herself in the eye knowing it was her fault.

It was her fault she couldn't save herself. It was her fault that she didn't make sure he was gone before opening her door. Her fault for letting him walk her up in the first place. For drinking too much and having to take an Uber instead of the bus she'd have usually taken. Police wouldn't do anything since she'd had too much to drink and brought it on herself. It wouldn't have been her first time going to them for help over... Sophie shook her head. She couldn't deal with the past and the present at the same time.

The nurses at the hospital were always nice when she would come in. They weren't any help either, though. All they did was call the cops who never seemed to care enough to get any actual justice. *Why even bother?* Sophie wondered. She wasn't going to waste her time on a system that found her to be a waste of theirs.

Sophie turned on the shower, turning the water as hot as she could stand it. She let it wash over her sore body. She scrubbed her body with an exfoliating scrub and a loofah, trying to wash away the night before. Maybe if she scrubbed hard enough she could wash the weakness away.

Once her skin was red and raw and stinging she moved on. She gently massaged shampoo into her scalp, taking extra care where it was sore from the strands of hair being ripped out. She was weak, not strong enough to push him away and force him out of her apartment. Sophie hated how small and meek she'd always been. She wouldn't ever be strong enough to be her own savior. Sister Meredith was right, she would always need someone to come to her rescue. If she had tears left to cry, Sophie was sure they'd be falling. She turned out to be exactly what Sister Meredith had said despite trying so hard not to.

Sophie sat on her bed wrapped in the biggest towel she could find. She stared off into the corner of the room for long enough that her skin had dried and her partly dried hair had begun to feel itchy against her back. She didn't want to move. Every small movement hurt. She felt like she'd been in a car wreck, but it was just her who'd gotten hurt. Broken. Again. Sophie stared into the corner until her phone rang.

It was still in her purse near the door where she'd dropped it. It vibrated against the hardwood floor, muffled inside the clutch. Who would be calling her on a weekend? Curiosity pulled her from where she'd frozen in place on her bed. She bent down to pick it up, her eyes glancing to the door momentarily. It'd remained unlocked all night. He could've come back any time. Sophie held her ringing phone in her hand as she rushed to the door. Relief washed over her once the deadbolt slid into place. Once it was locked, she answered the call.

"Hey! How are you feeling? Cage's hangover cure has saved my life, yet again. I couldn't imagine getting on a plane with one." Felicity's voice was chipper and excited. *As she should be.* She and her new husband were about to take off to Bali for two weeks on their honeymoon.

"I'm good, just a little sore from all the dancing," Sophie said quietly. Lying to Felicity about her pain was nothing new. Felicity barely knew anything about her past. Then again, Sophie didn't know much about Felicity's from the time Sophie left the orphanage to when they met again on the streets of Chicago. She loved Felicity despite the mystery her life posed.

"I'm glad you got home safe! Anyways, I gotta go. Cage is moving so slowly; he still isn't fully packed, and we have to leave in an hour. You're still good to handle the library for a couple weeks till I get back, right?"

"Yeah, of course. You can count on me." Sophie pulled at a string on her towel as she fought back tears. "Go have fun in Bali. I'll see you when you get back."

"Okay! I love you! See you soon!"

"See you soon," Sophie said just before hanging up. Felicity sounded so happy. It made Sophie's heart long for that kind of happiness. Could she ever be that happy?

The little voice in the back of her mind, that devil on her shoulder, whispered her greatest fears to her. She'd never be whole enough for that to be a possibility. That little devil seemed to grow bigger the longer Sophie listened. It grew and grew until it felt like a weight on her chest making it harder and harder to get a full breath.

"Oh no," she said to no one. She looked around her apartment. What she was looking for, she didn't know. Anything to help with the oncoming panic that was setting in. She hadn't gotten her meds refilled since she'd come back to Chicago. She hadn't even looked for a psychiatrist. Life had seemed to be going well. Her mistake had been trusting it would stay that way.

Sophie tried to think back to her therapy sessions. How was she supposed to help herself when her own body and mind worked against her? *54321! Use the 54321 method!* She thought to herself. *What can I see?*

"My chair, the clock, the coffee pot, the TV, my shoes." She made sure to list each out loud to try to help her control her breathing. She closed her eyes and listened to the world around her. "The cars outside, the neighbors walking upstairs, the TV next door, my own heartbeat."

She opened her eyes; she could feel the anxiety beginning to lessen. She had to keep going. Three things she could feel. She ran her hand across the cool Formica countertop. "The counter top." She touched her wet hair. "My wet hair." She ran her hands over the terry of the towel wrapped around her. "The towel, terrycloth."

What was next? Smell. Sophie closed her eyes again. What could she smell? "I can smell my shampoo. I can smell the bacon cooking next door."

Sophie opened her eyes and turned to find her jar of chocolate on the counter. She took one out and unwrapped it, careful not to rip the foil. She popped the chocolate into her mouth and savored the sweetness that coated her tongue and the relief of the panic fading. She let the chocolate melt completely in her mouth before she felt calm enough to look around her studio apartment and figure out what she needed to do next.

She'd take the day step by step. One thing at a time. She needed to get dressed. Something comfy. She walked to her dresser and pulled out an oversized t-shirt, a pair of sweats and her most favorite comfortable sports bra. After getting dressed, she also pulled on a hoodie and a pair of thick socks.

Doesn't matter what I wear. People take what they want anyways. Every time. I'll never be strong enough to save myself. She let her head hang down as she stood in the bathroom, the light still off but her hand rested on the switch. She'd planned on blow drying her hair, so it didn't dry in the ridiculous mess of curls it was already turning into.

Could she face herself? She stared at the dark mirror, only able to see the outline of herself as she considered just walking out. She closed her eyes and flipped on the light. She took a deep breath before slowly opening her eyes. She looked at the sink first, trying to build the courage to look in the mirror. *You can do this. Prove you're stronger.* She looked up and directly into her own eyes.

The same ugly, sad, blue eyes she was used to looked right back at her. They were rimmed by swollen red lids from the impressive amount of crying she'd done earlier that morning. Her cheekbone on the left side was swollen and a light purple from where he'd punched her. Her lips were pink and swollen from the forced kisses. The tip of her nose was still pink from the crying. She couldn't see anything else different, but she'd also covered the rest of her skin with clothing. She didn't want to know about anything else. She just wanted to forget it all.

She picked up her wide toothed comb and started detangling her lion's mane of hair. The platinum blonde was bright in the fluorescent light of her bathroom. She hated it but couldn't ever bring herself to dye it. She turned on her straightener. As she began to section her hair to make the process easier, she saw the scissors on the counter. Her hands fell to her sides. Why was she wasting so much time taking care of the entire reason she couldn't fight him off?

She turned off the straightener and pulled a pair of jeans out of her dresser. She changed out of her sweats and into the jeans. She pulled on a pair of black converse, grabbed her phone, and shoved it into her pocket, along with her keys and some cash from her wallet. She took the stairs down to the first floor. She'd never take the elevator again. She couldn't bear to.

She stepped out onto the sidewalk, her legs shaky from going down 9 flights of stairs, and took in a deep breath of the cool mid-morning air. She set off toward the salon down the street from her building. The city was still quiet, no car horns, no yelling, no blaring music coming from who knew where. Sunday mornings were like that - quiet. She found the small building she'd been heading toward and checked the hours posted in the window. *Perfect*. It was open.

Emotions bubbled up in her chest. She paused with her hand on the door. Did she really want to do this? She usually cut her own hair. Just trims every few months. That was probably one of the only useful skills she'd learned in her adopted home.

She pushed away all second thoughts - they were never helpful anyways - and walked into the salon. It was bright inside. The windows at the front let the morning sunlight in, and the white walls made it feel open and airy. A middle aged woman with dark brown hair and golden highlights stopped sweeping and turned to face the doorway Sophie stood in.

"What can I help you with today, darlin'?" Her voice was kind and had a slight, distant twang in it, as if she'd spent her formative years in the south but ran away to Chicago once she was old enough to get out. Sophie didn't miss how the woman's eyes kept going back and forth from her eyes to her purple cheek. *I should have covered it up.*

Sophie stared at the woman, unsure what to ask for. "I want it gone," she said, her voice flat and emotionless.

"Alright, come have a seat. How short are we talkin'? Shoulder? Chin? Pixie? Be a shame to chop all this gorgeous hair off." the woman held her gaze momentarily.

People always said that whenever she mentioned cutting it. What a shame it would be for her beautiful, blonde curls to be gone. Sophie looked anywhere but the lady in front of her. "Between shoulder and chin?" Sophie replied, but realized it sounded more like a question than an answer. "Please. I just want it short."

"Okay, doll. Let me grab a cape and I'll be right back." The woman walked to the back of the shop, brought back a black cover, wrapped it around Sophie's neck and got to work.

As the stylist washed Sophie's hair, Sophie tried her hardest to not wince in pain. The spots on her scalp where her hair had been ripped out were a painful reminder of what she'd brought on herself.

"You alright darlin'?" the stylist asked when Sophie did finally wince at a particularly painful spot.

"Yeah, just tender-headed, is all." Sophie closed her eyes and left them closed until she was done. It was all she could do to not cry as memories of the night before and other, equally terrible nights flooded her mind.

A very painful hour later the woman pulled the cape off. "You're done, my dear. Take a look."

Sophie opened her eyes and looked in the mirror. She'd lost a good 12 inches of hair. Her jaw dropped to the floor. Her hair sat just below her chin by an inch or two. The stylist had put loose curls in to accentuate the choppy layers. "It's perfect. Thank you so much." She turned her head to look at the whole cut. It was just what she needed.

"You're welcome. Come with me and I'll get you checked out." Sophie followed her to the register at the desk next to the front door. Her whole head felt lighter. She felt lighter. "That'll be $42.85."

Sophie nodded and handed her three twenties from her pocket. "Keep it," she said when the woman began counting out the change.

"You sure, dear?"

Sophie nodded and turned to leave. "Thank you, really. I love it. Have a good day," she said before pushing her way out of the salon. She felt better, strangely. As if she'd cut out the memories by cutting off her hair. Like she'd cut out the pain of the past by cutting off what held onto those memories she wanted to let go. With her heart and her mood lightened, she walked back up the street to her building.

She walked in the front door and took the stairs to the basement. She'd spent the last couple of days being so busy with Felicity's wedding that she realized she'd forgotten to check her mail. She found her box and pulled out her keys. After unlocking the door, she found only three envelopes. Two were normal junk mail, but the last was different. It only had her name on the front written in black ink. It looked like it'd been written with great care by someone who knew calligraphy. The lettering was beautiful and curvy and swirly, the kind of stuff Sophie wished she knew how to do.

She studied it as she walked back up the stairs to her apartment, wondering who would possibly have taken the time to create something so beautiful just for her. Who would know which mailbox was hers? Felicity, Cage. That was about it. Maybe Theo, if Felicity had given him her address?

Sophie tucked the mail under her arm as she opened her door, careful to check the hall down both directions. She'd never make that stupid mistake again. She locked the door behind her and threw away the junk mail. She looked at the envelope one more time, looking for any indication of who'd sent it, but there was nothing. Only a wax seal on the back holding the flap down. She noticed in the wax seal that there was an angel with a harp imprinted on the wax. Someone took a lot of time to make this work of art for her. She gently peeled up the wax to open the envelope, careful not to break it, and took out the letter concealed within.

Her eyes drifted over the page before she actually read the words. It was written in the same black ink and calligraphy that was on the front of the envelope, just smaller. Still definitely hand-written. It must have taken someone quite a bit of effort to make something so beautiful. It had to have been Theo. He seemed like the type to either know how to do something so fancy or the type to be able to pay someone to do something like the artistry she held in her hands.

Dear Sophie,

I must say, you do take my breath away. You were stunning last night. The blush pink of your dress made your flawless porcelain skin glow in the soft, romantic light of the crystal chandeliers in the ballroom. The way the satin flowed over your every curve could bring any mortal man to his knees, and the pout of your luscious lips would drive him mad. You certainly drove me crazy.

I hope you know how much you affect me. I wish I were brave enough to tell you, face to face but your presence steals my breath away. To hold your soft, delicate hands in mine and tell you that you make my heart beat harder than it ever has. That just the sight of you makes me want you more and more every time I see you.

I hope you know exactly how amazing you are. Your kindness knows no bounds, your heart is filled with generosity that most lack. I've seen the sadness in your eyes when you see the homeless people and stray pets around the city. I've seen how graciously you always tip the servers who take care of you. If only the people who could make true change happen had hearts like yours.

You make me want to be better. A better, less selfish, more giving man. I plan to start immediately. There's a homeless shelter near my house. Perhaps volunteering there will help show me how to have a heart like yours. I'll let you know what I learn about myself there. Until then, I hope you stay safe and keep being your amazing, generous self.

Sincerely,

Your Secret Admirer

Tears welled up in Sophie's eyes. Theo had said all the things she'd been thinking might not be perfect about him. Could she have really affected him so much? How could he possibly have noticed so much about her when he seemed to only talk about himself?

Maybe she had been totally wrong about him. Felicity had said he was a really good guy and to just give him a chance. Perhaps she was right.

Sophie smiled as she reread the letter a couple more times. She would have to pay more attention the next time she saw him. Maybe she'd even ask about his time at the shelter, see what he'd learned.

With a simple letter, he'd made the worst day of her life in a long time seem just a little bit better. She held the letter against her heart as she curled up in her chair. He'd dulled so much of the pain with simple words written on a page. Ink and paper. Could that be enough to heal her shattered heart?

The veil of sleep Sophie had been peacefully resting under was pierced by the shrieking of her alarm clock. Monday morning had come for her again, bright and early. Except today, she would be alone. She groaned and turned it off as she swung her legs over the side of her bed. Her body still ached, but as she looked in the mirror she was glad to see that the light purple shadow next to her eye had almost completely faded away. She would have had a hard time explaining that one.

Sophie looked in the mirror again, her mind jolted momentarily by the length of her hair. She had almost forgotten she'd had it cut so short. She did notice a plus side to the length, all she had to do was brush it and her hair was done. She added some light concealer over the remainder of the bruise, mascara, blush, and a light pink moisturizing lip tint.

Her brows scrunched together. She looked different. She spent so much time cultivating the image of this cute, happy, perky façade. What was she supposed to be now? She stared at her own image, thinking of the millions of possibilities. Did it truly matter what she did or how she looked? Predators took what they wanted no matter what, that was something she'd learned very well.

Perhaps if she looked tougher, she may seem less like prey. She shuddered to think of herself that way. As prey. A victim. That's what she was, though.

Weak and pathetic prey. She was an already wounded gazelle in a world of devilishly hungry lions.

Tears stung her eyes and she whipped around, turning away from the frailty she found in the mirror. Sophie searched through her clothing until she found what she was looking for. When she was able to bring herself to look in the mirror again, she no longer saw prey. She was a lioness in her black jeans, dark green t-shirt, and black ankle boots. She grabbed a black trench coat and pulled it on. *Perfect.* She would no longer be the cute, innocent prey that she had been for so long.

She shoved her phone, keys, and important cards into the pockets of her coat and headed out of her apartment to the John Arlington Library. The stairs provided safe passage to the ground floor. Would she ever be able to take the elevator again? Sophie avoided the thought by thinking about everything she needed to get done at the library that morning to ready it for the patrons, who were sure to show.

Ever since she and Felicity had been running the place, business had picked up. Felicity had mentioned once that she and John had upwards of twenty to thirty visitors per day. Sophie would venture to say that they averaged around seventy to eighty per day last month. They did a lot more community outreach to support the library. Whereas, Felicity said Mr. Arlington had relied on word of mouth.

The bus was crowded when Sophie got on, but her usual spot was open. Almost as if everyone already on the bus had expected her. She chose to stand next to the door. Cage had mentioned changing up her routine. She would have to look at different bus routes to the library, maybe some walking routes too, just to really change things up. Maybe it was time to start taking her bike out. *No that's stupid. I don't know how to ride a bike.*

The bus pulled up to her stop and she was the first out the door. She looked around the street, expecting to see the man who'd been following her. He was nowhere to be found. She rushed to the glass front door of the library, unlocked it, and pushed her way in. She didn't slow her rushed pace until the door was locked behind her and she was at her desk. Sophie forced her body to stop just behind her chair.

She closed her eyes and took a deep breath in through her nose and held it for a moment before exhaling through her mouth. She promised Felicity she could do it alone, that everything would be fine, and she'd call if she needed anything. Really, all she needed was not to be alone.

It was as if an angel had answered her silent prayer when there was a soft knock on the entry door. Sophie opened her eyes to see Theo there, smiling and holding two big white coffee cups. Sophie couldn't help the smile that broke out on her face. She ran to the door and unlocked it to let him in.

"Hey, you never texted back, so I thought I'd come check on you before you open today." His smile matched Sophie's. She'd completely forgotten to let him know she was safe, because ironically she wasn't and that's why she'd forgotten. She wasn't about to tell him that it was the Uber driver he'd ordered for her that was the reason she hadn't checked in. Her smile fell slightly, but not enough for Theo to have noticed. He handed her the cup and followed her to the central desk.

"Thanks, I forgot to make some this morning."

"It was fate," he said as he took Felicity's normal seat. "It worried me when you didn't check in, Sophie." Theo's eyes were sad with a hint of concern. Sophie searched for a reason to give him that would cover up why she'd never contacted him to let him know she was okay.

"I'm sorry. I meant to, but I was so tired I passed out the second my head hit the pillow and I was so hungover I slept most of yesterday."

"But you had time for a haircut? Not that I don't like it. It looks great, I was just really worried." Theo reached out and brushed a strand of hair away from Sophie's face. Sophie looked down at the coffee cup in her hands, angry with herself that she hadn't remembered to text him. It wasn't his fault what happened. It was hers for not being stronger, more able to take care of herself, but if he'd have come with her it wouldn't have happened either. *No, this isn't Theo's fault. It's yours.*

"I'm really sorry, Theo. I didn't mean to worry you. I was just really tired, and I forgot." Sophie braced herself for the shouting she was sure would ensue. She pressed her eyes closed and felt her shoulders tighten in anticipation of the fight to come.

"Hey, it's okay. Really, I should have just called you instead of waiting like an idiot," Theo told her as he pushed her chin back up with his finger. Sophie's blue eyes met Theo's and she saw the kindness in them that had attracted her to him in the first place. "Your hair really does look great. It fits you. Fierce," he said as he made a claw with his hands and growled like a big cat.

"You're ridiculous," Sophie told him.

"I just like to see you smile," he told her before he leaned in to press a kiss to her lips. Sophie flinched back just before their lips met and Theo stopped. "I'm sorry, I thought after the wedding and the dance floor that, you know..." his voice trailed off, hoping Sophie would fill the silence.

"No, I'm sorry. It's just me. I'm jumpy today. I don't know what's going on with me," she said as she finished the kiss. It was quick. A peck. Nothing like what had transpired on the dance floor between them two nights earlier. Sophie knew it was her fault. She was broken, shattered into even more pieces than before. It was only a matter of time before Theo realized it and left anyway.

"Okay, well, I've gotta get going to work. I'll see you later, okay?" Theo said as he stood from the chair, coffee cup in hand.

"Okay, see ya." Sophie watched as her lifeline walked out the door. If she wouldn't have been so dumb as to flinch away from him he may have stayed longer. She could have prevented the unavoidable for just a little longer. She dreaded being alone, which was unusual for her. Sophie paused on that thought. She usually enjoyed being alone, but all she wanted was someone with her, so she wasn't. *Am I really that desperate for someone to come save me? Good God, I'm pathetic.*

Sophie went about her usual morning opening duties and ran over the list Felicity had given her for the things she'd need to cover that she generally didn't, things Felicity managed on a daily basis. She started all of the computers, which were turned off over the weekend. She turned all the lights in the building on. She made sure the bathroom was stocked with soap, paper towels, toilet paper, and toilet seat covers. She replaced a couple of light bulbs in the small lamps placed throughout the library study area. She put away returned inventory. By the time she'd finished her morning To Do list, it was time to open.

It was a bright, sunny day so she propped open the door when she flipped over the 'Closed' sign to 'Open'. A breeze ruffled her hair at the door, and she took a deep breath of the fresh air. It helped her clear the thoughts of being alone she'd been drowning in for the last hour. She could do this. She didn't need anyone to save her or help her. She could do it on her own.

It was almost closing time when Sophie changed her mind. She was sitting at her desk, logging returned inventory and stacking it on a cart to be put away. She had closed the front door around lunch time, so when another visitor arrived, the bell alerted her. When she looked up the breath was stolen from her lungs.

The dark jacket and baseball cap gave him away. She couldn't believe it. Were stalkers usually so bold as to come into the workplace of their victim? Unless he knew she was alone, perhaps that would give him the courage to present himself. She felt like she was stuck in an episode of a police drama starring her as the victim.

He was unmistakable, but something about him seemed even more familiar. In her sitting position she could see his face. His eyes made something in the back of her mind perk up. The light hazel wasn't something she'd forget anytime soon.

How had he managed to stalk her so closely that he could pick her up in an Uber the night of Felicity's wedding? Near hyperventilating, Sophie stood and walked in long strides to the office. Her mind was acutely aware of the fact that she did not want to alarm the man who'd just walked in. She closed the door behind her and shut the blinds on the window. With her back pressed against the door, her mind began to race at the thought of being left alone in the library with the man who'd stalked and raped her. A sweat broke out all over her body. A physical indication of the anxiety pulsating through her. Not the worst one though, it was only second to the trembling that she was sure would start any second.

There was no way she could leave the library before closing. She was the only one who could close down the library. There was no way she'd let anyone else, but how was she going to leave the office when he was out there? Perusing the shelves like he had no idea who she was or that he knew she worked there! Sophie turned to peek out the window from between the blinds.

He was out of sight. *Shit.* How stupid was she to let him out of her sight?! She felt like an elephant was sitting on her chest. Air was hard to come by. Her fingers started to tingle as her heart hammered against her ribs and in her throat. She slowly slid down the door until she was sitting on the floor, her back pressing against the cool wood.

It was almost closing time. All she had to do was wait him out. He'd have to leave at closing, which wasn't for another 5 minutes. Sophie fisted her hands in her hair, trying to slow her thoughts down, trying to figure out how to get herself out of the mess she'd somehow found herself in, yet again.

She shifted her body, trying to get comfortable for her wait when she felt something in her pocket. Sophie scrambled to check her back pocket. She wasn't completely inept. She'd shoved her phone in her pocket! She pulled it out and unlocked it.

She found Theo in her contacts and pressed Call. It rang twice before his smooth, velvety voice answered. "Hey Soph, what's up?"

"Hey, I was wondering if you could maybe give me a ride home?"

"Are you okay? You sound shook up. Did something happen?"

"I'm fine. I just don't think it's safe for me to take the bus home tonight."

"I'll be there as soon as possible, okay? Do you need police or anything?" His voice was still calm but laced with hints of concern.

"No, there's just this creepy guy here. I'm safe in the office, I locked the door and everything. I just don't wanna walk home in the dark, you know?"

"I'll be there soon, okay? Stay in the office and don't come out till I knock on the door."

"Okay," Sophie said just before Theo hung up. His office wasn't far, maybe four minutes away. That's about how much time there was before closing. Theo would get to the library just in time to check everything out, clear the building, and make sure she got home safe. How pathetic was she calling him to come save her? Sister Meredith's voice bubbled up in Sophie's mind. *You'll always just be a victim, waiting for some man to rescue you.* The exact description of what she was currently doing. She was a victim waiting for a man to come and save her.

A tear slipped down Sophie's cheek. The cold trail intensified the memory. She felt the exact same tears roll down her cheeks when Sister Meredith had scolded her with words that cut deep into her and scarred her soul. Sophie would always be a victim, waiting for a man to come rescue her.

A few minutes later there was a knock on the office door. Sophie scrambled to her feet and peeked out the blinds to see who was knocking on the door. Her whole body relaxed when she saw Theo's deep brown eyes and always welcoming but dazzlingly bright smile. She unlocked the door and threw it open. She flinched at the sound the glass made when the doorknob hit the wall, a deafening rattle that almost had her thinking it would shatter. When it didn't, she threw her arms around his neck and squeezed him in a tight hug. He returned it by wrapping an arm around her waist and pulling her closer.

"You okay? You're literally shaking."

"I'm fine now. Thank you for coming to rescue me," Sophie said after she let go of her savior.

"Anytime, doll face. It's empty by the way. There's no one here anymore. You ready to lock up and go home?" Theo asked as he brushed a short strand of hair out of Sophie's face.

Sophie nodded in reply. She walked back to her desk and grabbed her keys and jacket. She told Theo to wait by the front door while she locked the back. She pushed open the door and looked all around the back parking lot. It was empty. Once she was satisfied, she pulled the door closed and locked it.

She met back up with Theo at the front door. "Ready?" he asked. Sophie nodded and followed him out the front door. She pulled it closed behind her and locked the large glass door. She followed him to a much less flashy Toyota Camry, to which she joked that he must have stolen it. She received a playful eye roll as Theo opened the door for her to sit in the passenger seat.

When they reached Sophie's apartment building, Theo parked the car right in front of the entry doors. "You good?" he asked after turning off the car.

"Yeah, just a little freaked out still, I guess." Sophie's voice was quiet as she tried to avoid the subject of why she'd been so afraid. She clamped her hands together just as tightly as she pressed her lips shut.

"Well, I couldn't find anyone in the library. Are you sure someone was there? I know you've been working really hard with Felicity gone, maybe you just need some rest?"

Sophie looked away from Theo as she squeezed her eyes shut, fighting back tears. "I don't know," she said as her voice trembled, and her resolve crumbled. No one had ever truly believed her, why did she think Theo would've been any different? She picked up her jacket and opened the car door.

"Wait, Soph, that's not-" his voice was cut off by the slamming of the car door. Sophie didn't look back to see if he was following her. She hoped he wasn't. She didn't know if she could explain her behavior without completely falling apart. She slammed her palm against the stairwell door. He didn't believe her. Why should she have assumed anything different? She got up the first flight of stairs fairly quickly. Sophie's mind raced as her feet pounded against the concrete steps. She felt her chest tighten and her shoulders involuntarily raise. Her heart started beating on her ribs as she opened the door to the 9th floor hallway.

She dropped her jacket on the counter and looked around for the small glass vial containing the shimmering blue liquid that she used to use to calm down as a child. A simple trinket given to her by Sister Gloria. She'd found out later on it was made with blue mica powder. She always wanted to make a bigger version but never got around to it.

Sophie shook the vial and set it on the counter in front of her. She bent at her waist and rested her chin on her crossed arms which she leaned on the counter in front of the vial. She watched the shimmering liquid swirl hypnotically in the round glass container. The longer she watched, the calmer she felt. Once the liquid stopped spinning, she had regained her grasp on her sanity. She took a deep breath and stood up straight, ignoring the twinge in her spine at having leaned on the counter for so long.

Sophie hadn't spoken to Theo for the last week since he'd picked her up from work. If she was honest with herself, she didn't really want to. But if that was the case, why did she feel so hurt that he hadn't even tried?

Because no one ever *tried*, Sophie thought. She knew that was why. No one ever fought for her, no one stuck around. No one wanted her. She walked down the stairs in her apartment building to the basement. She hadn't checked her mail in the last week either. She didn't usually get much mail anyways, so it didn't really matter. It was mostly junk.

She pulled out her key and opened the door. It was so squeaky, the pitch almost hurt her ears. *Maybe I should get some WD-40...* She pulled out the mail and was surprised to find a package with her name on it. She couldn't help but feel excited.

Who'd sent her a package? There was no name or return address listed on the package. She ran up the stairs, excitement coursing through her veins. Maybe Theo was trying to apologize with a gift. It had to be him, right?

She reached her apartment after what felt like forever as she took stair after stair, climbing up toward her apartment. She closed and locked the door behind her, making sure to try and open it to ensure the lock was working properly. She threw the junk mail in the recycling and set the package on the counter.

She studied it for a second, the same writing was on the front as was on the letter she'd gotten just over a week ago. The same stark black calligraphy made her name look so beautiful. She wondered how much Theo paid someone to do that.

She'd found when helping Felicity with the wedding that calligraphers were quite expensive. $5 per envelope was what she'd ended up paying, when you multiply that by how many envelopes you need for wedding invitations, it adds up quickly.

Sophie tore into the paper packaging, careful not to damage whatever was inside. She pulled out the paper first. A poem filled the page. Beautiful words written in the same script on the envelope pulled at Sophie's heart. Words of love and admiration filled her with a warmth she hoped would stay forever.

She picked up the item she'd left in the packaging and pulled it out. It was a small glass frame with dried, pressed flowers inside. She could identify the delicate white buds of the baby's breath and brilliant blue of the forget-me nots, but the red flower in the middle was unknown to her.

She pulled out her phone and took a picture of the flowers. She plugged the picture into Google's reverse image search. She scrolled past posts about the other flowers, searching for matches to the red one. When she found a matching picture, she opened the article.

"Known to symbolize love, passion, and deep desire, red camellias are the perfect gift for your beloved," she read out loud. Sophie's cheeks burned pink. Theo was really trying hard to apologize. She set the frame up on her counter against the wall so it wouldn't fall. She put the poem in her nightstand with the last letter.

Maybe I'll give him a call...

10

Sophie stared at the ugly metal doors that stood at the end of the hall. The easiest way to get into the basement was the elevator. *The damn elevator. It's just a damn elevator. Quit being a little bitch*, she told herself as she pressed the down arrow. Her heart hammered in her chest as she waited for the doors to open. *It's just an elevator.*

A loud, off key ding sounded the arrival of the car that would take her to her destination. *I can do this.* She stepped into the car and forced herself not to close her eyes as the doors closed behind her. She hit the B button to go to the basement. *It's just an elevator, I can do this.*

Sophie rode the rickety, groaning elevator down to the first basement level of her building where the mailboxes resided. She couldn't get out of the car fast enough. She had begun hyperventilating around the 6th floor and it got worse the lower she went. It felt as if the walls had begun to close in around her.

She pulled the skeleton mailbox key out of her pocket and unlocked the antique bronze door. As it creaked open, Sophie reminded herself that she really needed to get some WD-40 to grease the hinge. She grabbed the small bundle of mail and started to flip through it, unsurprised at what she'd received.

Bill, bill, credit card pre-approval spam crap, bill, cream-colored envelope labeled with only her name, "Sophie Martin" in beautiful stark, black calligraphy. There it was. That's what she was waiting for, the reason she'd been checking her mail daily.

The handwriting was the same as the two letters from weeks prior. Who was this mystery person? Why were they doing this?

Sophie ran up to her apartment. She wanted to be able to read the letter in private. She was convinced it was Theo trying to be cute, maybe playing a prank on her, that he obviously wouldn't know that there had been a man following her around the city every day.

Chills ran up and down Sophie's spine as she thought of the man that kept showing up on the bus. She ripped open the envelope the second she got inside her apartment and read the words on the page.

Dear Sophie,

I've watched you hold the letters close to your heart as you smile. I'm glad I can make you feel that way, makes me wonder how it would feel to be in your arms. How would it feel to be held by an angel like you? I wouldn't know, but I can imagine. You've captured my heart and I'm afraid it might break if you rejected me.

I never meant to keep my identity from you for so long, but you're so beautiful I haven't been able to bring myself to say hello. I love to watch you from afar, as you read in the library, as you sip your coffee and make that cute face when you get it with extra whipped cream, the way you like it but only get it once a month because for whatever reason you feel like you need to watch your figure. As if you could ever be anything but the most angelic, ethereal creature in the universe.

Sophie, you've ensnared my heart. It's yours and only yours. It's time, sweetheart. It's time for me to reveal myself. I've stood in the shadows of your world for far too long. You deserve a man to protect you. A man to sweep you off your feet. A man to destroy anyone or anything who tries to hurt you. Like the man who hurt you after the wedding. I've taken care of him and you never need to cry alone again because I will be here for you. I'll protect you forever. I'll be in the place where our eyes first met. Surely you remember the electricity that passed between us. I'll meet you there, my sweet Sophie.

Love always,
Your Secret Admirer

Sophie's whole body shuddered as she read the letter. She stumbled back two steps away from her front door, feeling the weight of her situation hit her in the chest like a balled fist knocking the wind out of her. She held her fingers over her mouth, her hand trembling.

He was watching her. It had to be the man on the bus. The man who always hid his eyes behind a baseball cap. She could picture the curve of his chiseled jaw covered with light brown stubble, the way his lips were always turned down at the corners in a frown. He always wore the same dark blue bomber jacket with zipper pockets on each side. Did he think he looked anonymous? Well, she had noticed him.

Apparently he'd been watching her for months. Sophie had gotten to the point where she could feel his presence, knowing he was there without even having to look. It chilled her to the bone to read the words he'd written on the page she held in her hand. He knew what happened the night of Cage and Felicity's wedding. The night he didn't leave the library when she was working alone. She had been terrified to the point that she had to call Theo to come pick her up played in her mind. Sophie's palms went clammy as she gripped the letter tight enough to wrinkle the pristine paper. It was all coming together.

Sophie felt tears stinging her eyes as she shook her head back and forth, and she wondered if this is what the universe had planned for her all along. If her current life was all it would ever amount to being. She was a hopeless, helpless little girl who couldn't even stand up for herself, just as Sister Meredith had predicted. She felt the darkness of the world creeping its way into her soul and shrouding her heart. Dread consumed her entire being.

It would never be better than what it was.

Sophie shoved the letter in the pocket of her jeans and walked out her front door, leaving it open behind her. It didn't matter anymore. She walked down the hallway of her apartment building, the one that always kind of reminded her of *The Shining* but did especially now. She pressed the small round button to call the elevator up to her floor.

She wasn't sure how long she stood there staring at the metal doors of the elevator. She was only snapped out of the trance-like state by the off-key dinging of the bell, signaling the arrival of the rickety car. She rode it down to the first floor and left out the front door.

Then...she started walking...walking, walking, and walking. She paid no mind to the street signs or lights as she let her feet carry her where they may. She passed by the salon she'd gotten her hair cut at, not noticing that the stylist inside had waved at her. She passed the coffee shop she visited every Saturday morning, where the barista knew her name and order based on the season. The world to Sophie was a blur, lost behind the shadows of the dark recesses of her mind she'd become lost in.

Soon, she found herself in the heart of downtown Chicago looking up at one of the tallest buildings around. She looked all the way up, her eyes scanning the windows, wondering what the people inside were doing. Was it an office building? An apartment building? Did the people have families? Friends? Were they loved? Were they cared for? Or did people hurt them like she'd been hurt her whole life?

Sophie thought back to the day she was adopted. The car drive home was quiet, save the sporadic babbling of her adopted sister. It wasn't until a few years later, Sophie realized just how bad, just how utterly fucked up her entire life had gotten on that day. She was taken from the generally loving and caring nuns at the orphanage and dropped in a rotten, stinking, shithole with an abusive "father".

It only took a few weeks for Sophie to learn how the house ran. The eldest of the girls took on the role of "mama", and ran the house, as the rest of them were beaten if they dared fall out of line. Her adopted father was a cruel drunkard, never showing love or compassion, only ever anger and resentment. He made sure the kids knew he was the provider, and they should grovel at his feet for each tiny privilege given to them all by his hand, basic necessities like regular meals and toilet paper.

Sophie swung open the tall glass door and walked into the luxurious lobby. She heard her shoes tapping on the granite floor and echoing all around the spacious room as she strolled towards the elevators. This one had the same bubble type buttons to call the elevator as her building. Without hesitation, she rode the elevator to the highest floor she could.

When the elevator signaled its impending stop she stood close to the doors, waiting for them to open. She caught a glimpse of her reflection in the shining metal before they opened. She looked pale and skinny, like a ghost version of herself. She had dark bags under her eyes and the hollows of her cheeks had begun to sink in. She brought her fingers up to touch her face to feel if that was really how she looked. Then, the doors slid open revealing an expansive hallway, which she stepped out into. She looked down one end, then the other. Searching until she saw a stairwell.

It didn't take her long to reach the roof. She was actually surprised that she didn't run into any locked or alarmed doors. The gravel that covered the rooftop crunched under her feet with each step she took. She reached the edge of the roof and rested her hands on the ledge. She let memories of her life flood through her mind. All of the painful traumas of the past came bubbling up and out of her.

"It's okay to be sad, you know," a small, sweet voice spoke from beside her. She whipped her head towards the sound. A little girl sat on the ledge, about twenty feet away from Sophie, with her back towards a fall that would easily end her life, the same one that would soon end Sophie's.

"What are you doing up here? You could get hurt." Sophie kept her voice firm, but cautious as she scolded the child for being on the roof alone.

"You could too. But that was your plan, wasn't it?" The girl's voice was blunt, all sweetness gone as she stared directly into Sophie's eyes.

"How-w-what? How'd you..." Sophie was so shocked by the little girl's words that she couldn't form a coherent thought. *How'd she know*?

"Because I'm omniscient." The girl fiddled with the skirt of her pink dress. A frown pulled at the corners of her pink lips.

"So, you're like God?" Sophie asked incredulously. *There is no way that this little girl could be anything but a child playing a prank.*

"I assure you I'm not playing a prank. I'm here to help you, Sophie."

"How do you know my name?"

"You know the definition of omniscient. I know you must, with your college degree and all."

"But you're just a little girl," Sophie said as her eyes grew wide. Could it be that this girl was telling the truth?

"And you're just a woman." The girl watched Sophie as she contemplated her response.

She was just a woman. And how could just one woman bear all that she had and still go on? How could Sophie continue living knowing there was another person out there that would eventually take her control away again?

The control of her life she'd fought to have for years, trying to get out of that house? The control over what happens to her body. He would take it away, again.

Sophie couldn't let that happen. She would die before she let that happen again. And that was what she planned to do. That's why her feet had taken her to the top of that building. "Tell me, Sophie, how can one woman change the world? How can one woman change everything? Or just the course of one life, even if just her own?"

"I can't change my own life. It's only ever been this way. Everyone else controls my life. So, I'm taking it back. I'm taking my life... back."

"Taking it back or just taking it?"

"I thought you're omniscient. You should already know."

"I do, but you don't."

"Don't what?"

"Know what it's like," the girl snapped. Sophie sat in silence as the girl turned to look out over the city. Sophie caught a glimpse of the look in her eyes. The girl's brown eyes were so sad, as if she were mourning the life she'd never had. "What it's like to watch everyone live their lives, while you're stuck behind the pane of a one-way window, and no one can see you or hear you. All alone."

Sophie watched as the little girl took in the sights of the city below them. "That sounds like torture," she replied. Sophie looked down at her feet, full of shame and embarrassment. She dug her toes into the gravel in front of her.

"And I'd do anything to save you from this," she said sadly. Sophie blinked at the girl. How could she be real? She couldn't be real. No child would've been able to get up to that roof. How did Sophie even get up there? Nothing was making sense.

"Well, you can't. I don't need saving anyways. I'm taking my control back. My life is *mine* to do with it as I please." Sophie knew she sounded like a petulant child at that point.

"Is this what your friends would want for you? Felicity? Cage? Theo? Endless nothingness? They want the best for you."

"They don't even know the real me. They don't see all the damaged baggage. That's all I am. Damaged goods. No one wants this in their life." Sophie felt her fingers dig into the concrete ledge in front of her. Her whole body felt so tense. What was it trying to tell her? To stay back. To not climb up like she'd planned on doing.

"Not many people in your situation would have been able to do what you've done."

"Oh, you mean survive the constant abuse from the moment I was adopted to the day I finally got emancipated? Just because it's taken this long for me to decide suicide is the best choice doesn't mean shit."

"You're just letting him win, Sophie," the girl shouted. Her voice was angry and dark.

"You know what? Fuck you. How could you even know anything about my life? You're not even fucking real!" Sophie shouted back as she pointed a finger at the girl. She felt a pang of guilt in her chest when she saw the girl's eyes go wide, the hurt apparent on her face.

"You're right. How could I be real? A child up on this rooftop? How did you even get up here, Sophie? Hmm? Is any of this real?" the girl challenged. Her voice was soft, but still holding an edge of anger.

"I-I don't know." Sophie looked out over the city. The famous Chicago breeze started stirring as she observed the constant motion on the streets below her. She wished deep down she was one of them, completely unaware of the situation up on the roof above them. "I can't do this. I'm damaged. I'm not strong enough. I'll never be strong enough," she whispered as tears began spilling down her cheeks.

"You've survived everything else up to this point. Please, don't give up now," all the sweetness had come back to the girl's voice as she begged and pleaded with Sophie not to go through with her plan.

"You don't understand. You could never understand."

"I understand much more than you know. You just need to believe in yourself, for once."

"I'm not strong enough anymore. I can't just keep picking up the pieces again and again when other people decide how they want my life to be. I need to take control. It's my turn to decide what happens, once and for all."

"It doesn't have to be this way you could be happy. Genuinely happy."

"No, I can't. I'm not who you think I am. You think you know, but you don't. You don't know me on the inside like I do. I'm out. I'm done. With everything. So just leave me alone please." Sophie glanced around the rooftop; the little girl had disappeared. Was her mental break over? Could she get on with her plan in peace? She looked down at the street again. A fire truck had stopped in front of the building. She had to do this soon. As she pulled herself up onto the ledge she could feel the ridges and bumps in the concrete press into her skin, the Chicago breeze rushing past her, blowing her hair around her face. Anyone else might be worried about not being able to see, but why did Sophie care? She wasn't about to see anything anymore.

Just before she could force herself over the edge she stopped. She closed her eyes, feeling the breeze caress her skin one more time. She listened to the sounds of the city she loved so much. The city that had saved her at one point in her life. *Thank you, Chicago.* The breeze died down and Sophie opened her eyes, taking in the last time she'd see her beloved city. *It's time.* Time for her to take control back from everyone she'd given it over to. Her life was her own and she would decide how and when it would end.

11

Angel ran the brush back and forth over the floor of the large, multi-stall bathroom, listening to the bristles scratch the tile floor as it cleaned away the soap scum from so many different kinds of soap over the years. He'd just about finished when the ear shattering alarm went off. He dropped everything and ran to the garage where all of his gear resided in a metal locker. His name was printed on a gold-plated metal plaque riveted to the black wooden frame.

The firefighters all donned their gear and piled into the truck. "Alright, there's a woman three blocks away on the roof of the Barlow building, possibly ready to jump. We are going to assist. If we're the first on the scene, Angel, I want you to go to the top. See if you can get her down. The rest of us will set up the net to catch her if she jumps. When we see you bring her down, we'll meet you up there for a physical assessment." The captain's voice was stern as he maneuvered the huge red truck around sharp corners, avoiding cars and pedestrians as he went.

"Yes sir!" Angel spoke through his mic. It only took a couple of minutes to reach the building. In a second he was out of his seat and on his way to the roof. He slammed through the first door. His boots made the metal steps ring and echo throughout the stairwell as he raced up the last flight of stairs.

When he reached the final door to the roof he hesitated. Angel laid his hands on the cool metal and pushed gently, trying to make sure he didn't scare the woman by making a huge ruckus slamming open the door. She didn't move.

He stepped toward the woman on the ledge, cringing at each step that caused the gravel to crunch under his heavy boots. Her short, curled hair was floating around her, carried in swirls by the breeze. He was reminded momentarily of the cartoon version of Pocahontas, except this woman's hair was platinum blonde and shining in the fading sunlight. He took his helmet off and set it on the ground, careful to be as quiet as possible. Any wrong move would send her careening towards Earth and her possible death if his crew didn't have the net ready.

He stepped closer. He could feel the breeze ruffling his own dark hair with the bulky helmet discarded behind him. He could feel his heart hammering in his chest and throbbing in his neck. How was he going to keep her safe? How was he going to get her back from the ledge she was perched on? Should he grab her hand and pull her back? No, she could jump forward, and he could drop her. Should he pick her up, bridal-style? No, he could drop her. Around her hips seemed to be the best option. Then what? She'd probably not be too happy with him. There wasn't much he'd be able to do at that point. He'd have to *establish rapport*.

Angel started unbuckling and unzipping his jacket. He dropped it next to him. He wanted to be able to have the best grip possible and he knew his jacket would get in the way. He stepped closer to the woman standing on the concrete ledge. She didn't seem to notice him. She was too lost in thought to hear his boots crunching as he crossed over the gravel, and he stepped closer to her. The breeze ruffled his hair again, also causing her blonde curls to be carried to the right of her. He saw faint yellow bruises on her left shoulder and her right wrist, almost like fingerprints. His heart ached for the woman. Someone had hurt her.

Once he was close enough to her, in one swift movement he wrapped his arms around her hips and pulled her body back from the ledge and into him. Her shifting weight as she realized what was happening knocked Angel off balance and they fell backwards. She screamed as they hit the ground and tried to get out of his arms, her nails clawing at his hands and forearms. He felt the gravel dig into his back and shoulders as she shifted back and forth, trying to fight her way out of his grip. "Stop! Stop!" Angel shouted at her. "I'm not going to let you go. I've got you."

"No! Let me go! Let me go!" She sobbed. She was almost incoherent from her hysteria.

"I can't let you go," he told the woman struggling in his arms. He shifted his body to sit them up so he could hold her in between his legs, hoping it would calm her and feel less restrictive.

"I don't want this! I don't want this life!" She tried punching and hitting his hands to break his grip.

"I'm not letting you go," he told her. He kept his voice calm, being careful to make sure he wasn't holding her too tightly.

"It hurts! Just let me go, please!" She begged and pleaded to no avail. Today would not be the day she would die. Angel would do everything in his power to make sure that was the case.

"No, you're not going to hurt yourself. I'm sorry you hurt, I'm sorry someone hurt you. You can't take this way out, though." He was calm, he was trying to be kind. He couldn't imagine what had driven someone like her to the lengths she was about to go to for her pain to end.

"Please," she whimpered as her body was wracked with silent sobs. Angel held her. She kept pushing at his hands, without being able to free herself from his grip. It felt like an eternity until she'd finally given up. It was maybe a minute or so, in reality. As soon as she stopped fighting him, she turned her head and looked into the eyes of the man who'd pulled her back from the silent salvation she sought.

Her eyes took Angel's breath away. They were bright blue and bore into his soul. A shockwave passed through his body the instant their gaze connected. The tears streaming down her pale cheeks broke his heart. He wanted to brush them away for her, help her heal from the pain she'd felt. She was so beautiful, he wondered why someone would ever want to hurt her.

"I can't let you hurt yourself, no matter how much you think it's the only way out." He kept his voice soft and reassuring. Her plump bottom lip trembled as she watched him. She had high cheekbones - one was covered in a faint, light yellow bruise - a cute button nose, dimples, and full, kissable, luscious lips. "It's okay, I'm here to help you."

The woman closed her eyes and shook her head, she pushed at his hands again. She realized the effort was futile and stopped. She dropped her head into her hands and cried, her body shaking against his. "It's no use," she sobbed. "You should've just let me go."

Angel held her against him, trying to steady her with his own frame. Her bare arms were growing cold in the fading sunlight and fierce breeze on the Chicago rooftop. When she stopped crying again she turned in his grip. Angel readied himself for a more intense fight to keep her safe in his arms.

He was surprised when she wrapped her arms around his neck and hugged him tightly. He held her close. It was what came natural to him. He tried to comfort the broken woman in his arms. "It's okay. You're safe. I'm here," he whispered to her.

"Don't let him hurt me. He's been sending me letters. Watching me. I can't. I just can't anymore."

"No one is going to hurt you, I promise." He winced at his own words. He didn't understand why he would promise that to a complete stranger. He knew he couldn't keep it. The last thing she needed was a broken promise. Legally, he wasn't even allowed to make sure she was okay after they both left the rooftop. He couldn't check the database for her name or phone number. Nothing. She would have to search him out.

The thought that he might never see this woman again made him want to hold her closer and never let go. His baser instincts were muddling his brain. Why would he be feeling so protective over this stranger? He'd saved beautiful women before in training and in chaotic real-life accidents he'd stumbled upon, but there was something different about this one. Something that told his soul he wasn't done protecting her once they left the rooftop. He felt her body tremble as she cried into his shoulder.

It felt like he'd held her for hours by the time the rest of his team made it to the roof. He knew it couldn't have been more than a few minutes from the time he'd made it up himself. They dropped their gear and started their exam to ensure she was uninjured. She wouldn't let go of him through the whole thing.

"She's okay. I've got her. It's fine. I'll get her down for the paramedics to take a look at her when they get here."

His roommate, Todd, met his eyes, an unspoken questioning. Angel nodded once, trying to reassure him that it was all okay. "We'll wait for you at the truck," he said as he touched Angel's shoulder for a moment before leaving the roof. Angel nodded in reply.

"Can you tell me your name?" Angel asked once it was just them, alone again.

"Sophie. Sophie Martin," she whispered.

The name sent a shockwave through his body. Sophie? His Sophie? From St John's? It couldn't be. This could not be the same bubbly blonde girl he knew from the orphanage. This broken woman in his arms *couldn't* be *his Sophie*... It wasn't possible. Her name was different anyways. His Sophie's last name wasn't Martin.

"It's nice to meet you, Sophie. Do you think you can walk down to the ambulance with me?" he asked. She looked into his dark brown eyes, almost pleading with him to not leave her, to hold her for the rest of time. He had to fight the urge to comply with her silent request.

"No, I can't," she cried as she wrapped her arms around his neck again. "I can't go back down. He'll find me, he will. I can't let him find me," she whimpered between sobs, vigorous head shaking, and more struggling to get away.

"It's okay. I've got you. You'll be safe with us. I'll stay with you till the ambulance comes, okay?" Angel said as he pulled away from her to look into her eyes. "I'm not leaving until you're safe, Sophie." His heart hurt for the woman. He wished she were his Sophie but didn't at the same time. He would take her home and keep her safe for the rest of her life, but he knew deep in his heart, this wasn't the same person. He would be able to mend her broken heart if she were his Sophie.

"Okay," she said as she let him pick her up in his arms and carry her to the door. He pulled it open, easily able to hold her slim frame with one arm. She was exhausted from the entire ordeal.

He didn't mind carrying her. She rested her head on his shoulder and closed her eyes. It was the first time she'd relaxed since he pulled her off the ledge and it had been about twenty minutes since then. He knew he could be wrong, time seemed to slow with her in his arms. It was like the universe was allowing him time to drink her in because he'd never see her again. The thought made his heart ache.

It was one of the hardest parts of his job. He never got to know what happened in the end. The problem most first responders had with their job was never knowing the ending. Would she be safe and turn her life around and find peace? He would never know.

He took the elevator down to the first floor. She looked like she was asleep by the time the doors opened again. Her breathing had evened out and he took the chance to study her face. Soft and peaceful in sleep, she looked like an angel with a halo of platinum blonde curls, messy from the wind on the roof. Sometimes he had wished he'd chosen to be a cop instead. Then, he could hunt down the person that hurt her. He would take great pleasure in locking the bastard away, leaving him to rot in jail for the rest of his life, but he'd taken a different course.

He wanted to save lives, just like his father. A second generation firefighter - kind of. Lester Harris was, of course, his adopted father but Angel walked in his footsteps and became a firefighter anyway. Lester was his idol. From the moment they brought Angel home, he wanted to be a firefighter, just like his dad. Camille, being the worry-wart she was, tried as hard as she could to get him to pick another career, but he never strayed. It was his destiny. He could feel it in his bones. For reasons just like today, saving lives was what he was meant to do. Pulling the woman in his arms off the ledge confirmed it for him.

He walked out the lobby door and was met by his captain who shot him a proud smile and gave him one stiff nod. One that said, "Good job, son," without saying a word.

Angel took the sleeping woman to the ambulance and laid her on the waiting gurney. The second he let her go her eyes shot open. She went nuclear, full hysterics. She screamed as if she were in the most horrific pain and flailed her arms as she tried to climb off the gurney and run away.

"Get me two and a half milligrams of droperidol!" the lead paramedic shouted at his younger partner. Angel helped the older paramedic restrain the woman as the other drew up the fast-acting sedative.

Once they were able to stabilize her enough, with Angel's help, the younger paramedic jammed the needle in her deltoid muscle and pushed down on the plunger of the syringe. Angel's heart broke for the poor woman. He wished he could keep an eye on her after she was packed in the back of the ambulance and driven away.

Sophie's eyes felt so heavy, as if they were covered in concrete. She tried so hard to blink, to see the world around her. The more she tried the more her whole body felt the same way. She tried lifting her arms to rub her eyes, but they wouldn't move, her range of motion restricted by something cold, and metal locked around her wrists.

She tried again to pry her eyelids open. Finally, the world came into view. It was bright and blurry, it made her eyes ache and she closed them again. Sophie felt like the whole platform she was laid on was dipping her from side to side. She'd have felt sick if she had anything in her stomach.

"Ms. Martin, you're waking up," a soft voice spoke from the corner of the room. "How are you feeling?"

Sophie whimpered, unable to form a coherent thought in her mind, let alone out loud.

"That's okay, you're just feeling the effects of the medication wearing off. Droperidol is great for when people can't calm down, but the recovery can be rough for some."

There were heels clicking across the tile floor, coming closer to Sophie. She tried opening her eyes again, this time she saw what she was sure was a woman in a white doctor coat with dark hair and eyes, but with skin as white as the coat. She squeezed her eyes tightly, trying to clear the blurriness.

"It's okay. You're safe here. Do you remember what happened? On the rooftop?" the female voice asked as Sophie felt a warm hand on her own.

She flinched away from the touch, not wanting it, not understanding what exactly was going on, why she couldn't move her hands.

"We'll get these off soon. We just need to make sure you aren't a danger to yourself, or others, first. Now, Ms. Martin, do you remember why you were on the roof?"

Sophie searched her brain for the right answer. The fuzziness of the medication made it hard to think. What rooftop was she talking about?

"Sophie, do you remember anything before that? What led you to go to the rooftop?" the doctor asked.

As Sophie shifted in what she'd come to realize was a hospital bed, she could feel it in her pocket. A balled up piece of paper with words that made her shudder right down to the deepest parts of her soul. The burning reason why she'd been driven to the breezy rooftop was concealed just beneath the fabric of her jeans.

They wouldn't believe her, not with her history. Sophie stayed silent. It was the best course of action she could think of.

"Ms. Martin, if you cooperate with me, we can get you out of here sooner and back to your life."

Sophie looked away from the pale woman in the white coat. She was just trying to do her job. Sophie could understand that. This woman wouldn't understand her, though, why she had been compelled to the rooftop not by her own volition, but by that of another. A sinister man who would take her as his possession. Take her will and choice away from her. The same way everyone else did. The same way that damn doctor did. And the firefighter who pulled her back.

But he was different. His intentions were pure. His heart was in the right place. He'd held her, calmed her, listened to her. He promised to keep her safe. His eyes told her it was the truth. His beautiful, shining brown eyes that had taken her breath away. Sophie bit her lip, determined to hold her silence. She held the image of the firefighter in her mind as she ignored the woman in the white coat.

12

February 2021

"I just can't believe she's been missing for three weeks!" *Ugh, Pamela is just so annoying. We get it. She was your best friend, get over it!* "We were supposed to get drinks last Friday. I'm her best friend, she would've told me if she was going out of town."

Guess it's time to turn on the charm. "Well, that's true, I suppose. Maybe she found someone and fell in love? After all, she was a very beautiful woman. Any guy would fall for her."

"Hey Pamela, isn't that Stacie right there?" *What is Walker talking about? That couldn't possibly be - What the hell!? It is! But how? Wait... something's not right...*

"Oh my God, Stacie! Stacie! Stacie, please! Stop ignoring me!" *Wow, she's really running up to that girl who clearly isn't Stacie. Some best friend. Doesn't even realize that this blonde looks nothing like Stacie. Pathetic. Although, she does look familiar...*

"Oh, hi! I'm sorry, I didn't realize you were talking to me. Unfortunately, my name's not Stacie, I'm Sophie. Do I look like a Stacie? I've never thought of it. I always figured if I changed my name it would be Erika with a 'k'. Oh no, I'm rambling, I'm so sorry, are you ok?" *Sophie, huh? She's so beautiful. Now, she really could get any man she wanted. I've never seen a woman look so angelic in a plain t-shirt and jeans. She's practically glowing...*

"Oh no, it's not you. We're sorry to have bothered you, Miss. Please, take this muffin for your troubles. Have a good day!" *Walker's a stand up guy. Though, I'm disturbed that a man of only thirty is balding. Stand up guy, but the genetics are far from it.*

"Oh, my goodness, thank you!" *I'm sure she gets free stuff all the time. Makes me sick, but her smile...*

"Well guys, I must be going. I have a client soon. Pamela, I truly hope Stacie turns up soon. I'm sure she's missing you as much as you miss her." *I truly do believe that.*

Now, where did that Sophie go? Ah, there she is. The Arlington, huh? I still need to head in there and check in with Felicity. That self-righteous b- Hold up, who's calling me now? Oh right, my ten o'clock.

"Hola Jenny, I'm on my way now..."

March 2021

It's been so long since I've felt like this. It feels invigorating. All the other women I've had...they were nothing. But this one... she's different. She's...special. She's...right on time. Ah, Sophie. You never disappoint. I'm so happy fate continues to bring us together. But I still have others in my life that I can't quite get rid of yet. So soon, Sophie, I'll have you.

"Hola! Yes, yes, I know... I'm glad you're back on your feet, Margaret... I don't think you should be propositioning such a dirty dance as the tango, mi amor, you've only just gotten out of surgery... Yes, I will be there tomorrow for our weekly meeting... Ok, mi bella... Talk soon."

Ah, Margaret. Such a sweet old lady. Harmless...except for those glorious chocolate chip cookies. Oh boy, I can't wait. They remind me of childhood...

As does she, my glorious Sophie. Why must you align yourself with that know-it-all librarian? Come to me.

Ah, well. I know when she's off. I'll be back soon.

June 2021

Well, this sure is interesting. I didn't think that stiff Felicity would ever be caught dead in a dance club, but I suppose that Cage fellow has changed her a bit. Oh, but Sophie... my Sophie, how lovely you look. Effortlessly elegant. So flawless.

Who the hell is this guy!? Kissing her hand!? No one should defile my Sophie's pure hand! Whoa, whoa. Calm down. He's just being a gentleman. But I swear, if he even thinks of touching her lips...

She even looks beautiful dancing. She really is perfect! Oh, don't you dare touch her! I swear, if you - Oh my god, did she just...back it onto him!? I...I think I need a drink.

"Ginger ale and Jameson, por favor." *This'll take the edge off a bit.*

Look at this drunk idiot. "Hey amigo, watch where you're going."

"Sorry, bud." *Why the hell did he pat my back? Creep. And whose voice sounds like that? He must smoke ten packs a day! He must not realize his body is a temple, like how I treat mine. He'll never get a woman as lovely as my Sophie - OH MY GOD! DID THEY JUST KISS!?*

"Agh!"

"Hey buddy, I think you've had enough. Time for you to leave." *This meathead really thinks I'm drunk. I might as well entertain him and just get out.*

"I'm going buddy, I'm going. Por favor, I don't want any trouble, amigo."

The next day

That sure is some fancy car. Some rich schmuck checking out a book on how to be a prick, I bet. Ah, there's my angel. Why is she going to the car...? Is that the same guy from last night? Why is she getting in the car!? Is this a date? Looks like it's time to take my evening jog a little early today.

Well, this sure is some fancy spot. So, Sophie's into the rich guys, huh? Never pegged her for a gold digger, but I can make it work. Should I try to get closer so that I can hear? No, probably not. No need to cause a scene, this place hates guys wearing athletic gear. That would only worry my Sophie, so perhaps I'll remain outside looking in.

Dear God, this guy smiles a lot. I get it, she's beautiful, but there's no way she's flattered by this. Right? There's no way... What the hell is she doing? She can't be leaning in for a -

"On your left!" *God, I hate cyclists.*

"Watch where you're going, you waste of three minutes and a bottle of corner store booze." *I can't believe I missed it. I hope she didn't kiss him...*

August 2021

Where is she? She should be home right now. I don't believe there was any plan to go out. She normally just stays inside on her weekends. I'll just have to wait for her to come back. Luckily the coffee shop on the corner is still open. Wait! Today is the day of the wedding! Thankfully that slut Felicity has such a big mouth. I know exactly where it is. Ah, let me go grab my nice watch...

1 hour later

Oh! Sophie, how I wish I could stay, but security here is just too tight. You look like an angel. I wish I could hold you in my arms...

5 hours later

Hmm...an Uber? Most of the people around here take the bus. Oh, Sophie! Why is she in an Uber? She seems a bit drunk. Something about this driver seems familiar. I'd better follow them inside.

Wow, so this is what it looks like from the inside... Sophie should be living in a palace, not this run-down excuse for an apartment building. But maybe her apartment is nicer... Oh there's the elevator. I should wait to take the next one. Don't want to startle her...Alright, it looks like the elevator has stopped...on the ninth floor. Perfect. I'll head up now. The driver should be coming down...

Hmm...no driver...

Oh, come on you piece of junk, go faster! That can't be a normal noise for an elevator. How does she ride this thing every day?

Ninth floor final- What was that crash? This way? I think there's a fight happening...

Here's the door. Wait...it's Sophie! There's that driver! What the hell does he think he's doing! What...am I...doing...? Why...am I breathing...so heavily? This is...turning me on? Not again. Stop it. Hands, stop it! Don't rub it! Fine, but only...for a little while...

Her breasts... they look so perfect. I never thought I would see them like this. My God, I'm so hard. Don't hurt her...but please hurt her. But make her scream. That should be me inside you, my love. Oh, how I wish it was me! Those other women were only a tease compared to your body. Such a firm and bubbly butt. I wonder what it feels to shove myself in between...

He's done. Good. Now, it's my turn for a little fun...

Wow, this backseat is surprisingly roomier than it appears from the outside. Ah, the door...

"Hey Mr. Uber Driver, I have a place you need to take me."

"What the hell? Hey buddy, if you want a ride, you're gonna have to use the app."

"Oh, I don't think so!" *I haven't had to do this to a man in years... I forgot how much stronger they are than women. But he's tiring out now. Luckily his windows are tinted. Now to just hop in the driver seat and...*

2 hours later

Now that he's all tied up, I should make it up to Sophie. I pleasured myself without her permission and that's just so wrong. I need to be better. I'm so ashamed. Maybe I should have stayed and kissed her wounds. Then, she'd be happy. Then, we could've made real love. That would've been lovely. But first...I should teach him a lesson about touching my dear Sophie. Actually...let's write her a letter first. Maybe I should tell her I love her?

"Oh, great, Mr. Uber man, you're awake. What should I say to Sophie?"

"You sick bastard! Where the hell am I?"

"I'm thinking about a confession of love. You think that's too much?"

"The police will come looking for me! The GPS on my phone will let them know -"

"Oh, you silly little man. You think I haven't already dealt with that? Your car is long gone, and that cell phone of yours happened upon a hobo fire. Now, back to the task at hand..." *Where's that old calligraphy set? Ah, there it is. Mother said I might need it someday, and sure enough...* "How should I start it? My...Beloved Sophie? No, too intense. Sophie, my darling? Definitely not. That's so eighteenth century. My Dearest Sophie... Yes, I like that! What do you think?"

"You're sick! Who the hell are you anyw-" *Ah, that should shut him up for a while. Now...*

"Oh, perfect timing! You're awake! I can read you my letter now. Tell me if Sophie will love it: 'Dear Sophie,

I must say, you do take my breath away. You were stunning last night. The blush pink of your dress made your flawless porcelain skin glow in the soft, romantic light of the crystal chandeliers in the ballroom. The way the satin flowed over your every curve could bring any mortal man to his knees, and the pout of your luscious lips would drive him mad. You certainly drove me crazy.

I hope you know how much you affect me. I wish I were brave enough to tell you, face to face but your presence steals my breath away. To hold your soft, delicate hands in mine and tell you that you make my heart beat harder than it ever has. That just the sight of you makes me want you more and more every time I see you.

I hope you know exactly how amazing you are. Your kindness knows no bounds, your heart is filled with generosity that most lack. I've seen the sadness in your eyes when you see the homeless people and stray pets around the city. I've seen how graciously you always tip the servers who take care of you. If only the people who could make true change happen had hearts like yours.

You make me want to be better. A better, less selfish, more giving man. I plan to start immediately. There's a homeless shelter near my house. Perhaps volunteering there will help show me how to have a heart like yours. I'll let you know what I learn about myself there. Until then, I hope you stay safe and keep being your amazing, generous self.

Sincerely,

Your Secret Admirer'. I say 'secret admirer' because I don't think I'm ready for her to know it's me yet. What do you think?"

"Oh my God, you're insane! You think some chick's gonna fall for you after you jacked off while standing in her doorway watching her get raped? I may be scum, but you're far worse, my friend." *Where is my stamp? I should heat it up and test it out. I hear right behind the ear is similar to wax...*

"Who asked you?" *Ah, that sizzle is soothing.*

"Agh, you motherfu-" *Ok, I'm bored of him now. I'll deliver this in the morning.*

The Next Morning

Alright, 969...970...971...972...now for the knife - wait, is anyone looking? Ok, perfect. Let's just gently open it so as not to scare her...here we go. Wow, she needs to lubricate that hinge. Place it underneath these two bills here. Hopefully she finds it with ease.

2 Hours Later

Yes, I knew she would like it! Oh, to make my Sophie smile, my life is complete. Now, what shall I say in my next letter...

A Week Later

More smiles. I think it may be time to reveal myself. Clearly, she loves me, too. And I am what every woman wishes to have. Yes, it is time.

Another Week Later

I know her schedule like I know my birthday. She should be home now. Probably reading the letter. How should I make my entrance? Well, hopefully this loud mouth Pamela doesn't give it away.

"Oh my God, flowers! Is this why you haven't been stopping by lately? Who's the lucky lady? Oh, so romantic, and right here at our shop! Stacie would love this..." *God, Stacie again? I should've chosen another place. Oh well, she should be here soon.*

An Hour Later

"Oh no, don't tell me she stood you up? So sad, I'm sorry, hun." *Shut the hell up, Pamela! But she is right, something is wrong. I should check on my sweet.*

"Oh, it's quite alright. These things happen. Mi corazon, please place these on Stacie's grave for me." *That'll shut her up.*

"Stacie's grave? She's not dead! How could you say such a thing? I'm so..." *Can't she see I'm walking away? And I thought blondes were supposed to be the dumb ones. Where's Sophie...*

30 Minutes Later

Her mailbox is empty, so she's definitely seen the letter. Maybe she's waiting for me upstairs...Why is her door open? What the hell happened here?

"Sophie, mi amor?" *Hmmm, no answer...* "Are you here?" *She's gotta be here...* "Sophie, where are you?" *What kind of game is she playing?* "Sophie!" *Something has happened to my angel! I must go find her!*

---

48 hours later

"WHERE THE HELL IS SHE? I've been searching this city for two days! She's nowhere to be found! No one has reported her missing...maybe she left me...no, no... she wouldn't do that. All of her stuff is here... It still smells like her in here... What if I..."

I can't believe I'm taking my clothes off in Sophie's room. I should be looking for her! But her smell is so enticing. Are those...yes, her dirty panties. I knew she would wear something classy and sexy like this lace thong. Inhale. "Ooohhh wooow...that...oh that smells so... Oh my God, I'm so hard. I can't...take it..."

I can't believe I'm really defiling Sophie's bed with my naked body. I should stop. But the feeling of her lace around my erection feels so... "Oh God I can't hold it in... aaahhhh..." *No, no, don't do it. You don't deserve a climax. You need to find Sophie. Now, NOW! Get up! That's it. Put the panties down. Shake it off. Now get dressed. You've got work to do.*

---

24 Hours Later

"Of course, she's in the last place I'd expect. Keep an eye on her for me, would you? I can't go back there just yet, I recently noticed someone's been watching me. You'd better get back before they notice you're missing," *Sacred Heights, huh? She'll be in good hands there. Now, to find out why...*

13

Seventy-two hours of the same questions.

Seventy-two hours of being stuck in the same, uncomfortable, pristinely white room.

Seventy-two hours of pure Hell.

They wonder why people go insane. *It's because of things like this*, Sophie decided. She had been ready to leave for seventy-two hours.

She hated hospitals. They reminded her of the worst times in her life. It was better to stay calm and ignore everything around her and focus on channeling her thoughts towards getting the hell out of there. It smelled like bleach and other disinfectants, with a trace of blood and urine. The smell made her a little nauseous.

Where am I going to go, though? Sophie wondered as she waited on the nurse who was supposed to be bringing her discharge paperwork any minute. She obviously could not go home to her apartment. The stalker knew where she lived, knew which apartment she'd been renting, and even which mailbox was hers.

How did this person know *so much* about her? It's not like she posted her every move on social media, and even when she did post, her accounts were private. Only visible to those she chose to let see them.

She couldn't go to Felicity's. She was newly married, and Sophie was not about to barge in on their life like that. She needed a new place to live. They didn't need to take in someone like her.

Sophie couldn't even go back to the library. The stalker must know where she worked and must have followed her home. She worked in a very public place, so finding her wasn't hard.

Sophie closed her eyes and tried to focus on the memories she had of the man in the dark jacket with a baseball hat covering his eyes. She couldn't even pick him out of a lineup. He was careful not to show too much of his face, but she could remember the curve of his lips and the light, ashy brown stubble that covered the lower half of his face, and the light, creamy color of his pale skin. She'd almost swear he was attractive if he wasn't the scariest person she'd ever encountered. Or rather, not encountered.

The chubby nurse with auburn hair came back to her room and handed her a packet of information. "Here's your discharge paperwork. Here's the list of medications prescribed to you. If you start feeling any sort of way again, please give us a call, okay hun?" The nurse gave her a sad smile.

They'd tried to convince her to stay and get treatment. Sophie couldn't risk the man finding her here. Who knows what would happen if he found her?

Sophie took the packet from the woman and nodded in agreement, trying to silently let the nurse know she really wouldn't be back any time soon.

Sophie wondered briefly what happened to the man with the curly, brown hair who usually walked her out. She couldn't remember if he was an orderly or a nurse. Whatever he was, he made the effort to check on her each time she'd been admitted. An effort she appreciated. No one else had tried to establish a connection like he had.

Sophie stood from the hard mattress and followed the nurse out. She didn't need directions. She'd been to Sacred Heights and knew her way around, but she let the nurse lead the way. Sophie's eyes trailed along the familiar walls, doors, and windows as she was lost in thought again about where she would go next until a ruckus broke out in the hallway behind her. Her head snapped around to see exactly what had caused it.

A burly, older man she recognized from TV, some FBI hot shot who'd murdered his superior last year. He was pushing the orderlies surrounding him away. He shouted something about being needed.

Sophie's heart sank as she thought about the man's past. He'd obviously been pushed over the brink by too much stress. She knew the feeling, which is why she herself was so familiar with the mental hospital she was about to leave, in the city she couldn't wait to run away from.

How would she get out of Chicago without this stalker knowing? She needed money, clothes, and her important documents. That was all that was necessary. How would she get those without anyone seeing her going to her apartment? Sophie walked out the front doors and took a breath of fresh, clean air - air that didn't smell like antiseptics.

It was late summer; the days were starting to get shorter. The sun was just setting below the trees that lined the drive up to Sacred Heights. Sophie set off down the path. It was near a half mile long walk to the main road, then another mile to the bus stop she needed to be at. The walk would generally only take her about thirty minutes, but since it was starting to get dark she kept a quick pace. Twenty minutes if she could power walk the whole way.

The wind started up shortly after she made it to the main road. She only had on the tank top and jeans she'd been admitted in, and it didn't do much to cut the chill of the breeze that shook the trees now behind her - their leaves rustling against each other. She rubbed her hands up and down her arms as she walked. Maybe it would encourage some extra blood flow to keep her warm.

She had hope, until she watched the dark clouds roll in from the east. Nasty, gray, monstrous clouds. If only she had her phone, she'd order a taxi. She'd left it in her apartment the day she'd been picked up and taken to the hospital.

Sacred Heights had been kind enough to give her a bus pass, though. At least she wouldn't have to walk the seventeen miles it was to her apartment. She needed to pack and leave that place. She hoped that no one was watching her building. She'd be quick. Grab a bag, pack her clothes, grab her purse and her file of important papers, shove it in the bag and go. She'd give herself ten minutes. Max.

With a plan in place, she felt a little better. Sophie took a deep breath as she reached the bus stop. She needed to fill Felicity in, just so she didn't sic Cage on her. He could find anyone - a talent he'd gained while he was with the bureau, Sophie had learned.

What would she tell Felicity? That she had a family emergency? No, Felicity was smarter than that. She wouldn't believe it. She couldn't tell Felicity the truth. That could put her in danger; or worse, Felicity would make Cage track this person down. That was something Sophie could never allow. She could never repay him. She knew his and his company's services were unbelievably expensive.

How was she going to convince Felicity that she was okay but that she needed to leave - especially with her recent disappearing act? That would take some thought. Sophie had the whole bus ride back into the heart of Chicago to think about it.

Once the bus stopped in front of the John Arlington Library, Sophie was on alert. She looked up and down the street, searching for the familiar but unknown man that haunted her nightmares. He was nowhere to be found.

The light inside was still on, just as she'd expected it to be. She knew Felicity would still be at the library. She rarely left before seven o'clock most days and she assumed it couldn't be much past six. Sophie pulled in a deep breath and blew it out, drawing in the courage to tell Felicity what she needed to hear, the courage to break her heart.

Sophie pulled open the glass door and walked inside. She spotted Felicity immediately but had gone unnoticed by the owner. She watched Felicity run a hand over her face, pushing her glasses up for a moment; something Sophie had watched many times when the woman had come to a seemingly insurmountable issue. Every time she'd done so, she would fix her glasses with renewed strength and conquer said problem.

Sophie was envious of Felicity's strength; she'd aspired to be like Felicity her whole life. Strong, brave, intelligent. Sophie had never felt like she quite matched up, though. Felicity was one of a kind. Sophie's heart ached in her chest, almost stopping her in her tracks. She could just stay. Ask for help.

No. She needed to do this on her own. She had to do this on her own. She'd always had help. She was always the weakest one. She could do this.

"Felicity," Sophie spoke softly, her voice almost a whisper but clearly audible in the empty library. Felicity's head whipped towards her so fast, Sophie thought it just might turn all the way around.

"Oh my God! Sophie! Where have you been?" Felicity ran around the desk and up to Sophie. She wrapped her arms around the smaller woman as their bodies collided, nearly sending them tumbling to the floor.

"I needed to take a break from everything, that's all." Sophie's voice was weak. Did she really have the heart to lie to the one person who'd put so much effort into her life to help her succeed, the one person who had always believed in her?

"You could have told me you needed some time off! I was so worried about you!" Felicity was squeezing Sophie so tight that it hurt her shoulders.

"I'm fine, I just need some more time. I just came to let you know that I'm okay. I'm not coming back though. I gotta go home and deal with some stuff. Okay?"

Felicity let go of the woman but kept her hands firmly on her shoulders as if to make sure she didn't disappear again and studied her for a moment. "You're not okay, Soph. What's wrong?" Felicity took in the differences in her best friend's demeanor. The confident, perky young woman was now distant and cold. The warmth in her eyes was replaced by a sadness so deep Felicity could drown in it.

"I'm fine, I promise. Like I said, I just gotta deal with some things. It'll take a while though, okay?" Sophie felt the tears prickling in her eyes.

"Sophie, you have a home here. You can't just up and leave. What's going on? I can help you. Cage and I can help you get through whatever it is you're going through. Please, don't leave." Tears welled up in Felicity's green eyes.

"I gotta go, but I'll keep in touch, okay?" Sophie pulled away from Felicity's hands. She had to leave now, or she wouldn't be able to. Breaking Felicity's heart was a lot harder than she thought it was going to be. "I'm sorry, but I gotta go. I'll keep in touch," she promised, knowing full well it was a lie.

Sophie walked out of the library. She did her best to ignore the sound of Felicity sniffling behind her as she walked away. She ran to the building her apartment was in and took the elevator up.

Once in the small studio, she packed everything she would need to get far away from Chicago. She paused at the coat rack on the wall. There was a letter perched on the top.

She dropped everything she was holding and reached out to grab the letter but hesitated just before she could pick up the familiar, cream-colored envelope with stark black calligraphy. She stood there for a moment; her arm outstretched as if frozen in time just before she picked up the letter.

No. He had no hold on her life anymore. This person would not control her anymore. Her life belonged to her and no one else.

Sophie picked up her bag and purse, loaded with her most important possessions, and left the apartment she'd called home. Ready to leave behind the life she had built with the woman who had become her best friend. She had to leave it all because of *him*. Sophie glared at the letter and left it in its place as she rushed out the door and down the hallway to the elevator.

Her knee bounced nervously as she sat at the bus stop, waiting for the next bus to arrive. According to the app, it wouldn't be there for another fifteen minutes. A lifetime for the woman who sat there in the rain, which had just started pouring down on her. She should own a rain jacket of some kind but had never brought herself to actually purchase one since she moved back to Chicago. A silly mistake.

She sat on the metal bench, soaked to the bone. Her blonde hair stuck to the sides of her face and her clothes rubbed the wrong way on her skin every time she moved. Fifteen minutes of agony is all she had left until the bus would come.

She was surprised when a pair of headlights pulled up to a stop in front of the bench she sat on. The window of a beautiful red truck rolled down and a familiar face greeted her with a smile. "I thought I recognized you. We met the other day. Do you need a ride?" the man asked.

Sophie was amazed he'd pulled up in front of her at that very moment. He was like a guardian angel or something. "No, I'm okay. Just waiting for the bus. Never got a rain jacket, silly me." She waved her hand as if to dismiss the man she'd spent the last few days praying she'd see again.

"Are you sure? It's getting pretty nasty out. I wouldn't want you to get sick or hypothermic."

"I'm okay, I assu-" but she was cut off by a bright flash of lightning and an ear-shattering roar of thunder that made her jump so high that her body came up off the bench. Of course, the first storm of the summer was the one time she really needed to get out of town.

"Please, get in. I really don't want you to get struck by lightning." He unlocked the doors for her and reached over to push the door open.

"Okay, fine." Sophie stood and climbed into the large truck, finally out of the rain.

"Where to? Home?" The firefighter asked her.

"Uh, no. I can't go home..." Sophie didn't know where to direct him. She was just going to ride the bus as far as it took her, then stay in a hotel for the night. Then, rinse and repeat the next day.

"Do you need a place to stay for the night?" he asked. Sophie's heart leapt in her chest. She looked up at him and bit her bottom lip, not knowing how to answer.

Yes, she wanted to tell him desperately, but she knew what his next offer would be; with him. That she couldn't do. She had just refused Felicity's offer. She couldn't turn right around and take this stranger's offer for a warm bed. His dark brown eyes searched her face for a clue as to what she needed.

"It's okay, I have a house. You can stay with me if you need to. My couch is comfortable. You can even have the bed if you want it," he smiled as he joked. Sophie felt paralyzed. She knew she needed to answer but he'd just asked what she didn't want to hear.

"Um... I mean, I can go to a hotel or something..." she said feebly, knowing somehow this man wouldn't let her do that. He was too kind to make her sleep in a disgusting hotel in the middle of Chicago when he had a nice, warm, clean bed she could borrow for the night.

"No need. My roommate is on vacation, so it'll be nice and quiet. Not gross like a downtown Chicago hotel room," he said as he made a face then smiled.

"Okay, I guess. If it's no problem. But just for the night," she said as she buckled in.

"I realize this is all probably weird. I just couldn't leave you out there in the rain, you know. I don't think I've ever actually introduced myself. I'm Angel, Angel Harris."

"Sophie Martin and thank you for doing this. Regular people aren't usually this nice. So, thanks, I guess."

They remained in silence the rest of the quick drive to Angel's house on the outskirts of downtown Chicago. It was a small, white house with blue shutters, a blue front door, and a literal white picket fence around the front yard.

How could he have such a perfect little house in Chicago? Sophie didn't think they existed. It was so cute and somehow fit him perfectly.

She glanced back over to the man, whom she now knew as Angel, the firefighter who'd saved her life three days prior. She almost laughed out loud over the fact that she'd just thought of him as a guardian angel and his name was just that. Angel.

After he parked the truck in the two-car driveway, he hopped out and jogged around to open her door for her and take her bags. Sophie's cheeks burned crimson. She'd never been treated that way. She muttered a thank you and followed him into the house, eager to get out of the rain and her wet clothes.

He set her bags down on the dining room table and left her alone as he went to a different room in the house. Sophie glanced around at her surroundings.

It was an open living space that housed the kitchen, living room, and dining room. All of the areas of the room flowed perfectly into one another. It did not look like a regular bachelor pad. He mentioned a roommate, but Sophie was amazed that the house really looked like it was designed to be homey and perfect. That word. It kept popping into her head. It was all perfect. Too perfect. The house, the man, the timing.

No. He's just being helpful. Besides, he looked nothing like the man who'd been stalking her with the jacket and baseball cap.

Angel had a darker complexion, like warm honey. His lips were fuller, and his face was clean shaven. While the stalker's hair was covered by a hat, what peeked out from under it was an ashy brown. Angel's hair was jet black, full and looked so soft.

He reappeared holding a dry shirt and a pair of blue plaid pajama pants. She would have refused the clothes, but as she looked at her bag she realized it was soaked.

So, she took the dry clothes and asked where the bathroom was. Angel directed her down the hall he'd just come from, the first door on the left. As she changed, she tried to figure out what her next move would be tomorrow morning. She needed to leave the city somehow. Only, she didn't know where to go. She pulled on the dry shirt after removing her soaked tank top and bra.

Sophie heaved a sigh, feeling the weight of indecision pressing in on her chest, making it feel tight and hard to breathe. She held her cold hand to her chest to remind herself that there was nothing actually restricting her breathing. Her lungs were healthy. *Breathe in. Breathe out.*

She removed her wet jeans and pulled on the pajama pants. Her skin was so cold that the fabric felt warm. She felt better without the soaked clothes rubbing her skin raw. She paused when she caught a whiff of amazing food, which prompted a grumbling in her stomach. She hadn't eaten since noon and it was probably nearing nine o'clock, or even later.

Sophie picked up her wet clothes and opened the door to find that the aroma of cooking food was even stronger in the hallway. She followed her nose back to the kitchen.

She wasn't surprised to see Angel standing at the stove. One of his hands was on the handle of the pan, holding it still, while the other held a spatula that flipped around the sizzling ingredients that must have been what was giving off such a heavenly aroma. Warm and spicy herbs filled her senses, making her whole body feel warmer. The anticipation of the meal to come was almost too much to bear. Her stomach growled loudly.

Angel turned to see Sophie walking toward him from the hallway. He chuckled when he heard her stomach, but looked back to the pan he was cooking in.

"What are you cooking?" Sophie asked as she took the space next to the cook and peered into the pan.

"Fajitas, I haven't had dinner yet and apparently we could both use it." Angel smiled at the woman next to him. Her hair was still damp, making it look darker than it was - almost silver, rather than the perfect shade of platinum blonde it was. He looked back to the pan, still stirring the peppers and onions.

He felt her presence leave his side, creating an empty coldness he hadn't expected. He gazed over at the dining table on the other side of the kitchen and found her waiting patiently. Her hands were folded in her lap, and she watched him, silent like a statue. "Do you like fajitas?" he asked curiously.

She hadn't said anything. Her brows knitted together, as if she were confused by his question. "I've never had them before."

"Oh, well, it's kind of like chicken tacos with bell peppers and onions and a warm spicy seasoning." He was suddenly conscious of the fact that he had brought a stranger into his house. He knew absolutely nothing about this woman except the fact that she had a mental breakdown three days ago and was about to jump off a building, yet here she sat at his kitchen table, wearing his clothes, waiting for the food he was cooking. He felt his cheeks turn pink. *I hope she likes it.*

"Sounds good," she said quietly. She didn't move until he brought the sizzling pan, a stack of tortillas, sour cream, salsa, and two plates to the table.

Sophie waited until Angel made himself a plate, not wanting to be rude to the man who'd taken her soggy ass in for the night, not even knowing who she was except for one terrible encounter on a rooftop that made her look absolutely insane.

She watched as he piled fajita fixings onto the tortillas and topped them with sour cream and salsa, the fillings steaming until covered by the cold condiments. She followed suit and made herself a plate in silence. She took the first bite and the flavor exploded on her tongue. It was amazing! She couldn't stop the food-gasm moan that slipped out. She could cook, but it was never that good. She smiled as she and Angel locked eyes.

His eyes crinkled at the corners as he chewed the bite of food he had in his mouth. *She's cute when she smiles.*

Sophie swallowed the delicious bite. "This is so good! I'm gonna have to learn how to make it," she told him before taking another bite.

They ate the rest of their meal in silence. A contented silence where neither felt the need to fill an awkward void. Sophie generally couldn't stand such silences, but in Angel's presence she felt herself easing into his relaxed state. Her shoulders dropped and her smile came easier. Life didn't feel so overwhelming in the presence of this complete stranger. Until they'd both finished their meals.

"So, do you wanna take the bed for the night? It's more comfortable than the couch," Angel told her as he scrubbed the pan he'd used to cook dinner.

Sophie felt a shock go through her body. *Sleep in his bed?* No, she couldn't do that. She couldn't take his bed away from him when he'd already been so kind. She had started to shake her head to turn down his offer and take the couch instead, but he stopped her.

"I insist. Especially if you're going to be traveling tomorrow. Please, take the bed." He led her to the first bedroom, his bedroom. He assured her she would be warm and comfortable there. Angel grabbed a pillow from the bed and left the room.

Sophie stood at the edge of the large bed. It looked cozy enough. She pressed a hand down on the mattress to test the softness. It was a memory foam mattress, the kind she loved; soft but not too soft. She pulled back the comforter and top sheet and climbed in.

It was so soft and warm. She felt like she was lying in a cloud on a warm summer day. She could live in that bed for the rest of her life and die a happy woman. It smelled divine - like a rain shower in a forest, fresh and clean with a little bit of Angel mixed in. Sophie soon drifted off to sleep, lost in a dream world where she was cuddled by clouds.

14

Angel was woken by the rays of sunshine streaming in the window of his living room. He sat up and swung his legs off the couch. *Definitely not the best place to sleep.* He stretched his neck from one side to the other and rubbed the back of it. He was happy to help Sophie out for the night, but damn. That couch was terrible. He got up, stretched his arms out wide, and yawned.

The oversized clock, the one Angel's mom picked out which she put above the small fireplace in the living room, told him he'd woken earlier than usual. 6:30 was early for the first day of his 48 hours off. That was one thing he liked about being a firefighter, his schedule. 24 hours on, 48 off, generally. Unless he picked up extra shifts like he had been the last few weeks. Angel padded to the kitchen to start a pot of coffee before going to take a shower.

He pulled the dark roast out of the cupboard above the sacred pot and set it on the counter as he grabbed a spoon and filter. He thought back to the night before as he prepared the hot brew. He'd recognized her instantly even though she was soaked and shivering, hunched over at a bus stop. He knew he'd never forget her, but what he hadn't expected was the pang of sadness in his heart when he saw her on the bench.

He didn't think it'd be as hard as it was to convince her to let him give her a place to stay for the night, and for free at that. She was definitely guarded. It made him wonder even more what had driven her to the top of that building. She'd seemed so strong and independent when she'd first refused his help.

What could possibly have driven her to such lengths as taking a swan dive off a building?

While he'd felt empathy for the woman, he was also relieved, even happy, to see her again. She'd been a constant worry in the back of his mind ever since he watched the ambulance take her away.

As Angel was lost in thought while making coffee in the kitchen, Sophie began to stir in his bedroom. She left her eyes closed in hopes of falling back asleep, but after a couple attempts to reposition in a comfortable spot, she knew that was not going to happen. She opened her eyes and looked around for a clock. She found one on the end table on the far side of the bed. It read 6:32. Too early. Sophie sighed, her body still felt heavy and tired.

Just as she was about to get out of the bed she'd been so comfortable in a few minutes ago, she heard cabinets closing in the kitchen. She froze. Someone else was awake. Who was it? Probably Angel. They'd been up pretty late last night, though.

Maybe someone broke in? *No, Sophie. That's dumb. He slept on the couch. He'd have heard someone break in.* The only thing she could do was exactly what she'd yell at a character in a horror movie not to do: go check it out.

She stepped carefully and slowly towards the door, trying as hard as she could not to make a noise, just in case. She turned the door knob and pulled the door open. Once she was in view of the kitchen she relaxed. Angel stood in front of the coffee pot, which was emitting a wonderful aroma that filled her nose. She instinctively took a deep, savoring breath. She loved the smell of fresh coffee. There was nothing like it.

Angel turned toward the soft sound of someone enjoying the smell of the coffee brewing. He smiled when he saw Sophie. Her hair was messy from sleep - curls poking out at different angles - and her eyes were closed, but there was a slight smile on her lips as she took in the smell of the dark roast brewing. She was just as beautiful as the night before and the day on the rooftop. Perhaps even more so, seeing as how she had just gotten out of his bed.

"Smells delicious," Sophie told Angel once she opened her eyes. She took the same seat at the dining room table she'd sat in the night before.

"Just wait till you taste it," Angel replied with a smile playing on his lips. "How'd you sleep?"

"Good. Your bed is way more comfortable than mine," Sophie confessed with a chuckle. "Thank you, for letting me stay, or rather convincing me to." Sophie twisted her fingers together and fiddled with her nails as she avoided Angel's gaze.

"Of course. I couldn't let you stay out in the cold or sleep in some creepy, gross hotel room when I have a perfectly good bed." Angel pulled an extra coffee cup out of the cupboard. It was his mom's favorite; the watercolor flowers and vines had reminded her of her garden, so he bought the cup for her for Mother's Day. She, of course, insisted he keep it, so she has a cup at his house when she comes over for coffee with her son.

"Well, I appreciate it. I'll be out of your hair soon, though. I've gotta be on my way."

"You can stay for coffee and breakfast if you want? I have plenty of both; food and fresh coffee." Angel poured steaming hot coffee into both mugs. He hesitated for a moment when he realized he didn't know what Sophie wanted in her coffee.

He picked up her mug, along with the sugar and set them on the table in front of her. He pulled the heavy cream out of the fridge as well as the peppermint mocha creamer he kept on hand for his mom and put them on the table next to the sugar. Angel liked his coffee black.

As long as Angel could remember he'd liked black coffee. When he was twelve, his dad had even tried to dissuade him from liking it by giving him a drink of black coffee. It backfired. Angel had been hooked ever since.

"Oh, thank you. I appreciate all the help, really, but I need to get going as soon as possible."

"Where are you going to go?"

Sophie opened her mouth to reply but found herself frozen in place, her mind without answer. She closed her mouth as she contemplated where she was going to go. She grabbed the peppermint mocha creamer and started pouring it into her coffee. "I'm not sure yet."

Where could she go? *Out of Chicago,* was the first thing to come to mind. She didn't have a huge savings, but she had enough for a bus ticket to wherever she wanted to go and a motel room for a few weeks, which would be about as long as she needed to find a new job and apartment. Chicago was home, though. Sophie desperately wanted to stay. She loved her job at the library. She loved Felicity and her other friends. She loved the city. Could she really leave all of that behind forever? Did she really believe leaving would help? Who knew how obsessed this crazy person was? Would he follow her wherever she went? Did leaving the city matter? Did leaving the state matter?

Angel watched the gears in Sophie's head spin as she thought about her options. He had to help. He couldn't just sit by and watch her struggle with nowhere to go and no one to help.

"You don't have to leave until you at least have a plan, you know?" Angel couldn't stop himself before he said the words. Why did he feel such a strong urge to help her, to take care of the woman in front of him? Yeah, she was gorgeous but that wasn't the reason. He could feel the tug in his heart that told him it was deeper than that.

"Thanks, but no thanks. You don't want me here. Not for an extended amount of time. I just need to do this on my own."

"What makes you say that? You need help and I'm in a spot to be able to provide that." What was her problem? He had a house, plenty of food, and a place to sleep. It was safe, just far enough outside the busy city streets to lessen the risk of being a target of crime, but close enough to be within walking distance of anything they needed. It was perfect.

"I'm not some charity case that needs a knight to come rescue me." Sophie could feel her heart thumping in her chest, anger making it beat harder and harder like a drum against her ribs. Why did everyone think she needed to be saved? Sophie was DONE being a victim. She was done being the little girl who cried as she waited for a knight in shining armor to come save her, yet again! She definitely didn't need a guardian Angel. If she wasn't so mad, she'd have laughed at her own internal joke.

"I don't think you-"

"And I definitely don't need to be stuck in a stranger's house while he takes care of me. For all I know, you're the creep who keeps sending me letters!" Sophie's grip on the handle of the mug tightened.

"What? Why would I do that? I'm trying to help you!"

"Well, I don't need it. I can do this myself." Sophie stood up, leaving her coffee mug on the table as she stalked into the bedroom where she left her belongings. She set her still damp bag on the bed and put the few remainders of her belongings into it that she hadn't last night before falling asleep.

"Sophie, I didn't mean to upset you. All I meant was that if you need somewhere to be that doesn't have your name on it, somewhere that no one can track you to, you can stay here for as long as you need to." Angel stood in the doorway, his shoulder resting on one side as he crossed his arms.

"You don't have to help me. I'm not your obligation. I'm not a child, I can take care of myself." She closed her bag and turned toward the doorway.

"I just want you to be safe and to help you if you want it."

Sophie looked into the man's eyes as he spoke softly to her. An unspoken apology passed between them, and Sophie felt as if he'd defused her anger with just his soft brown eyes. Her heartbeat slowed and she dropped her bag on the bed. What sort of spell had he put her under?

Angel saw her brows relax and her mouth fall out of the hard line it'd been in since she left the table. She was coming out of her angry cloud and was coming back to Earth. "I just want to help you, if you want it," he repeated. "If you don't, that's okay too. It's up to you. I'm not going to force you to do anything you don't want to."

The choice was up to her. It was truly Sophie's choice. She could leave if she wanted to. When had she ever truly had the choice over her own life? She had a taste when she moved back to Chicago and started working for Felicity. Then, the stalker had taken her free will away from her. Again, it had been taken from her. All Sophie truly wanted was to be free from the dictatorship of not having the option to choose what happened to her own life. That was all she wanted. To be able to choose. Here stood a man giving her a choice. She could do whatever she wanted.

"I don't know where I'm going to go." She looked at her bag on the bed as she crossed her arms. Her heart ached. All she wanted to do was go back to the library and see Felicity and tell her everything. She wanted her apartment back. She wanted that little glimpse of freedom she had.

"That's okay. You can stay until you know," Angel offered. He stood up straight and let his arms fall to his side. "Now, do you want any breakfast?"

"Yeah, I guess."

"You like country gravy?" he asked as he turned towards the kitchen and left the room. Sophie quickly followed at the mention of gravy.

"It's my favorite."

"Perfect!" Angel said as he got started in the kitchen. Sophie took her spot at the table again and looked at the coffee she'd left untouched after pouring the creamer in. She took a drink and savored the warmth that spread inside her. It was delicious. *Is there anything he makes that isn't? Maybe his gravy will suck.*

Sophie watched Angel work. He moved effortlessly about the kitchen as if he were on skates, gliding across the tile, floating like a ghost. She tried to ignore the way his t-shirt hugged his shoulders, but it didn't leave much to the imagination with how tight it was across his upper back as he cooked. Sophie looked away before she was caught staring. She focused her energy on her coffee.

"What happened after we first met?" he asked as potatoes sizzled away in the pan in front of him.

"They took me to Sacred Heights, a mandatory 72 hour hold."

"Yeah, I figured that's what was going to happen. I would have visited you if I would have been allowed to."

Angel was different. *Who would want to visit a mental hospital full of crazy people, just to see someone they've never met before*? Angel puzzled Sophie. Why did he care so much? Why did he want to help her? She was just another crazy person trying to figure out what life meant.

"I don't see why. It's not like it's a fun place."

"Just to make sure you were okay. Most people don't find themselves in your situation and I was worried about you."

Sophie let his words sink in. A stranger worried about her. Did people actually do that? Worry about strangers? Obviously. He was proof, Sophie supposed. Proof that good people still existed. How could she know he was a good person? They'd had so few interactions. Sophie decided it was gut instinct that told her so. Maybe it was time she started trusting it.

15

It had been a week since Sophie had agreed to stay with Angel until she was back on her feet. In just that short amount of time she found herself in sync with him. They both woke up at 6:30 each morning when he was home. They'd have coffee and breakfast, then go on their way for the day. He let her decide what she wanted to do, then shift any plans around hers. He'd given her rides to interviews at various places over the last week. He'd also fed her and let her sleep in his bed, without complaint about sleeping on his uncomfortable couch.

Everything was about to change, though. His roommate, Todd, and his girlfriend, Melody, were coming back from their vacation. Sophie couldn't help the nervous trembling she felt in her hands. What would Todd think of Angel just inviting some crazy lady to stay with them for who knows how long?

Angel had told her a little bit about Todd and Melody. They'd been together for three years. Todd was a firefighter at Angel's station. Melody was a nursing student in her last few months of school. He'd assured her multiple times that they would be fine. Still, Sophie couldn't stop the shaking. What if they demanded she leave? Where would she go? She couldn't go to Felicity.

Oh, Felicity. Sophie's heart seized in her chest at the thought of her best friend. She'd called a few times, but Sophie couldn't find it in herself to answer. She eventually stopped calling. Sophie couldn't help feeling extremely guilty at the fact that she was ignoring Felicity. Angel had been kind enough to not ask about the ignored calls, but Sophie could tell he was curious.

"So, I was thinking we could do burgers and salad for dinner. How's that sound to you?" Angel asked as he looked through the fridge. Sophie sat at the chair she'd taken over at the dining room table.

"Sounds good to me. Do you really think Todd is gonna be okay with me staying here?"

"Yeah, he's a good guy. He wouldn't make you leave with nowhere to go. And Melody is awesome. I think you'll like her a lot. She makes sure we don't break ourselves, at least not permanently." Angel set the buns out on the counter, then the ground beef he planned on turning into burgers right next to the buns.

"Okay, I just don't want to be a burden. I haven't gotten a job yet, so I feel like I'm about to overstay my welcome."

"Don't worry about it, Sophie. You're my guest as long as you want to be." Angel shot her a cheesy grin before turning back around to root through the cabinets for the rest of the ingredients he needed. "They should be here any minute. Wanna grab a bottle of wine from the garage for me?"

"Yeah sure, be right back." Sophie wandered out to the living room and out the front door to go to the garage, which stood on the other side of the driveway. It took her a minute to find the wine, Angel's garage was a disaster. All the stuff they had that didn't fit in the house was stored out there and they were obviously not the best organizers in the world.

With the wine in hand, Sophie made her way back to the door that would lead her to the driveway. She hesitated with her hand on the door knob as she heard a car pull into the driveway. It had to be Todd and Melody. She waited, her hand still on the knob until she heard their voices fade as they made their way into the house.

Sophie pulled the door open to follow them in, making sure they were fully inside the house before she opened the front door; she hoped Angel would have told them she was staying there before she came in. She held tight to the wine bottle, determined to not let the shaking in her hands make her drop it. She took a deep breath before pulling open the front door and walking inside. She made her way to the kitchen where she heard laughing and joking.

Todd was the first to turn toward her. He smiled before he introduced himself. "Oh, hi. I'm Todd, Angel's roommate," he said as he held out his hand for her to shake. She took it, wishing that he hadn't because she was entirely certain that her palms were sweaty and gross from how anxious she was.

"Nice to meet you, Todd."

"And I'm Melody, Todd's girlfriend. You must be Sophie? Angel was just telling us about you. How long have you guys been dating? He never mentioned you before." Melody's hazel eyes radiated warmth as she smiled at Sophie. Sophie had gotten good at reading people over the course of her life. Melody felt like the kind of person to give the shirt off her back to a stranger in need, it made sense to Sophie that she was studying to be a nurse.

"Oh, we're- "

"Mel, we're not dating. She is just... Staying here for a little while." Angel glanced over at Sophie and smiled at her, like he was trying to silently tell her it was okay, that he would handle this.

"Oh, I'm so sorry. I shouldn't have assumed. You would just be so cute together. God, I'm sorry. I'll shut up now." Melody blushed as she held her hand over her mouth and laughed at her mistake. Todd wrapped an arm around her shoulders as he chuckled at his girlfriend.

"Oh Mel, you're so sweet. Let's go unload the car." He led her outside, an arm still holding her close, leaving Sophie and Angel alone in the kitchen. Sophie could tell they were happy together. Perhaps it was the post-vacation bliss, but she was sure it went deeper than that.

Sophie and Angel's eyes met, and they laughed together. "She's funny," Sophie said as she set the wine on the counter and leaned her elbows on it to settle in. She liked watching Angel cook. It was like watching an artist paint. He was so sure of all the right moves to make and ingredients to add without having to check and double check a recipe like she did.

"Mel's great. Even better once you get to know her. I told you they wouldn't mind. They're good people. Like you and me."

"You barely know me. How could you possibly know I'm good people?" Sophie asked as she smiled. Angel was such a refreshing person to be around.

He wasn't darkened or corrupted from a world filled with anger and hate and violence, like Sophie had been.

"Because you've been here for a week and you've only been kind, helpful, and apologetic about being a burden even though I've tried to remind you over and over that you're not. I can just tell, you know?" He tapped his temple as he smiled slyly at Sophie. "I'm psychic."

Sophie barked out a laugh as she threw her head back. He seemed to always find a way to make her laugh. What would she do when she had to leave, and he wasn't around anymore? Sophie pushed the thought out of her mind. She'd enjoy this while she could. Before it ended, like everything else good in her life.

Dinner went smoothly as they all drank, laughed, and joked. Melody had already convinced Sophie that they were going to be good friends by the time Sophie was ready to turn in for the night. She reminded Sophie of Felicity in the way she immediately accepted her and brought her into the small circle of the household. They'd planned to grab coffee and donuts in the morning. Todd and Melody had gone to bed about an hour before Sophie and Angel did. They cited they'd usually stay up but that they were wiped from the long drive.

Sophie stayed up with Angel until she could feel her eyelids starting to become heavy. "I'll see you in the morning," she said as she gave him a small smile.

"Goodnight, Sophie."

"Goodnight, Angel." She slipped down the hallway to his bedroom. She heard snoring coming from the other bedroom down the hall. Sophie chuckled while wondering how Melody could sleep with all that noise right next to her.

She knew Angel didn't snore. She'd checked on him a few times in the middle of the night when she'd get up for water or to go to the bathroom. He always slept soundly and peacefully. Sophie laid in bed staring up at the ceiling. She'd had a good night and didn't want it to end but she was exhausted. All the anxiety about meeting Todd and Melody had faded once they'd had time to get to know each other. She could feel her body relaxing as she let her eyes drift closed, sleep wasn't far off. She could feel it coming on. Soon enough, she was deep asleep.

Sophie awoke to a ragged scream tearing at her throat and her body shaking so hard she'd started sweating. It felt so real, the pain was real. She sobbed into her hands. It'd been so long since she had a nightmare that bad.

The door to the bedroom flew open and Angel rushed in. He sat next to her on the bed and held her arms in his hands. "Sophie, are you okay? I heard you scream. What's wrong? Please tell me," he asked her quietly.

Sophie shook her head as she continued crying. Angel wrapped his arms around her trembling shoulders and pulled her into his chest. He gently shushed her, trying to calm her in any way he could. He whispered to her that she was okay, that he was there and wasn't going to leave her alone. He slowly rocked her back and forth as he held her close to him. Nothing else in the world seemed to matter as he calmed the broken woman in his arms.

"It's okay Sophie. I'm here. I'm not going anywhere." Angel didn't know how long they sat like that, her curled in a ball and him holding her as she shook and cried. He felt instant relief when she picked her head up to look at him. Her eyes were puffy, and the tip of her nose was red, but she was still one of the most beautiful people he'd ever seen. It broke his heart that something could terrorize her so much that she'd make the horrible noise she had. She sounded like she was dying. He was surprised it didn't wake up anyone else.

"I'm so sorry. I didn't mean to wake you up." She sniffled as she pulled away from Angel. She wiped at her eyes to clear them of tears.

"I don't care about that. Are you okay?" he asked as he watched her closely in the dark room.

"I'm fine, just a bad dream is all." Sophie tried to play it off like it was nothing. She could tell Angel knew better. He was not about to leave her alone after she screamed in the middle of the night like she was dying. She was glad he cared, but still felt the shame and embarrassment of being such an inconvenience for scaring him awake when she was fine.

Angel didn't think she was fine, though. People don't scream like that when they're fine. "I'm not going anywhere until I know for a fact you're okay, Sophie." He placed his hand over hers as he scooted closer to her. "What happened?"

"I was just having a nightmare, I'm fine. Really, you don't have to stay with me." She turned her head away from him when she felt another wave of tears threaten to shatter her façade.

"Please tell me, you don't have to worry. I'm here and I'm not going anywhere until you tell me to," he told her as he watched her bright blue eyes fill with tears. She looked back at him, and her eyes pierced through his soul. The pain and sadness he saw there was so deep he wondered how she wasn't completely lost in it. When she didn't say anything he asked her, "Do you want me to stay?"

Sophie couldn't bring herself to speak. Her voice failed her when she tried to open her mouth to tell him she was fine. She nodded. All she truly wanted was to not be alone for once. She was always so alone. Ever since she was a little girl. She'd been alone since before she could remember. An orphan, an unwanted adoptee, a burdensome girlfriend no one wanted. But Angel was different. Sophie didn't feel alone with him. She felt like he cared, like he had a space reserved just for her.

When the tears receded, she spoke in a soft, squeaky voice from crying so hard. "Yes, please stay." She'd been sitting in the middle of the bed but shuffled over to give him room to lay down. She held up the blanket and sheet for him to get in his own bed she'd taken over.

He moved slowly, cautiously, like he was testing the waters with each move to make sure he didn't scare her away. He didn't know she wasn't about to go anywhere. He was the only person who made her feel safe in the way he did.

Angel laid in the bed next to her. He was on his back with his hand comfortably tucked under his head, staring up at the ceiling when he felt her shift next to him. He didn't move or even look at what she was doing, he didn't want to scare her or make her uncomfortable. He didn't look down until he felt a warm body laying next to him. She had pulled her pillow closer to his so she could be near him in the large bed.

"Is this okay?" she asked when their eyes met in the darkness.

"If it is with you," he told her quietly. "Whatever you need, I'm here Sophie."

"Would it be okay if you held me?" she whispered, never breaking their eye contact.

"Of course. Come here," he said as he rolled onto his side. He shifted the hand he had under his head to a comfortable spot under her pillow and he brought his other arm over her waist, and he pulled her close. Her soft, small body fit perfectly against him. She pressed herself into him and relaxed as much as possible. Her forehead rested against his chest as he rubbed her back until he was sure she'd fallen asleep.

He wondered what could have happened to her that had traumatized her so much. All of the possibilities he could come up with only made him angry, which was something he tried to avoid. Angel wasn't an angry person in general, but when something set him off he usually saw it through. He hoped whoever hurt her never tried anything again, especially not in front of him.

He looked down at Sophie, whose breathing had slowed to a deep even pace that told him she was asleep. Her silvery blonde hair had fallen into her face, which was still snuggled into his chest.

He stopped rubbing her back to brush it away so he could see her. She shifted closer to him in her sleep, but her head fell back enough to show him her face. He hoped that she would be okay in the morning. No one should have to feel the way she obviously did deep down, where she wouldn't let anybody see.

She was broken and needed help to put herself back together. Angel only hoped she would let him help. He'd done his fair share of healing in therapy as a kid. He had gone through so much before he was adopted by his parents that he'd been broken too.

A kid couldn't watch their parents die right in front of them and be okay after that. Especially not how his parents had died. He'd blocked the memory out for most of his childhood until he'd started experiencing behavior problems and his adopted parents refused to take no for an answer. They helped him so much.

So, Angel knew he could help her, she just had to let him. He had to push away the thoughts of anyone wanting to hurt someone like Sophie before he kept himself up the rest of the night. Her face was so peaceful, lying next to him. So different from the pain and anguish he'd seen minutes before when her gaze ripped through his soul. He watched her sleep as long as he could before he slipped into a peaceful sleep himself.

16

Sophie shifted in the comfy bed, but something was wrong. She sat up right and rubbed the sleep from her eyes. She was alone. Where had Angel gone? He'd been there when she fell asleep. Had she overstepped by asking him to hold her? She knew it was a weird request, but she felt like she'd needed the comfort he'd provided when he hugged her as she cried. She'd even told him he didn't have to stay, but he insisted he be there for her. The sound of the latch on the door shifting caught her attention. Someone was about to come in.

Angel peeked his head in, hoping he hadn't woken Sophie when he got up to start the coffee pot. He'd intended to slip back in the room unnoticed. He found that that was not the case. Sophie looked panicked as she sat in the bed. He rushed in and closed the door behind him.

"Hey, I'm here. It's okay. Just got up to start coffee is all." He sat next to her as she calmed herself.

"I just didn't know where you went. I'm sorry about last night. That wasn't fair for me to ask you to stay or hold me, I just, I don't know." Sophie went quiet. She was so embarrassed she'd asked him to cuddle her back to sleep.

"I was just trying to help, however you needed it. Did you sleep okay after that?" Angel asked.

"Yeah, surprisingly. Usually, I can't fall back asleep after nightmares like that." She avoided Angel's gaze. She didn't want to know what she'd see there. "I forgot to tell you yesterday when Todd and Melody showed up, I got an interview for today. I was wondering if you could take me. It's that little café next to the fire station, Sam's I think? It's not until 10 o'clock, though." She glanced at the clock on the bedside table. It was 8:00 already? She never slept past 6:30 anymore.

"Oh, yeah. Of course, we go there for coffee all the time. Sam is a good guy; I think you'd like working there." Angel stood up once he heard the coffee pot beep, signaling that it'd completed the brew cycle. "I'll go get us some coffee." Angel felt the environment shift into an awkward silence. Sophie still felt like a burden and as if she'd done something wrong. He left the room without saying more.

Sophie smacked her palm to her forehead. Why couldn't she just be a normal person for once and not feel so awkward about everything. He was just trying to help her through a tough time. She was grateful, really. She just couldn't get over the fact that he didn't expect anything in return for helping her. She really needed to start making money again so she could at least pay him something for letting her stay. Would he even let her? She had to try. She'd nail this interview with Sam and get a job. She had to.

She got out of bed and dressed into a pair of black pants and a nice blouse she'd managed to stuff in her bag as she was leaving her apartment. Something she figured she'd need for a case like this. An interview outfit. All she had shoe-wise was the black flats she'd stuffed in the bag too. They would work. Once she had some more cash, she'd get new clothes and another bag. She checked her hair in the mirror on the dresser. It still had some controlled waves, so once she ran a brush through it, it was ready to go.

Some mascara and tinted lip balm were the finishing touches to her look. She didn't want to go too heavy on the makeup or the outfit. It was a coffee shop after all, not a corporate nightmare. She left the bedroom and met Angel in the kitchen. He sat at his usual spot at the table, the spread of coffee additives in front of him - laid out just for her - like he did every morning. Did he still not expect anything in return for his kindness?

"If I get this job, I'll pay you back for everything you've done for me."

At that moment, Sophie heard footsteps behind her. Melody padded out into the kitchen as she yawned. "Nonsense," she said. "We'll help as much as we can. Don't worry about it."

Apparently, it had been decided among the household that she'd stay as long as necessary. Sophie smiled as she poured the creamer into her coffee. She glanced up at Angel who was grinning at her. He took a seemingly triumphant sip of his coffee. Sophie chuckled quietly to herself. He was a goof. She couldn't help but feel all warm and fuzzy inside; she was wanted somewhere. They wanted her to stay. All three of them.

With the boost of confidence of feeling accepted by all three household members, Sophie rocked her interview and was offered the job on the spot. Although, she couldn't have said Angel dropping her off and walking her in wasn't helpful in her landing the job. Sam seemed to have a soft spot for the rookie firefighter.

It was her first day and she was beyond excited. It wasn't a glamorous job, mostly making and serving coffee and other beverages, but it was a job. A job with a good boss. It was also the start of Angel and Todd's 24 hours on. Sophie felt comforted by the fact that they were still close by, just in case. Not that she'd be able to call on them if needed, but they were there and that's what mattered.

Sam had spent the morning teaching her how to use the espresso machine, which she'd managed to pick up rather quickly. He'd let her have some freedom and let her try brewing her own coffee, with the promise that she wouldn't let it go to waste.

She must have done well since Sam had trusted her enough to leave for an hour to go home for his lunch. It was something he hadn't done in a long time, she assumed. He'd mentioned being the only one there for the last two years during her interview. She stood behind the counter as she waited for customers. It was a slow lunch hour that day. She served two black coffees and one sandwich, totaling $9.85. It was a moderately busy area. She was surprised the firefighters hadn't come by.

Sam made it back before any other customers came in, something Sophie was secretly glad for. What if they'd asked for something more than black coffee and sandwiches? Something she had no idea how to make? She didn't have to worry about that anymore, though. She smiled and waved at him through the window.

"Any trouble while I was gone?" Sam asked as he made his way behind the counter.

"A whole two coffees and a sandwich. Very troubling," she joked.

"Slow day. Maybe it'll pick up. Let me know if you need anything, I'll be in the kitchen getting tomorrow's food prepped."

"Will do." Sophie leaned back on the counter and started flipping through the espresso machine manual, again. She had to learn how the heck the monstrous mechanism worked eventually.

The bell on the door alerted her to another customer arriving. When she looked up she stopped in her tracks. Her heart hammered against her ribs and her jaw fell in horror.

It's him.

Dark bomber jacket, light stubble, baseball cap. He was unmistakable. Her heart pounded so hard she could feel it in her throat. Was she about to throw up? Run away? Scream? Fight for her life? There were so many options, so many possibilities she couldn't choose between them. She froze instead.

"I'll have a black coffee, please." His voice felt so familiar. It raked at her soul and tore it to shreds. She couldn't move. "Ma'am are you okay?" he asked. She still couldn't see his eyes. She imagined them as deep black pits. He was the monster of her nightmares.

Sophie forced herself to move, to pour him a cup of coffee. "$2.00," was all she could say. He handed her two $1 bills and turned to head toward the counter that housed the sugar and cream.

The second he turned away and couldn't see her anymore it was like the spell broke. She ran to the back, through the office and out the back door. It slammed closed behind her. She found herself looking around the lot behind the café, waiting for the man to appear and slice her throat, end her, take her away, something, anything. He was coming for her. He found her. How did he find her?

She glanced toward the firehouse. She desperately wanted to call Angel, but he was in the middle of his shift. He couldn't leave. Could he? What were the rules? Did firemen have rules about when they had to be at the firehouse during their shifts? Did she have any other choice? The door next to her opened and Sam appeared.

"Sophie, are you okay? I heard the door slam; I've been looking for you. What happened?" Sam's voice was dripping with concern. How could she explain that man and what he'd done to her? How he'd ripped her whole life away? How she'd almost jumped off a building just to break free from him and he'd just found her again?

Tears welled up in her eyes, she couldn't even bring herself to speak. She sobbed into her shaking hands as she fell down to her knees on the concrete. "I can't, I can't stay here. I'm so sorry, Sam."

"Just tell me what happened, please!" he asked as he kneeled next to her and placed a hand softly on her shaking shoulder.

"I can't. I have to go, I'm so sorry. I can't come back, Sam. I'm sorry," Sophie cried as she got up and ran to the firehouse.

She stood in the parking lot next to Angel's truck for way too long, hoping he might come outside and find her and save her. What was she doing? Sophie angrily wiped tears away from her eyes. She was waiting for someone else to come save her again. The shame grew in her chest until she was sobbing again.

With her back against Angel's truck, she slid down to the ground and curled up in a ball. How long could she hold herself together this time? If that's what she was even doing. How long until he found her? It's not like she'd gone far. He'd already found her when she thought it'd be impossible. How could he have found her?

Her body hurt from the painful sobs leaving her chest. She couldn't breathe anymore. Maybe he really would kill her this time, but he wouldn't be there to even do it. Her own body had turned against her at the thought of him. Was that his trick?

Her chest heaved as she tried to catch her breath. The weight of everything was so heavy, it had robbed her of all thought other than attempting to breathe. Why couldn't she breathe?

As if by divine miracle, she heard familiar footsteps heading her way. "Sophie? Oh my God, Sophie!" She felt hands grab her shoulders, then one brush her cheek. She couldn't focus enough to comprehend what was happening, but she was sure it was Angel who was touching her, she felt it in her bones. She heard other voices, but they were speaking in gibberish. Her vision was starting to tunnel. She had to get a hold on herself, or she was going to pass out.

"Angel," she gasped. "Please," she said as she gasped for breath.

"What can I do?" the voice in front of her asked.

"Home," was all she could manage. More gibberish followed, then she was being lifted into Angel's truck and buckled in. She wrapped her hands around the restrictive seatbelt, it was crushing her already heaving chest.

"Keep it on, I'm taking you home. Just try to breathe. In through your nose, out through your mouth. You're just having a panic attack. It's okay. I'm here. Just breathe for me, please," Angel told her as he started the truck and pulled out of the parking lot and began racing home. He kept walking her through breathing techniques and exercises until they pulled into the driveway. He shut the truck off and unbuckled himself so he could turn to face her. She felt her own belt be unbuckled.

How long would the feeling of suffocating last until I do actually suffocate? Sophie wondered. She felt her body be turned and the familiar hands cupped her cheeks. It shocked her into taking a full breath.

"That's it, more. Take another deep breath."

She tried as she closed her eyes and focused on her aching lungs.

"That's it, good. One more, please, for me."

She squeezed her eyes shut harder and pulled in another deep breath before letting it out. Her lungs started working on their own, then. Slowing their sprinting pace. Her heart began to slow as well. She opened her eyes to see Angel staring right into her soul.

"There you are, I was starting to worry about you. Take another breath."

He'd saved her. Just like she'd silently prayed for. Sophie's heart leaped in her chest, but not from anxiety. This was a different pounding. It resonated throughout her whole body, an electric thrumming in her veins.

"Wanna tell me what happened?" Angel's hands still cupped her cheeks, his thumbs brushed against her cheekbones, making the electric feeling even stronger. Not just electric, but magnetic.

The feeling coursing through her scared her almost as much as the panic she'd felt mere moments ago. What was it? What did it mean? What was wrong with her?

"Sophie, you're worrying me. Please tell me what happened," he asked.

Sophie couldn't help it. She couldn't stop herself. She leaned forward and pressed her lips against Angel's. He'd saved her. His soul called her closer. She felt safe. She felt comforted. She belonged somewhere. She belonged wherever he was. Her soul sang out to her and seized control of her body. Pushed her forward. She closed her eyes and felt the softness of his lips pressed against hers as she kissed him.

But it was wrong. He wasn't moving. He wasn't kissing her back. Sophie pulled back, tears springing up in her eyes again. That was not how she'd expected that to go. With her soul crushed and defeated, she bolted from the truck and into the house. She slammed and locked his bedroom door behind her. She couldn't face Angel again. She was mortified. She'd read the situation totally wrong. He didn't feel the way she had. He didn't feel the magnetic electricity pulsing between them like she had.

Sophie laid face down on the bed just as she heard knocking on the door. "Sophie, please open the door!" Angel called out to her. "Please come let me in, we need to talk about this!"

There was no way in hell that was happening. Sophie was going to be swallowed whole by the Earth for the rest of eternity, or at least she hoped that's what was about to happen. She buried her face in the pillow he'd used last night. It still smelled like him. She was pathetic. How could a guy like that ever feel anything for someone as broken as her? She'd never make someone as amazing and kind as Angel happy when she couldn't even find a way to be happy herself.

Sophie ignored the knocking and the pleas that came from the other side of the door. She wondered briefly if he had a key to his own bedroom, then wondered why he didn't use it. Then, she felt even more like an idiot. He probably did have one, he was just waiting for her to open the door for her sake. Could he be any better of a person? Why did he have to make her feel like such shit by being so perfect?

Sophie zoned in on the clock. She watched the minutes tick by as she listened to Angel keep knocking and asking her to come to the door. Eventually he stopped. It had begun to get dark, but Sophie left the light off. She hoped she'd fall asleep sooner rather than later. Maybe that would wake her up from this nightmare?

17

Sophie tried to go to sleep, but the guilt and embarrassment wouldn't let her brain slow down enough to rest. She just laid in the big, lonely bed, staring at the ceiling, eyes wide open in the darkness.

Her brain replayed the moment she'd pressed her lips to Angel's, feeling the unmoving softness of them. Replaying the scene in her head. Analyzing it over and over and over. Looking at it from every angle she could, from every lens.

I'm an idiot.

What kind of idiot would think someone like him would ever want someone as broken as her? She couldn't count the number of times she had rolled her eyes at herself. She was so dumb. Of course, he wouldn't kiss her back.

Resigning to the fact that she just wasn't going to be able to sleep, Sophie decided she would get a late-night snack. Something to appease her grumbling stomach. Maybe some of the leftover fajitas from the night before. She'd never tell Angel, but his fajitas were her all time favorite meal she'd ever had.

Sophie opened the bedroom door around midnight, many hours after Angel had stopped trying to coerce her to open it. She looked down before taking a step into the hallway, glad that she did so because Angel had fallen asleep there on the floor. His back was resting against the wall next to the door with his legs stretched out before him.

Despite the embarrassment she'd felt earlier, she was touched by his willingness to sleep somewhere so uncomfortable, just to be there for her if she needed him. She found that in that moment, she did need him. She needed him to be there for her. The room had become too lonely, but also too full of her own thoughts for her to be able to sleep.

As she watched him sleep, she thought back to the night before and how he'd held her in his arms, and she fell asleep curled against his chest. She'd needed the comfort he provided. He hadn't made her feel embarrassed or uncomfortable, she did that all on her own. He simply protected her from the nightmares when nothing she'd done to try to help them go away had worked.

With all thoughts of food abandoned, Sophie reached out and shook his shoulder. "Angel, wake up. You shouldn't sleep on the floor." She felt guilty she'd locked him out of his own bedroom. He was kind enough to let her borrow it. The least she could do was let him sleep in his own bed.

"Hmm, Sophie? You came out." Angel rubbed his eyes, trying to clear his brain of the fog of being awoken from a sound slumber.

"Yeah, to see you on the floor. C'mon. Come sleep in your own bed. I'll take the couch tonight." She grabbed his hand and helped pull him up.

"No, really. Sophie, I'm okay. You can have the bed." He tried to turn away from the threshold of the bedroom, only to be stopped by Sophie grabbing his hand to pull him in the dark room.

"Angel, you've been too kind to me already. Just... please, take the bed," Sophie insisted. She watched as he thought about it for a moment, contemplating the best course of action for both of them.

"We can share the bed. It's more than big enough. Last night proved that. Come on." Angel led Sophie into the bedroom by the hand he hadn't let go of as they'd discussed sleeping arrangements.

Sophie conceded and let him guide her to the bed. It wasn't as if they hadn't shared a bed before. He was right.

We can share, but just for the night, Sophie told herself. She would take the couch tomorrow night.

After she laid down in the bed, facing away from Angel and trying to give him as much space as possible, she felt the bed shift under his weight. She had forgotten completely about the way her stomach had been grumbling when he wrapped his arm around her waist and pulled her close. She wanted to ask what he was doing, to ask if this was okay, but she didn't want to do anything that would make him move. Angel had a way of comforting her soul with everything he did. She couldn't help but wonder if that was why she'd felt so compelled to kiss him and his soft lips.

"I'm sorry about earlier," he whispered in her ear, his breath tickling the hairs on her neck making her whole body break out in goosebumps. Sophie couldn't understand what made her body react this way to the man cuddled up behind her.

"What?"

"I'm sorry. I didn't mean to embarrass you. I was just shocked. I wasn't expecting you to kiss me at that exact moment."

"Don't be sorry. It was dumb. I shouldn't have done it," she said as she shook her head.

"If that's the way you feel, it's not dumb, Sophie."

"But it was, because you obviously don't feel... that way." Sophie could feel the embarrassment building in her bones again. She could feel her cheeks flushing crimson and her heart pounding in her chest. She was glad Angel couldn't see it in the dark room.

"I never said that," he whispered as he intertwined his fingers with hers and pressed a light kiss behind her ear.

Sophie could swear her heart was about to explode out of her chest. Had the most perfect man she'd ever met really just say what she thought he did? Did he just admit to having feelings for her? "But... you di-didn't kiss back," she stumbled over her words, not knowing what to say.

Angel placed his fingers under Sophie's chin and guided her to look at him. "Sophie, I never expected someone like you to kiss someone like me," he said as she fully rolled to face him. He rested his hand on her cheek and rubbed his thumb along her cheekbone. She avoided his gaze, looking down at his chest instead.

"Someone like me?" she asked. Her brain was all muddled in confusion, his touch was turning it to melted candle wax. He was turning her whole body into a melted mess.

"Yes, someone as beautiful, kind, funny, and intelligent as you. I thought I was dreaming, and I never wanted to wake up," he mumbled, his lips a breath away from hers. He pushed her chin up just enough, then closed the gap between them and melded their lips together. He held the back of her head with one hand tangled in her short, blonde curls as he held her body close to his with the other hand on her lower back.

Sophie let his kiss melt away everything she'd ever felt before that point. His lips were so warm, so inviting, so blissfully numbing. She could kiss Angel for the rest of her life. She wished she could feel the butterflies dancing around in her body forever. She snaked a hand into his soft, thick hair and deepened the kiss, parting her lips slightly, allowing him access to every part of her mouth. His tongue caressed hers, bringing it to life. She couldn't help but let out a little whimper.

Everything he did made her whole body burn with need. A need she hadn't ever felt before she'd met him. She hooked her leg around his, bringing his body closer to hers. She was left breathless when he pulled away. He brushed her hair away from her face and let his thumb trace the outline of her cheekbone again.

"Sophie, amor, is this what you want?" he asked, his voice low and husky, but patient and soft. Angel pressed his hips forward on instinct, wanting *so much* to be inside the woman he held close to him, the woman who held him just as closely. He was ready and aching for her, but he would stop if she couldn't. He'd do anything she needed. After the one kiss, he was hers to command. She moaned, her kiss-swollen lips parting in the most sensual way as he ground his hips into hers.

She could feel him, feel the desire he had for her. She hadn't opened her eyes since Angel had kissed her. She did then when she felt him pressed against her. She could see the passion burning inside his normally dark chocolate-colored eyes lit up by the moonlight shining in the window, making them glow like whiskey in firelight.

Sophie trembled as she contemplated her next move. She ran her hands down the soft cotton of his short sleeved shirt and clenched it in her fists, trying to get a grasp on something to anchor her in reality. Angel held her gaze, scorching her from the inside out as he continued rocking against her slowly and carefully.

She knew it would come to this eventually. Two adults of the opposite sex, cohabitating in the same house, one having saved the other's life - forming an inseparable bond between the two souls. She should have known this would happen. But if it was so inevitable, why did she feel so shocked by his lips on hers? Why was she so *scared*? He'd never given her any reason to think he might hurt her; despite the verbal clashes they'd shared in the weeks prior.

She felt his fingers brush the skin of her lower back as he trailed them along the edge of her shirt, sending embers shooting through her veins. He was waiting for an answer. *What had he asked again?*

"Sophie, are you sure?" That was it. That's what he asked. She had gotten so lost in his eyes and her thoughts that she'd forgotten to answer. Was she sure? Did she want this? Did she want him? What if she didn't want it? What if she was too scared? What if she was too broken, too scarred by the violence of her past?

She could feel the embers smoldering in her soul, pushing her to leave the pain and shame behind her, to let the man in front of her love her back to life, love her until the broken pieces of her soul fit together again. "Sophie?" His soothing voice interrupted her stream of thoughts again. She had to answer him, fast before he assumed she didn't want it.

"Yeah, yes. I'm sure," she replied hastily. It was true, *mostly*. She wanted Angel more than she'd ever wanted anything before. He'd taken care of her, picked up her broken pieces, loved her when she felt like she wasn't worth it.

"Because if you aren't ready, I'll wait as long as you need me to, mi amor," he whispered to her softly as he traced the shell of her ear with his warm fingers and tucked another rogue strand of hair behind her ear. His touch sent a scorching trail through her veins by brushing his fingertips over the skin of her lower back once more. He was reigniting the fire she'd felt the second she'd kissed him earlier that night. Angel pressed his lips to the soft spot where her neck and shoulder met, making goosebumps erupt all over her body again.

"No, I'm ready." Her voice was wavering and uneven, but her resolve was solid. Sophie let go of his t-shirt and twisted her fingers into his luscious hair once more and pulled his lips to hers in a wanton kiss.

Angel pulled her closer to him, as if he were protecting her from her own thoughts. He only broke away to make sure she understood he was hers to command.

"You stop me anytime. I won't force you to do anything you don't want," he told her. It needed to be her choice. Every step closer had to be taken by the one who'd suffered too much for one lifetime already. He vowed silently in that moment never to make her suffer on his account.

Angel pressed a kiss to her lips before he slowly traced his fingers up the back of her shirt. He watched her icy blue eyes drift closed as he released the hooks of her bra. He ran his hand across the newly freed skin of her back, feeling the softness paired exquisitely with the goosebumps that covered her from head to toe.

He would do everything he could to make this an experience she would never forget, something she could think of to erase the painful memories of the past. Keeping his left hand concealed beneath her shirt softly caressing the newly revealed flesh, he held her neck with the other as he pressed a slow, gentle kiss to her swollen pink lips. He held her close to him as he rolled onto his back, pulling her on top of him. She needed to know she had full control of his body, mind, and soul.

Sophie opened her eyes to see Angel below her, a small, sensuous smile graced his lips. She felt him shift beneath her, pressing up, grinding his hardness into her. "Angel, do you love me?" Sophie asked. He gave her an amused look before he answered.

"Sophie, I've loved you since I pulled you off that ledge." Angel smiled at her as he ran his hands up and down her sides.

She pressed her lips to his in a searing kiss before sitting back up and pulling off her shirt and bra together. She saw his lips part as if he were about to say something, but no words escaped. His hands followed the curve of her waist up to cup her breasts, stopping just below them.

"Is this okay?" he asked, his voice barely above a whisper.

All Sophie could do was nod. She was too anxious for words. She sank her teeth into her plump bottom lip as he cupped her breasts, admiring the fullness of them.

He brushed his thumbs over her nipples, testing her boundaries, seeing where he could touch her, what she would allow. When she gasped, he did it again as he watched her carefully.

He could see every curve of her perfectly toned body. The moonlight lit up her skin. The flawless canvas was covered in an ethereal glow. She looked like Selene, the Goddess of the Moon, her platinum blonde hair turned silver in the night; her skin was glowing in the pale moonlight. She took his breath away. Angel sat up and took one of her nipples in his mouth, circling it with his tongue, bringing it to a stiff peak before letting it go to give the other the same treatment. All the while, listening to the small moans and gasps Sophie was gifting him.

She had never been touched that way before. Always, it was taken. It was forced. She'd been the one to give pleasure, never to receive it this way. She ground herself onto his hardness again as his simple touch gave her almost too much pleasure. She could hardly contain herself. There were only a few layers of fabric between them. The most offensive being his shirt, but Sophie was not about to tell him to stop whatever magic he was doing to her with his tongue. He was making her whole body tingle.

As if he had read her mind, Angel let her nipple go with a soft pop and leaned away from her to remove his shirt. He would not let her be the only vulnerable one. He wrapped his arms around her and pulled her body close to him to feel her silken skin against his. Her soft, flawless, glowing skin. Angel peppered kisses across her collarbone to the crook of her neck where he nipped at her and lavished the bite with his tongue, soothing the mark he'd made. He felt her dig her nails into his shoulders, deliciously painful. He knew she was almost completely taken over by the sensations he was causing. That was his plan, to make her feel everything in the best way he knew how. He lifted her up, his hands under her thighs, and laid her down on the bed. He shimmied out of his jeans and boxers but let her keep her bottoms until she was ready to discard them.

"Angel," she whispered as he kissed a path down her neck.

"Yes, amor?" he mumbled as he kissed the valley between her breasts and trailed even further down.

"Don't stop," she gasped as he sucked on a sensitive patch of skin on her hip. Her hands fisted into his hair. Sophie could barely breathe. Her mouth had gone dry long ago from her heavy breaths and occasional gasps and panting. She couldn't get an even breath to save her life, but if this was how she was meant to go, she'd die the happiest woman on Earth.

Angel came up to lay beside her. He pressed his lips to hers again, feeling the throbbing need deep in his chest. He'd make love to her, but not before he was sure she was ready. He held her face in his hands as he kissed her, only breaking it to watch her body react to his touch as he trailed his fingers down, down, down until he met the small patch of hair that hid her most sensitive skin.

Angel's fingers brushed over the sensitive bundle of nerves at her core, eliciting a breathy moan from Sophie. He watched her face for any sign of discomfort as he pressed a finger into her. He curled his finger, searching for the spot he knew would bring her some of the most intense pleasure.

Sophie had never felt the sensations rushing through her body by someone else before. He knew the right place to touch and tease to bring her the most pleasure. She grabbed onto his shoulder, unable to stop herself from digging her nails into his skin. How did he know just where to touch? Sophie didn't care. She only cared that he didn't stop.

And he didn't. Not until the sensations became stronger and stronger, until something inside her exploded. A loud moan slipped from her lips. His fingers stilled inside her, letting her ride out the waves of her orgasm before withdrawing them completely.

"Oh my God..." she whispered over and over through heavy breaths. No one besides herself had ever given her an orgasm.

"Do you want me to stop?" Angel asked again. He brushed a wet finger over her nipple, pulling another moan from the still recovering Sophie.

"No, please don't stop," she nearly begged. She pulled him into a rough kiss, trying to show him how much she needed him by wrapping her leg around his and pulling him as close as she could. "Please."

"Tell me if you want me to, okay?"

Sophie nodded in reply. She was sure he'd broken her in some way. Her body hadn't ever felt so loose and relaxed before. She was tired but didn't want him to stop. Ever.

Angel eased Sophie onto her back and lifted her thighs above his hips. He pressed a kiss to her still kiss-swollen lips. He couldn't believe what was happening to him. She was the most beautiful woman he'd ever seen, and he was about to be inside her. He positioned himself at her core and pressed forward. She was so warm and wet from her orgasm it didn't take much pressure for him to bury himself fully inside her.

"Fuck." He couldn't stop the obscenity before it tumbled from his lips.

Sophie had been so caught up in the feelings Angel was stirring up inside her body, she barely caught what he'd said.

"What? Are you okay?" she asked, suddenly worried about the man inside her.

"You just feel so good..." he whispered in Sophie's ear before he took her earlobe between his lips and lightly sucked on it. The sounds she made were almost too much for him, but he had to at least give her another orgasm before reaching his own. He had to hear *that* noise again. He pulled back and thrust into her, taking his time to let her feel everything. He didn't know how long it had been for her - he wasn't stupid enough to think someone as gorgeous as she was could possibly be a virgin - but he could tell what she was feeling was new to her.

Sophie's body was covered in goosebumps again as Angel brushed against the bundle of nerves deep inside her, over and over. Bringing her closer to another mind-blowing release with each stroke. He kissed her neck, cheeks, and shoulders as he filled her over and over again. She couldn't help but think how perfectly they fit together, like they were made for each other. Two perfectly shaped puzzle pieces coming together in the most satisfying way.

But, as Angel and Sophie became lost in each other's touch, neither noticed the dark silhouette just outside the window. Watching everything unfold in front of him.

18

The second Sophie's eyes opened the next morning, guilt filled her heart. Angel had made everything else in the world melt away the night before. When the morning sun filtered in through the window, thoughts of how messed up she was filled her mind. She'd never officially ended things with Theo. *Had they even really started?* He'd never asked her to be his girlfriend, but she'd assumed they were at least exclusively dating. Maybe she was wrong, but he'd seemed to be interested in her to the point where it'd be mutually exclusive.

Sophie sat up, letting the covers fall into her lap. The cold room was a reminder of the warm, fiery bliss she'd experienced at Angel's hands. Goosebumps erupted all over her skin as she thought of his hands exploring her body the way they had, soft and gentle in their caresses but also calm and confident, the exact opposite of how she'd felt. She was jittery and scared, but excited and comfortable with the man who'd somehow found his way under her skin. The things he'd made her feel...

Sophie shook her head. She was supposed to be angry at herself, not thinking about Angel and all of the wonderful things he'd made her feel.

She hadn't even told Theo why she had disappeared. He wasn't even a second thought before that moment. The guilt burned deep in Sophie's chest. He was probably worried sick. Any normal person would have been.

Maybe he hadn't really cared that much? Considering his job, she assumed he'd be able to find her pretty easily if he'd wanted to. So, maybe he didn't want to. She ran an anxious, trembling hand through her hair. Her anxiety dampened palm pulled at the strands of her hair.

What would Angel think of all this? She asked herself. She looked to the other side of the bed and found it empty. She listened to the sounds in the house for a second. She heard rustling in the kitchen cupboards and then the beep of the coffee pot. Angel must be making coffee, like he did most mornings when he was home.

Sophie swung her bare legs over the edge of the bed and shivered. Why was it so cold? She pulled a short sleeved t-shirt and a pair of leggings on before heading to the kitchen. She found Angel exactly where she'd thought she would; he was right next to the coffee pot, waiting for it to finish brewing.

Thoughts of the night before started flowing through her mind when she noticed he hadn't bothered to put on a shirt. His pajama pants hung low on his waist, showing off his muscular shoulders and the sexy dimples in his lower back.

She stopped at the threshold of the hallway just to watch him. She watched the muscles of his shoulders flex as he reached into a cupboard to pull down their coffee cups. She couldn't tear her eyes away from him. She chewed on her bottom lip, an unconscious effort to pull herself out of the trance-like state Angel had stuck her in.

As if he'd sensed her, he turned toward the hallway and smiled brightly at her. "Good morning," he said before turning toward the fridge to gather the creamer and half and half then took them to the table.

"Morning," she said curtly. Sophie took her seat at the table and clasped her hands together on her lap, nervously wringing her fingers. She watched as Angel went back to the coffee pot and filled the cups before bringing them to the table. *How could he be so calm? Is he not wondering what the hell is going on? What was last night? What are we?*

"Are you okay?" Angel asked once he sat down across the table from Sophie. His dark eyes held a soft concern in them.

"Yeah, I'm fine." Sophie said quickly as she began preparing her coffee. She abruptly stopped as she picked the coffee cup up to take a drink. She looked back up and her eyes met Angel's again.

He was quiet, waiting for a truthful answer without accusing her of lying openly. He gave her a soft, knowing smile before he took a sip of his own coffee. He knew. He knew she wasn't. That she was a complete mess. *How did he know?* Sophie set her cup down and groaned as she dropped her face into her shaking hands. She couldn't face him as she told him. She couldn't meet his eyes as she was filled with shame.

"No. I'm not. I'm freaking out. Before I went to Sacred Heights, I was dating this guy, Theo. The last time I saw him we got in a fight because he didn't believe me when I said there was someone stalking me. I just walked away. I didn't tell him we were through dating, nothing. Now, this thing with you – I just feel so guilty, but I don't even know if I should because he never officially asked me to be his girlfriend or anything like that, but I assumed we were somewhat official since it had been a couple months and now I feel so so so guilty for sleeping with you without calling it quits officially with him even though I don't know if we were even official and I just don't know what to say or think or how to feel and –" Sophie stopped when she felt a warm hand pull hers away from her face. She glanced up at Angel with her one uncovered eye. Angel gave her another warm smile before he replied to her anxiety-fueled rant.

"Sophie, I'm not sorry about last night, and I don't think you should be either. If this guy was serious about you he would have made you his girlfriend, but he didn't. So, last night wasn't something to be ashamed about. It was amazing, and so are you."

Sophie wished she could feel so sure about things the way Angel did. She let her other hand that was covering her face fall back into her lap, realizing she probably looked silly only covering half her face. No one had ever said anything like that to her before. Sophie studied Angel for a moment, deciphering whether he meant what he'd said. She ran through a checklist in her mind; He was leaning towards her, his eyes holding contact with hers, his breathing was steady. "I'm not, though." Sophie looked down at the hand in her lap. He had no idea about her past. He didn't know about the terrible things she'd done, or that had been done to her. If he knew everything he'd change his mind like everyone else. She had to tell him before he was too invested if he wasn't already. She had to be fair to this warm, caring, loving person in front of her.

"You are, you just can't see it through all of the pain in your past. You don't have to take that pain with you into your future, though Sophie."

Sophie's heart thudded against her ribcage as she combed through some of her less traumatic memories. She needed Angel to know exactly what he could be getting himself into. "I'm an orphan. I have no family. No one that means anything, at least." She blurted out. Angel's hand gave hers a reassuring squeeze. "I was adopted by a piece of shit, abusive, greedy asshole who abused all of us, except his biological son who we had to treat like a fucking prince, but he was just as bad as his father." The threat of tears pricked Sophie's eyes. She took a deep breath and looked up at the ceiling, trying to fight them back.

"I'm so sorry you went through that, Sophie. You know, I was an orphan, too. Before I got adopted by my parents. If you got out of your own head every once in a while you'd have seen the picture on the wall in the living room." Angel smiled as he got up and walked to the living room, grabbed the picture off the wall - that Sophie had honestly never paid attention to - and set it on the table in front of her. He chuckled as he said, "We're different colors."

Sophie felt like such an asshole. How had she never paid attention to the picture? Nope. She knew why. Angel had said it. She never gets out of her own damn head. "Oh my God. Angel, I'm so sorry."

"Don't be, you have a lot going on. They adopted me right after I turned 9, in 2004. They're amazing people. I'm sorry you weren't so lucky, Sophie." He left the picture on the table. "But you're here now, and I intend to help you make your life better as long as you want me to. Just like my parents did for me. Although, I sincerely hope you don't think of me as a dad because that would make last night weird," Angel joked as he sent a dazzling smile Sophie's way.

She couldn't help but laugh. How did this man know exactly what to say every time to make her feel better? "I was adopted in 2004 too, when I was 9. The month before my 10th birthday." Sophie thought back to that day.

She watched as families brought new children into their lives. She heard the awful things some people said about her, right in front of her. "Too pretty, she'd cause trouble, looks spoiled." Sophie looked back up at Angel, she could see his mind working over an idea. "What?" she asked him, curious to know what was going on in his brain that had puzzled him so much.

"Sophie, where were you adopted from?" Angel's face had turned serious, his brows knitted together, his lips no longer turned up at the corners.

"St John's Catholic Church and Orphanage, why?" Sophie was completely lost. Why did that matter? What was going on?

"Sophie, it's you." Angel's eyes lit up and he grinned. He grabbed her hands. "We were there, together. Do you remember me?"

Sophie often tried to forget her time there. Sister Meredith was still an ever-present demon in her nightmares. A voice that never left her subconscious for long. Sophie closed her eyes as she thought back to the time she'd blocked out. Nights reading with Felicity. Days avoiding Zachariah. Running around the forest with the twins whose names she struggled to recall. Her protector, a boy a little younger than her who would go everywhere with her that he was allowed. Always there, rescuing her. Playing with her when she was lonely.

Sophie looked at the man in front of her. His eyes hadn't changed one bit. The same they had always been, warm dark brown fringed with perfect thick eyelashes any girl would kill to have. How had she not realized her protector from the orphanage was the one to save her from herself on top of that building? Could that have been why she'd felt the connection with him as he held her still, keeping her safe from the jump she had intended on taking? Her mind was taking her through so many thoughts at once she couldn't figure out exactly how to feel.

"Sophie, are you okay? It's okay if you don't remember." There was a hint of worry in Angel's tone. He'd hope she did. He'd been waiting his whole life to find her again. She never let go of his heart. Even as young as he was, he knew she was his soulmate. He knew better than to lead with that at the moment, though.

Angel felt it in his heart the day he'd pulled her off the ledge. He'd tried to deny the familiarity he felt when he first looked into her clear blue eyes again after so many years, that it couldn't possibly have been *his* Sophie he saved that day. It's hard to forget the person who holds your heart. She'd held his since he was very, very young. He could remember following her wherever she went, fighting off that horrible boy who would harass her, hugging her when she cried the lonely tears of an orphan with no family to speak of.

He watched her then, just as he was now. Her blue eyes darted back and forth between thoughts. Since he'd found her at the bus stop he could tell she got lost in her thoughts, a lot. Her mind never seemed to stop, the wheels forever turning and trying to make sense of everything going on around her.

Angel briefly wondered what had made her so aware of everything all the time. He stopped himself. He didn't know if he actually wanted to know. Even the thought of someone hurting her broke his heart and she'd already confirmed that had been the case with her adoptive family. Her soft voice snapped him out of his own thoughts.

"No, no. I do. I remember you. I was just... thinking. Stuck in my head again," she said with a self-deprecating chuckle.

"I can't believe it's you. I always wondered if I would ever see you again. I told myself I was crazy when I saw you on the roof. That it couldn't be you, but it was. Like fate, if you believe in that kind of stuff."

Sophie couldn't tear her eyes away from Angel. Here sat the boy who'd protected her and kept her safe for years in that orphanage she'd tried so hard to block out. She found memories pouring back in. It almost brought tears to her eyes. She never thought she'd see him again after he'd been taken away with that nice looking family. The family who loved him and helped him grow into the man he was; the one sitting in front of her who was so full of compassion and kindness.

"Me too, I never thought I'd see you again."

Angel reached across the table and took her hand in his. "I'm really glad you're here, Sophie."

"Me too, Angel." The warmth grew in her chest as she thought of all the impossible things that had led them back to each other. The universe had a mysterious way of making the impossible possible. For the first time in her life Sophie felt like she belonged somewhere. She felt like she was home, that she had a home. A home with Angel.

Tears welled up in her eyes as she saw the warmth radiating from his eyes again. Sophie had found her home, with the one person who had always made her feel as though she had a place in the world, a place to belong. The one person who had never expected anything in return for everything he gave her.

19

Sophie and Angel had spent two weeks together since they realized they had known each other since long before that day on the roof. They were completely inseparable when he wasn't working. Todd joked about them being attached at the hip when he found Sophie sitting on the kitchen counter as Angel was cooking dinner. Melody swooned over how cute they were with their whole crazy story about being orphans together, that they were fated to find each other again. Both of which, of course, made Sophie blush like a little school girl whose crush was just discovered.

Angel noticed each time and would wrap a comforting arm around her shoulders and give her a quick squeeze, almost like he was physically telling her that everything was okay, and she didn't need to worry or be embarrassed. He was so good at noticing how everything affected her and knowing just how to respond. It was like a mental connection had formed between them when they'd figured out who they were to each other.

Sophie often wondered who *exactly* they were to each other. Angel had never asked her to be his girlfriend, but she knew deep down he was way more serious about her than Theo ever was. Could that have just been because of their past? Perhaps, but Sophie was sure it went beyond that. They still shared Angel's bed but hadn't been together in a biblical sense since the first time. She didn't want to think about why. So, she distracted herself any way possible.

Sophie spent most of her days reading the books on the bookshelf in the living room. In just two weeks, she had already finished the first row of books, eight books to be exact. She also spent time weeding the small garden in the backyard, until there wasn't a stray weed in sight. She touched up the white paint on the picket fence. She had even tried to make fajitas for lunch for Angel on one of his days off. It was a mess and she ended up throwing it away. Inedible. She wished she could cook like Angel, but it seemed no matter how much she watched to learn, she couldn't get it quite right.

Angel was working the day it was all turned upside down. The perfect life and routine they'd created, ruined.

Sophie sat on the couch, in her usual corner leaned comfortably against the arm with her book propped on it. She was flipping through the pages she'd thought might entertain her long enough to distract from watching the hands of the clock turn slower and slower each second she spent watching them.

She was waiting for them to hit 6:30 when Angel should get home from his shift at the firehouse. She'd been having a hard time controlling her anxiety all day. Her mind jumped from one worst case scenario to the next. Each one was worse than the last. It was one of those days she would wish Angel was home to let her know everything would be okay. Since he wasn't, she did her best to picture his face and his calming voice telling her so.

Being cooped up in the house for weeks wasn't helping anything either. Although, she had started learning the patterns of the neighbors. The young couple next door would take their dog on a walk every morning at 6:30 and then leave for work 30 minutes after returning. The man came home at 4:45 and the woman at 5:20. Sophie had learned the sound of the man's old Toyota; it had a distinct hum that told her it was going to die soon. She wondered if the man knew he needed a new car too.

The older couple across the street also had a pattern. They'd take a walk every day at 9:30 in the morning, holding hands as they strode down the street in a comfortable silence. Sophie hoped to be like that when she was their age. The school bus passed by the house each weekday at 7:45 on its way to the nearby middle school, kids shouting and laughing audible even over the sound of the rumbling diesel engine carrying them.

Everything about the world outside her windows felt so achingly normal. Sophie wished she fit in to that. Angel made her feel at home in his house, but she didn't fit into the normalcy of the rest of the world around her. She couldn't even leave the front door without the worry that he'd find her.

Sophie looked up from her book and out the window. She saw the elderly couple from across the street pass by the front yard, their faces stretched in wide grins as they chattered while they walked together. She thought again about how she hoped for a happy future like that. Walking hand in hand with her love, talking about anything and everything as they enjoyed the fresh air that came with the inklings of the coming change in seasons.

Fall was just around the corner. *Someone should tell the Chicago weather that*, Sophie thought. It was the second week of September, and it was still sunny and in the mid-70s without the slightest hint of rain in the last month or to come in the near future. She glanced at the clock again. 6:00. Time was going so slowly. Sophie could have sworn she looked an hour ago and it was 5:45. She decided long ago that time was not on her side.

She groaned as she put the book down. She hadn't understood a single word she'd read for the last 15 minutes. The same paragraph, over and over and it still wasn't making any sense. Looking up at the clock every 10 seconds probably didn't help. She just wanted Angel to get home.

She put the book back in its place on the shelf and began pacing. She walked around the living room, into the kitchen, down the hall, into Angel's room and all the way back to the living room. She was so glad Todd was working and Melody was too. They'd think she was crazy. They'd been fortunate enough to not have experienced any of it first-hand. Sophie paused in the kitchen. She put her hands on the counter and leaned against them, the edge pressing into the heel of her palms. She took a deep breath in and slowly let it go. *Just 30 more minutes. That's all. Then he'll be home.*

She pressed her eyes closed and focused her breathing into an even pattern of calm, steady breaths. Breathing in for 4 counts and out for 8. She felt her shoulders relax and her heart rate begin to slow down to its regular cadence. Angel would be home soon. Sophie walked over to the front door and looked out the peephole, hating that she had to stand on her tippy toes to see out of it properly. 30 more minutes.

She paced for 27 of those 30 minutes all the way through the house, only avoiding Todd and Melody's room. She spent the last 3 watching the front door from the couch. She'd been stuck in her head, as Angel would say, the whole time. Each minute seemed to bring on a new wave of anxiety.

It had been 31 minutes. Where was Angel? He was never late. If he ever thought he was going to be, he would reach out. Text, call, something.

Relief washed over her when she saw a shadow pass across the window. Angel was home. *Finally*. Sophie waited for him to come in, ready to give him a huge hug and welcome him home from his shift.

Sophie waited. The doorknob turned but the door didn't open. Her whole body froze. Why wasn't he coming in? Sophie stared at the door, still waiting for Angel to come in. The confusion clouded her mind. When the shadow appeared in the window again she felt her body reel with panic. She could see through the gauzy curtains, she knew exactly who was trying to look in.

Hat. Bomber jacket. Angular features.

It was him.

He'd found her.

Sophie wanted to scream. She wanted to fight. She wanted to stop him. But she couldn't move. She was frozen in complete terror. Could he see her? It didn't seem like it. Sophie stayed completely still. Movement may tip him off to someone being in the house.

The man left the window, but Sophie couldn't see where he'd gone. She mentally checked all of the ways into the house. The windows in each room. All locked on a regular basis. The front door was locked. The back door!

She'd left it unlocked earlier when she'd gone out to water the plants that morning. Sophie couldn't find it in her to move. Why couldn't she move? *Damn it, Sophie! You have to get it together and go lock the fucking door!* Her consciousness screamed at her.

Sophie looked to the back door. It was in the kitchen. She could see it from her place in the living room. There was a shadow in the window next to it. Something about the possibility of him coming in gave her body the shock it needed. She darted across the room and slammed the deadbolt in place. She sat with her back against the door and her knees curled up to her chest, hoping he hadn't seen her.

The door knob jiggled as it was checked and turned. Tears poured down Sophie's cheeks at the thought of what could have happened if she hadn't acted as quickly as she did. At the thought of what could still happen if Angel didn't show up soon.

Angel pulled up two minutes past 6:30, hoping Sophie was able to contain her anxiety in those couple minutes. He knew how quickly she could go from zero to infinity in split seconds. He got out and walked up to the door, but hesitated. Usually, she would have opened the door for him, since she usually watched out the peephole for him at 6:30. Something was wrong.

Angel looked around the yard and to both sides, looking for any hint as to what could be out of place. He walked across the porch and looked around the corner of the house that led to the backyard, a small walkway lined with concrete pavers. He saw movement, a shadow thrown across the pavers. Someone wearing a hat and much too large to be Sophie.

Before it rounded the corner, Angel ducked back around so he couldn't be seen. He waited until the last second to ambush the person rounding the corner. The man was taller than Angel, and stronger. The leverage belonged to him, even though Angel had gotten the jump on him. The man propelled Angel past him, using Angel's own momentum against him. Angel slammed into the fence.

He whipped around to see the man sprinting away, already out of the front yard. "Fuck!" Angel shouted. He couldn't reach him in time for him to disappear. Angel dug his keys out of his pocket and rushed back to the front door. He let himself in to find Sophie on the floor in front of the back door, shaking wildly and bawling.

"Sophie!" He dropped to his knees in front of her and pulled her into his arms. "Are you okay? Did he get in?"

Sophie shook her head as she dropped her knees to be able to hug Angel back.

"It's okay. He's gone. I chased him off. I'm so sorry I couldn't catch him. I need to call the police and file a report, okay?"

Sophie nodded. She let him lead her to the couch, after closing and locking the front door. Tears were still falling down her cheeks, her nose, and lips bright pink from crying. Angel sat next to her and wrapped an arm around her shoulders to pull her close to him. He pulled his phone out and called the police. He filed a report over the phone and the operator promised an officer would be around to check out the neighborhood within five minutes.

Once he'd gotten off the phone he shifted towards Sophie. He brushed a thumb down her cheek. "Sophie, are you okay? I'm so sorry I was late." Angel's heart ached at her silence. He needed to know she was okay; he couldn't know unless she told him.

She didn't say anything. What could she say? He'd found her. Everything was ruined. She wasn't safe anywhere. He'd always find her. No one could protect her.

"Sophie, amor, please talk to me." His voice was pleading. He pressed a kiss to her forehead. "It's okay now. You're safe with me." He pulled her into his chest and let her cry, her tears wetting his t-shirt. He didn't care. She needed to let it out.

Sophie hadn't said anything since he'd gotten home. It was nearly 7:30. Angel couldn't stand the silence. They were still sitting on the couch when Melody got home.

"What's wrong?" she asked as she rushed over to the couch.

"Someone tried to break in. Sophie was the only one home. He didn't get in, but she's totally freaked out."

"Oh hon, let me get you some tea." Melody shuffled off to the kitchen to start the water.

"Sophie, please talk to me. I need to know you're okay," Angel said softly, making sure Melody couldn't hear him. "What's going on in that head of yours?" He looked into her teary blue eyes. They were starting to turn red from the sheer amount of crying she'd done. She looked so tired, so defeated and broken. "Do you know who it was?" Her eyes widened in terror, and she buried her face in Angel's chest again. She did know, Angel realized. It must have been the man who found her at the café. How could he have found her here? Did he stick around to watch Angel take her home?

Overwhelming guilt filled Angel. If he hadn't convinced her to stay with him she'd have been out of the city away from that monster. "Sophie, I'm so sorry. This is my fault. I wasn't here to help you. I kept you here in Chicago.

I was selfish. I should have let you leave. Please, I need you to talk to me. Please?" Angel asked.

"I can't," Sophie whimpered. She didn't have words to tell him. She couldn't articulate the feeling inside her. She felt like she was dead already. She knew Angel could tell she wasn't okay, but she couldn't bring herself to lie and tell him she would be.

"Just talk to someone. Please? It doesn't have to be me. Anyone. Tell someone," he asked as he squeezed her. Sophie just nodded to placate him. Could he tell she didn't plan on talking ever again?

Angel just held her. He'd do whatever she needed to help her. That was what it seemed like she needed. He couldn't know for sure since she barely said a word for an entire week after the incident. He took the week off, he switched shifts with Todd and another coworker, to spend time upgrading the security around the house and to be there for Sophie in case she did decide to talk. When she hadn't, Angel couldn't help but feel like everything that happened was his fault and that Sophie blamed him too. Why else would she not speak to him?

20

"Angel, do you think you can take me to the Arlington?"

Angel stopped pouring coffee in the mug in his hand and whipped around, almost fast enough to spill the contents of the mug. "The Arlington? As in the one you worked at with Felicity?" he asked.

Sophie nodded. She needed to talk to someone, like Angel had said. She couldn't bring herself to talk to him though. He wasn't wrong when he pointed out his hand in everything and as much as Sophie didn't want to blame him or be angry with him, she was. She needed to talk to Felicity.

"Yeah, of course. When do you want to go?" he asked.

"Felicity won't be there for another couple of hours, so maybe then?"

"Yeah, totally. Just let me know when you're ready." Angel finished preparing his coffee and sat across from Sophie at the table. "You know, Sophie, you can talk to me, right?"

"Yeah, I know. I'm just still figuring it all out." It made Sophie's heart ache to keep Angel at arm's length like she was. She really did need to figure out how she was feeling about what was going on, and she couldn't do that with Angel. She needed to do it herself. He couldn't protect her from it all.

A couple of hours later, they endured a silent car ride to the library. Sophie could barely stand it. She wanted so badly to say something. Anything. What could she say?

All she said was, "thanks," when they pulled in front of the stone building. An architectural wonder she'd missed so much. "Would it be okay if I call you when I'm ready to come home?"

"Yeah, I'll be waiting," he said with a small smile. Sophie hoped he wouldn't give up on her. She just needed a little time. If he meant what he'd said, he wouldn't. Sophie got out of the truck and stared at the building in front of her. She never thought she'd come back. A shiver ran down her spine as she thought of the last time she was there.

She pulled open the glass door and walked in. She looked straight to the central desk, hoping to find Felicity there. When she was disappointed, only finding the desk empty, she looked around the library for the woman she needed to talk to. The light in the office was on and the door was closed, which told her exactly what she needed to know. Felicity was knee-deep in paperwork. It also meant she was alone. She never closed the door when she wasn't.

Sophie knocked on the door, her heart hammered in her chest, as it had been since she'd decided she had to come back. The familiar voice called out, and Sophie felt like she was right back where she was before everything that had happened.

"Come in!"

"Hey, it's been a while..." Sophie said when she opened the door and walked in. Felicity's head snapped up as their eyes met.

"Oh my God," Felicity muttered as she climbed over the desk and closed her arms around Sophie so tightly she thought she might not ever breathe again. "Sophie, where have you been? I've missed you so much!" Felicity cried into Sophie's shoulder as the two women hugged each other.

"I've missed you, too. It was time to come back. I needed to talk to you. About everything." Sophie didn't have any more tears left to fall. Felicity did though. When she pulled out of the hug, Sophie's shoulder was damp. Felicity pulled a chair out for her and sat in the office chair on the other side of the desk.

"You came to talk, so talk." Felicity said as she folded her hands, guarded but ready to listen to whatever Sophie had to say.

"Well, it all started before your wedding. This guy, I kept seeing him on the bus. I thought it was whatever at first. Then, I started seeing him following me around town. Like, to the flower shop when we had the signing for that author, Scarlett Phoenix. He followed me back from the flower shop. I thought I was crazy, he'd just disappeared into thin air. Then, he started getting off at my stop.

"I even talked to Cage about it. After you asked me to be your maid of honor. He told me to change up my routine, different routes home."

"You talked to Cage without even telling me what was going on?"

"Felicity, you were so busy with the wedding I didn't want to worry you! There's more, though..." Sophie hesitated before starting again. It was such a painful memory. She could feel her heart twinge, like an old wound being reopened. "The night of your wedding, I got drunk, like most everyone and I uh – I took an Uber home. The driver, he walked me up to my apartment," Sophie's voice broke in the middle of her sentence. Tears stung her eyes; she knew they'd come eventually so she just let them fall. She couldn't look Felicity in the eye. Sophie took a breath to center herself before continuing.

"Soph, you don't have to tell me unless you want to. I can't even imagine how much pain you went through."

"That's not all."

"There's even more?"

Sophie nodded and continued. "I got this letter the next day. It was so sweet, I assumed it'd been from Theo. Then, that guy showed up to the library. I was so scared, I called Theo to come take me home. He didn't believe me, though. The guy was gone by the time he showed up and we got in a fight, and I walked away from him. That's when I got a poem, with some dried flowers in a glass frame. Again, I assumed it was Theo."

"Was it?"

Sophie shook her head. "When you got back from your honeymoon a week later, I got another letter. This one was different though, creepy, possessive, almost angry. I lost it. Completely lost it. I was gonna jump off a building." Sophie chose to omit the part where she talked to a little girl who she was pretty sure never existed in the first place since she disappeared into thin air.

Felicity had started crying again, her quiet sobs barely audible. Sophie had to get through it though. She needed to get it all off her chest.

"Obviously, I didn't. A firefighter pulled me back. You'll never guess who it was. We'll get to that in a minute. I got stuck in Sacred Heights for 3 days. Ugh, it was hell. I hate hospitals. The day I came and quit my job was the day I got out. I was gonna leave Chicago for good. Get the hell out of this place so that piece of shit would never come for me again. He couldn't hurt me if he couldn't find me."

"But you're still here."

"Yeah, I was taken in by someone. A really good guy. The firefighter who pulled me back. He happened to drive by the bus stop I was waiting at as it was pouring rain and I was soaked with no jacket."

"Sounds like the beginning of a sappy rom-com." The women laughed through their tears. Sophie wiped her face dry for the moment.

"Oh, God. I wish it was. He convinced me to stay and get myself back on my feet before I left for good. Gave me a place to stay, helped me heal a bit. Until a week ago."

Sophie took the moment to look back at Felicity. She was fully entranced by Sophie's story. "What happened a week ago?"

"The guy on the bus tried to break in. He found where I was staying. Angel chased him off."

"Wait, who's Angel?"

"The firefighter I've been staying with, that pulled me off the ledge. He's like my literal guardian angel, though."

"No way! So, it is a sappy romance!" Felicity smiled at Sophie, trying to bring some levity back to the conversation. "Tell me everything about him!"

"Are we forgetting about the creepy stalker who wants to kill me?"

"No, but Angel is a lighter subject."

"You're not wrong. The only problem is, I wouldn't still be dealing with this guy if he hadn't convinced me to stay. If we hadn't..."

"You didn't!"

Sophie blushed a deep pink, from her neck all the way up.

"You did! How was it?"

"I couldn't even describe how amazing he is."

"So, what's the big deal?"

"He's the reason that guy found me," Sophie argued. "I'd be long gone if it weren't for him."

"Maybe, but...he helped you more than you realize. You're here. In the library where he stalked you. Would you have ever come back here if you hadn't met him?" Felicity argued back. Sophie took in her words. Felicity wasn't wrong. "I think being with him has helped more than you know."

"This is why I came back here. I needed an outside perspective. I've been stuck all this time, ever since I left. I'm so sorry I left."

"Sophie, you have nothing to be sorry about. Well, maybe the fact that you didn't talk to me about literally any of this before you dipped out on me."

Sophie looked down at her hands. She had been wringing her fingers, looking for an escape for the anxiety she'd been feeling about the exact moment she was stuck in. "I'm so sorry. I wish I would've done things differently. Let Cage and his company help me. He offered, you know. I didn't want to be indebted to you guys. I didn't want to worry you. I wanted to be able to take care of myself, for once in my life. I see now how wrong I was to not let you in and let you guys help."

"Sophie, stop. You don't have to apologize for trying to save yourself from that psycho. Were there better ways to do it? Yeah, sure. But what's done is done. Now, we can only move forward. So, in the spirit of moving on, will you be coming back now?"

"I don't know. He knows I'm connected to you and to this place."

"The neighborhood has been dangerous as of late, my husband happens to own a security company. I don't see why he wouldn't beef up security to protect his wife, do you?" Felicity said, her voice calm and confident.

"You don't have to – "

"I want to. If it makes you feel safer, I'd do anything for you to have the life you want. I couldn't bear to replace you, so your old position is open if you still want it..." Felicity hesitated, waiting for Sophie to accept her offer.

"Only if you're sure. I won't take off again."

"I'm sure!" Felicity rushed to answer, not leaving Sophie any chance to back out. She grinned at Sophie, glad her best friend was back. That they were back together again. She felt like her life was complete. "I'm gonna have Cage send a team out to install cameras tomorrow, and a guard to stand at each door, the whole time we're open. You'll get armed escorts to and from your house. We could even have someone watch your house, if you want."

"Whoa, whoa, calm down. I don't want an armed guard at all times."

It dawned on Felicity then, her mouth opened in a little circle as it hit her. "This is why you didn't tell me, isn't it? Overboard? I just care. I don't want you to get hurt."

Sophie smiled at her best friend. She couldn't have wished for someone better than Felicity to help bring her back down, and vice versa. "I'm so glad you do."

"Now, what are we gonna do about this stalker guy?" Felicity asked. "Cage still has FBI contacts. We could pass everything over to them and see if they know anything?"

"One life change at a time. Thank you for everything you've done for me, Felicity. I can't tell you how much I appreciate you." Sophie's phone rang, then. She picked it up and Angel flashed on the caller ID. Sophie showed Felicity, who urged her to answer at once. "Hello?"

"Hey, you just about ready? I have a surprise for you." His voice conveyed his excitement.

"Yeah, we were just finishing up. Are you on your way?"

"I'm actually outside."

"Oh okay, I'll be out soon." They hung up and Sophie looked at Felicity who was grinning like a Cheshire Cat.

"Lover boy is waiting for you. Go, go!" She said as she shooed Sophie away, waving both hands at her.

"Alright! Alright. I'm going. When should I be back, boss?"

"Monday. 8:00 sharp. Don't be late or I might have to fire you," Felicity joked as Sophie stuck her tongue out at the woman before leaving the library.

On her way out, Sophie ran straight into a hard body. Sophie's eyes shot up to see the face of the man she kind of hoped to never see again. Theo smiled at her, a sad but friendly smile.

"Hey Sophie. How have you been?" he asked.

"Been better," she replied shortly. She felt the anger rise up in her chest. He hadn't believed her when she needed someone to be there for her.

"I'm sorry I haven't called. Work's been crazy," he said, which they both knew was a complete lie. He rubbed the back of his neck as he waited for her to respond.

"That's alright. I spent some time doing some work on myself. I actually met someone else. He's right over there." Sophie pointed to Angel's truck which sat just outside the front of the building, right where he'd dropped her off at. He stood waiting to let her in, holding the door open and everything. "Anyways, it was good to see you, Theo. Have a great night," she said as she strode confidently over to the truck that awaited her.

"Your chariot awaits, mi' lady. Who was that?" Angel asked as he held his hand out for her to grab as she climbed into the truck.

"Just Theo. He officially knows I've moved on." Sophie couldn't stop the smile that spread across her face. "What's all this about?" she asked when he got into the driver's seat.

"It's a surprise." He grinned before he started the truck and drove them back to his house. It wasn't a long drive, but long enough for Sophie to get all up in her head and work herself up to near panic attack by the time they pulled into the driveway. Angel turned off the engine and looked at her. "It's okay. I promise, it's nothing bad. You deserve a nice night after all you've been through." Angel got out of the truck and opened Sophie's door for her and helped her down.

"What did you do?" she asked as she eyed him suspiciously.

"Follow me," he said as he took her hand in his and gently pulled her forward to the front door. "Would it be okay if I covered your eyes? I don't know if I trust you to keep them closed," he joked.

"Yeah," Sophie said. Her breaths were coming in shorter huffs. What was he doing to her? Angel's warm hand covered her eyes as she heard him open the door. Once it was swung open, she could smell the fresh-made food and hear the sounds of a crackling fire and light piano music drifting from the speakers in the living room. What had he done?

"Keep your eyes closed, okay? I want to see your face when you open them."

Sophie nodded in reply, agreeing to his terms. His hand left her eyes, but not before he pressed a kiss to her cheek. Her chest swelled with warmth that radiated all throughout her body. She kept her eyes closed.

"Okay, open on three. One... Two... Three!"

Sophie opened her eyes to find the house lit by candlelight, a feast prepared on the dining room table for them. The fire in the fireplace was indeed lit, which she had actually yet to see in the time she'd lived in the house. "Angel, it's gorgeous. You did all this?" she asked.

"With some help. Melody may have set everything up for me while I was out on a very special errand. We'll get to that later. For now, come sit and dine with me. It's Mel's special. Coq au vin, with roasted broccoli and herbed potatoes, and a delicious bottle of red wine to go with it."

"It smells heavenly," Sophie said as she sat in the chair Angel held out for her. "Angel, this is all so amazing. It's all for me?" she asked. He'd gone through so much trouble, just for her. Why?

"You've gone through so much, lately. I just wanted to help you take your mind off of everything and have a nice night." Angel smiled brightly as he sat then poured her a glass of wine.

"You sure there's no ulterior motive?"

"That's for me to know and you to find out," he joked as he sipped his own glass of wine.

After they finished their meal, they sat on the couch together in front of the fire. Sophie held her third glass of wine, the alcohol warming her from the inside made her cheeks feel warm and her body relaxed and comfortable, leaning against Angel who had his arm resting on the back of the couch.

"Sophie, I'm really glad I found you. In life, you know. I'd been waiting since I left the orphanage to see you again. I didn't believe in fate before you came back into my life."

"Me too," she told him. The wine was emboldening her, letting her do what she wanted for a change. Letting her do what she wanted without fear of the consequences that may come after. Was it the wine? Or was she finally letting go of all that miserable pain from her past. Whichever one, she was glad to be present there, in the moment, with Angel, who was also on his third glass of wine.

"So, I was thinking, since you feel the same, then maybe you might want to stay. With me? Like for real. For good. Maybe as my girlfriend?" he asked as he looked into her clear blue eyes, his heart about to beat right out of his chest.

"You want me to be your girlfriend?"

"Yeah, I do. I think we're cute. Todd and Melody think we're cute. I mean, the universe even thinks it, why else would it have brought us back together like this? When we needed each other?"

"Are you sure you want me to be your girlfriend? I'm a little unstable," Sophie said as she turned her body towards Angel after setting her glass on the coffee table. Angel set his glass down too and shifted to match Sophie.

"Meh, not really. Not when you think about all the stuff you've been through. I don't care anyways. I care about you, though. I want to be there for you when you need someone, I want to make you laugh and smile as much as humanly possible. I want to make you forget all the bad stuff and leave it in the past so you can be happy, here with me. So, if you want to, I'd be thrilled if you would be my girlfriend and move in with me, officially. In a whole romantic capacity, not just what we've been doing for the past couple months." Angel leaned closer to Sophie; a fraction of an inch closer for each second that passed between them.

Sophie glanced down at his deliciously plump lips, hoping he was going to kiss her very soon, but he stopped just before their lips touched. He was waiting, she realized. He was waiting for her answer before he moved another inch closer. "Only if you promise one thing," she said as she leaned closer still. She could feel his warm breath against her lips.

"Anything you want," he whispered.

"Promise not to leave me?"

"I promise to stay until you tell me not to," he told her. He always knew the exact words she needed to hear.

Sophie pressed her lips against his. It was so easy to get lost in his touch as he snaked a hand into her hair and pulled her closer. She couldn't help but whimper into his lips as they kissed.

Angel pulled away, much sooner than Sophie would have liked. He picked up her hand and pressed something cold and small into her palm. Sophie looked down to see a small, shiny brass key laying there. She looked up into Angel's warm, dark eyes. Eyes that brought her home wherever she was.

21

"Ready?" Angel asked Sophie as he held her hand in his. She nodded in silent reply. Their eyes locked as he pressed a warm kiss to her knuckles before releasing her hand and letting her out of the car. Once Angel reached her side of the car he wrapped an arm around Sophie's slim waist to keep her close and warm in the chilly mid-October evening and led her to Felicity's front door.

As soon as they approached the door, Cage flung it open and welcomed them inside. Angel chuckled next to her as he let her lead the way. Sophie's heart skipped a beat as she realized she hadn't introduced Angel to anyone before and wasn't sure what exactly she should introduce him as.

"This is my..." Her what? Boyfriend? She looked back and forth between the two handsome men wondering what she should say, but was saved by Angel, yet again.

With one glance in Sophie's direction, he could see her internal panic and knew it would probably be easier for him to introduce himself. "Angel, Sophie's boyfriend. Sorry, I've been keeping her all to myself lately. Just can't seem to get enough of her," he joked. He felt a gentle squeeze from her hand in his, a silent thank you for taking the reins.

Sophie could tell he wasn't sure what all he should reveal about what had been going on with her in the last few months. "It's okay, Angel. They know everything. Cage is the owner of Priority One Security. His guys set up the system at the library." Sophie could see Angel's features soften as he relaxed, feeling the same sense of safety that she did around the Murphys.

"Thank you, for everything you're doing to keep Sophie safe," Angel said as he stuck out his hand for Cage to shake.

"She's like family. We'd do anything for her." Cage gave Angel's hand a stiff shake and a smile before excusing himself to go check on Felicity in the kitchen.

"You're doing great," Sophie assured Angel, who in return gave her a smile and a peck on the lips.

"You too. You're brave for even leaving the house, amor." Angel pressed his lips to Sophie's forehead. They were startled by a gasp from the other side of the room.

"Sophie!" Felicity squealed as she ran to her friend and wrapped her arms around the woman. "I know I just saw you today at work, but it feels like a million years."

"I don't plan on going anywhere anytime soon, thanks to you guys," Sophie said as she hugged Felicity just as fiercely back.

"Promise? No more ditching me, okay? We've got you. Whatever you need, hun."

"Need...to breathe," Sophie choked out as she tried to pry herself out of Felicity's tight grip.

"Okay, fine. I suppose you can breathe."

Once Felicity let go, Sophie introduced the two strangers in the room. "Felicity, this is Angel, my boyfriend. Angel, this is Felicity, my boss slash best friend."

"So glad you're here!" Felicity shook Angel's hand then grabbed Sophie's. "Come on, let's catch up," Felicity babbled as she led Sophie to the kitchen about the fun details that come with preparing to sell a house. She and Cage had been discussing selling their one bedroom to upgrade for room for children. The second they reached the kitchen Felicity stopped abruptly, put her hands on Sophie's shoulders and looked at her straight in the eyes. "He is gorgeous, Soph! You didn't tell me that part!"

"Well, it wasn't really - I mean we weren't - We didn't mean to end up together, it just kinda happened."

"Spill; everything that you're comfortable with, that is."

Sophie had missed Felicity dearly, way more than she thought she was going to. Being in her kitchen again, laughing with her, gossiping like nothing had ever happened. Sophie knew she couldn't leave ever again. This was her home. Chicago was her home. Felicity and Cage were her family. She'd gone her whole life wishing she had a family that cared about her and loved her, she hadn't realized it had been staring her right in the face ever since she ran into Felicity that day she came back to Chicago.

The two couples sat down to dinner soon after the women had disappeared into the kitchen, which had apparently given Cage and Angel ample time to get acquainted as they were chatting away about government jobs and their fantastic benefits. Felicity had cooked up an amazing pot of Cajun chicken with fettuccine alfredo, garlic bread, and sauteed green beans - a favorite of Sophie's.

"Oh, Felicity. You've outdone yourself," Sophie said as she shoved more chicken and fettuccine into her mouth.

"Sophie's right, this is amazing," Angel agreed.

"Why do you think I married her?" Cage joked. Felicity shot him a playful glare as Angel choked on his noodles momentarily before swallowing them. "Wouldn't you marry her for this food? Every meal she makes is this good!"

Felicity smacked Cage's bicep as he laughed boisterously. "So much for soul mates. Apparently you only love me for my food!" she chided.

"Oh, no babe. I definitely love you. It's just a bonus that you're such a great chef." He blew her a kiss as he started eating again.

The warmth that filled Sophie's soul threatened to pour out in the form of tears. Happy tears. She took a sip of her wine and observed the scene before her. Cage and Angel were scarfing down their food like they had been starving to death for the last week and Felicity was chuckling as she took a bite of her own garlic bread. She wished she had a photographic memory to keep this moment in her mind forever. It was how she'd always wanted her life to be.

After dinner they found themselves sipping wine as they talked in the living room. Felicity had started a fire in the fireplace and poured her and Sophie each a glass of wine.

"So, Angel, you saved Sophie from the rooftop, right?" Cage asked. He knew the basics of what had happened, but Sophie could tell he'd wanted more information since they stepped foot in the front door.

"Yeah, we got a call about her. My chief sent me up to try to talk with her, try to get her down, you know? I didn't know exactly who she was until much later."

"What do you mean who she was?" Cage asked. He was thoroughly confused; it was written all over his face.

Sophie smiled, knowing what came next. Felicity wasn't wrong. Their story was pretty much a sappy romance movie plot, with a lot of angst added in.

"That we met long before the rooftop."

"Oh wow. Did you go to college together? No offense, but judging from that truck, I can't imagine you're a huge Ducks fan," Cage laughed quizzically.

"Well, actually, there are a lot of -" Sophie realized that that wasn't the point of the conversation. "Sorry, never mind! Angel...?"

"No, it's quite alright, amor." Angel chuckled, knowing that what he was about to say was really going to blow Cage's mind. "All three of us - yes, Felicity, you too - were at St. John's together. Sophie and I were inseparable - or rather, I was like Sophie's shadow. I didn't recognize her until she'd already been staying with me for a while." Angel knew exactly what to say and how to say it. Sophie would've fumbled all over the place and totally clammed up when she got to the sex part.

"I KNEW IT! I have read far too many stories in my life to not pick up on the parallels. Had you asked me eighteen months ago whether I thought those stories had a place in the real world, I would have skeptically laughed and explained how stories are an escape from reality, thus have no place in it. However, after everything that has happened in the last year or so, there is literally nothing that surprises me. When Sophie first told me your name I had thought of you, but obviously there are thousands of Angels in Illinois, and probably hundreds in Chicago. Honey, I think we should become a crime fighting team. Your brawn and my brains? Huh? Huh?" Felicity joked, clearly more entertained by her joke than anyone else.

Sophie gave her a pity laugh, which turned into a real laugh, which made Angel smile, then laugh. Finally, Cage joined in on the laughter, which made everyone laugh even harder. After everyone had calmed down, Felicity took a sip of wine.

"You know, Angel, I can't believe you guys found each other again," Felicity said. "I definitely never thought I'd see Sophie again after she was adopted." Felicity stood up. "You know, I still have some pictures. Sister Gloria - God rest her soul - gave me a box some years ago before she passed. Let me go grab it." She turned quickly, nearly knocking over a lamp, rushed off down the hall, and soon returned with a box that she set on the coffee table, and started rifling through the pictures inside. "Ah!" she exclaimed as she pulled out a small picture of a little boy, who bore a striking resemblance to Angel. "I know who this is!" Felicity said as she handed the picture to Angel.

"I remember that little boy so well. He was my protector. As I got older, I eventually forgot the name of the little boy who saved me constantly from that asshole Zachariah. I can't believe you saved me again," Sophie said as she rested her head on Angel's shoulder.

"Ugh, I remember *him*! Hold on. Here!" Felicity said as she fished out a picture of a lanky pre-teenaged boy whose eyes lacked any sort of depth. They were flat brown and devoid of any emotion besides pure evil. It made chills run down Sophie's spine. She remembered him very well.

"What about the other kid?" Angel asked. "What was his name? Creek? No. No, what was it? Something about water," he wondered out loud.

"River?" Felicity asked. "The kid whose sister died?" She fished out two more pictures. A set of twins, both with blonde hair. One boy, one girl. *But the girl!*

Sophie and Cage gasped as they leaned forward to try to get a better look at the pictures. "Who's that?" Cage asked, shock laced his voice.

"Her name was Brooklyn. They were twins. I remember when she died. We were just kids. She was what? 10? She was really sweet. This picture was taken the day before she went missing. The tragic thing is, when they found her body, the dress was nowhere to be seen...if you know what I mean. River was never the same after that. How could you be? Your only family ripped from you like that?" Felicity asked as her face fell. She knew exactly how he must have felt, except she was the cause of her father's demise. River had no part in his sister's death.

"It can't be..." Sophie grabbed the picture from the table where Felicity had set it down. She studied the picture carefully. The young, blonde girl wore the same pink dress she had on when Sophie had seen her on the rooftop. Her hair was in the same braids, tied off with the same pink bows. Her eyes held the same sadness they had when she'd tried to stop Sophie. *It can't be her*, Sophie thought. She was completely baffled. *How could it be the same girl?* There was no denying it. It was her.

"Soph, you okay?" Angel asked as he softly rested his hand on her shoulder.

Sophie nodded, realizing she was acting really weird. She quickly set the picture back down. "Huh? Yeah, I'm fine. Just thought she looked really familiar. Makes sense now. She was with us at St. John's." Sophie looked up and caught Cage's gaze. He'd been taken aback by seeing her too. *How did he recognize her?* He wasn't at St. John's with them. He had a family. He gave Sophie a look that just said, *later*. Sophie looked away from him and back to Angel.

"Well, it's been so great seeing you guys and having dinner again, but that wine is hitting me hard and I'm exhausted. Angel, is it alright if we head home?" Sophie asked. Angel gave her a slightly quizzical look but didn't argue it. Felicity gave Sophie a look, a silent questioning of why she suddenly needed to go home.

"Of course, let's get you home." He helped her up off the couch and waited as she gave Felicity a big hug before following him out of the house. Once they reached the car, Angel opened the door for her. "Are you okay? You made a weird face when you were looking at Brooklyn's picture," Angel asked. He waited for an answer, standing in the way of the car door closing.

"Yeah, I'm-" Sophie was cut off by a dark figure appearing behind Angel. He was knocked out with one blow to the back of the head and before she could scream Sophie's face was covered with a cloth. The last thought she had before everything went black was, *I thought chloroform would smell worse.*

Angel groaned as he felt hands shaking his shoulders. The ache at the base of his skull was making his ears ring. It hurt so bad his whole head was throbbing.

Angel and Sophie were leaving the house. Angel opened the door for Sophie but stopped to talk to her. A larger dark figure came up and struck him from behind, knocking him out instantly. The man watching the Murphy house from down the street with binoculars sat up straight in his seat.

Fuck!

He threw the binoculars down on the seat next to him. He leaped from his car and raced toward the house as he watched the entire scene unfold in front of him. He ran so fast that the wind whipped the dark ball cap off his head. He had to get to them before it was too late.

The dark figure reached into the car for Sophie and pulled her out to toss her limp body over his shoulder. He watched as the woman was dropped into the back of a van, the doors slammed closed concealing the unconscious woman within.

Fuck! He's gonna get away!

He pushed his arms and legs as fast as he could but the second he reached the van the dark figure had dropped the woman into, it was gone. Already moving too fast to catch on foot. He had to make sure the man was okay, but his gaze was locked on the speeding van.

Shit! Of course, the license plate is covered. He knows how to cover his tracks. He isn't as stupid as he likes to pretend to be.

He really needed to check on Angel, who'd been hit from behind. He rounded the car and just as he did, he heard the door of the house open behind him and two pairs of footsteps run out to the sidewalk he was crouched on. He shook the man's shoulders, trying to wake him up.

"Come on, wake up," he growled.

"What the fuck happened?!" shouted a woman's voice from behind him. Another man crouched next to him, also attempting to rouse the man laying on the sidewalk.

"Angel, what happened? Come on, wake up," the man ordered.

"Sophie, where's Sophie?" asked the man laying on the sidewalk. His words were slurred, as if he were drunk. *Must have been one hell of a blow to the back of the head.* "Where did she go?" he asked as he started to sit up. He held his head in his hands.

"He took her, I saw it." The man in the dark bomber jacket told Angel, his voice absolute and unwavering.

Angel picked his head up and tried to open his eyes. When he was able to focus, blood-red rage flooded his vision. He knew the man in front of him. He launched himself at him, tackling the man to the ground. Screaming as he slammed his fists into his face. "What the fuck did you do with Sophie, you sick fuck?!" Angel had never felt such rage before. If it hadn't taken over his entire mind, he'd have been scared. But all he could see was red, even through the pain in his skull. Angel pushed the pain aside to make room for the redness that overtook him.

"Angel! Angel, stop! What are you doing? He didn't take her!" Felicity cried out as she watched the man try to protect his face from the fists flying at it.

"Bullshit! I've seen him stalking her! He tried to break into our house!" Angel shouted; each sentence punctuated by the sickening blow of Angel's fist in the man's face.

Cage struggled to pull Angel off of the man he'd attacked, adrenaline fueling Angel's strength. Cage held him by his arms from behind. Angel struggled to get away and return to beating the man who'd been terrifying his girlfriend for the last few months.

The man on the sidewalk checked his mouth for blood, which he inevitably found. Angel knew what he was doing when it came to throwing a punch.

"I wasn't stalking her," he said as he sat up and spit out a glob of saliva and blood. "I was trying to make sure he didn't take her. And clearly I fucking failed." He stood and leaned against the car behind him.

"What the fuck are you talking about?" Angel shouted as he tried to get out of Cage's iron grip.

"Angel, calm down. We need to know what he knows. If I let you go, are you going to stop?" Cage asked. He waited until he felt Angel's body relax out of the rage-fueled state it'd been in.

"I'm fine," Angel grunted. He was pretty sure he was in control enough to not attack the man in front of them.

"It's not the first time he's taken women. I've been watching him. He led me to you all."

"What do you mean?" Cage asked, his investigative instinct kicking in.

"I'm a Private Investigator. The police quit looking into the case a long time ago, so I picked it up. They tried to say there wasn't any connection between the murders." The man rubbed his thumb across his nose, checking it for any blood. He'd gotten lucky. No broken nose.

"Murders?!" Angel roared as he began to lunge forward. Felicity put her hand on his shoulder, stopping him in his tracks.

"Angel, please."

"What connections?" Cage questioned.

"It's not the first kidnapping. Doesn't usually end well, though. Eight, now nine, blonde females, ages ranging from 10 to 25. All with delicate, feminine features. Sweet girls, all taken. The last four showed up around a year after disappearing, all dead. Starved to death."

"And you think the same person just took Sophie?" Cage asked as he glanced at Angel, making sure he wasn't going to attack the man again.

"How could you possibly know that?" Felicity asked. Now that the excitement had subsided, she was able to get a good look at him. He was exactly how Sophie described him. However, though she hadn't seen him before, he looked eerily familiar.

"He always stalks them first, sends them letters. Similar to the ones he sent her. He's been going all out for her, though. I know why, and I think you'll all understand soon."

"So, you *have* been stalking her?!" Angel shouted as he lunged at the man but was stopped by Cage. Rage rippled throughout his body yet again, setting every nerve on fire, making him see red again. He seethed but stayed in place.

"Garbage rummaging is hardly stalking. I'm a PI. Licensed and everything. Wanna see?" he asked as he fished in his pocket to pull out his license. He handed it to Cage, who looked back and forth between the man and the license.

"River Bridges?" Cage read out loud.

As if lightning had struck her in her place, Felicity jolted to attention, eyes wide. "Wait, River?"

"Yeah...it's me." He looked at his feet and sighed. Felicity could see the anger with himself for not getting there in time. It was clear on his face. It was the same look he had almost two decades ago, one she was very familiar with.

"But...how?" Felicity's mind was racing as she tried to rationalize the situation through the fuzziness of the wine she'd had. Her best friend had just been kidnapped. By a murderer. Not just a murderer. River was sure he was a serial killer. And River himself, there in front of her, after how many years, almost twenty? And why hadn't Sophie asked for help from Cage sooner? Why hadn't she let Priority One keep an eye on her at all times? She was missing, and Felicity couldn't help but blame herself for not pushing harder to get Sophie more protection.

"It's a long story..."

Stoke the Flames

Did you love *Stoke the Flames*? Then you should read *Secrets of the Arlington*[1] by Monica Misho-Grems!

[2]

Secrets of the Arlington is Monica Misho-Grems' debut novel and book one of *The Orphans of St John's* series.

Content.

Felicity felt like the luckiest woman in the world, working for her favorite place in the world: The Arlington. The John Arlington Library was not just a hub of international knowledge; a collection of history's greatest tales, heroes, and villains; a star map to all of the possible worlds in the universe – but a safe haven for bookworms and introverts alike.

Until it all changes.

This is what the young, orphan Felicity Johnson loved about it – and why the adult Felicity chose to be a librarian. Well, that and her boss, John Arlington. A man who became a father to her once she discovered The

---

1. https://books2read.com/u/bpakng

2. https://books2read.com/u/bpakng

Arlington. That is, until one day when he doesn't return to lock up the library.

Whirlwind.

Worried and confused, she searches for answers. Felicity soon uncovers why he never made it back, and that he may not have been the man that she once thought he was. What other secrets will Felicity unearth as her world crumbles to pieces while she tries to escape the past she never knew she had? Can heartthrob FBI agent Cage Murphy help Felicity figure out her past and ensure she has a future?

Read more at https://authoratheart.com/.

Also by Monica Misho-Grems

The Orphans of St John's
Secrets of the Arlington
Stoke the Flames

Watch for more at https://authoratheart.com/.

Also by Alessandro Williams

The Orphans of St John's
Stoke the Flames

About the Author

Monica Misho-Grems is a young and budding author from Portland, Oregon. As a child, she split her time between many hobbies, including dance, reading, and writing. At a young age she showed a deep passion for literature - both reading it and writing it - but it wasn't until her teen years that she began to dream of doing it professionally.

Monica got her start writing more serious content by writing fanfictions on various message boards late in her teen years and early twenties. Once she became more comfortable, with herself and her writing, she began dabbling in more erotic literature, and eventually found the style that we see.

Nowadays, Monica Misho-Grems lives in Southeast Portland with her husband, John, their three daughters, and her father. She is a full-time mother, wife, daughter, friend, and Clinical Trainer for a local OB/GYN company; she hopes to add "writer" to the full-time mix.

Read more at https://authoratheart.com/.

www.ingramcontent.com/pod-product-compliance
Ingram Content Group UK Ltd.
Pitfield, Milton Keynes, MK11 3LW, UK
UKHW022024190726
13853UKWH00005B/2103

9 798201 435196